My Viking Alpha

Immortal Love Saga

J. R. Froemling

My Viking Alpha: Book I of the Immortal Love Saga

Printed in the United States of America

This is a work of fiction.
Names, characters, places, and incidents are used fictitiously.
Any resemblance to actual events, locales, or persons, living or
dead, is entirely coincidental.

Published by The Great Yarn Dragon, LLC
Effingham, IL 62401

ISBN: 978-1-957393-08-7

First Edition: 2022

This book is for my sister and brother-in-law.
Their love is eternal and inspiring.

Other Books By J. R. Froemling

The Wolfe Legacy
> Mistress Giselle - Book One of Hope-Marie
> A Devil's Hope - Book Two of Hope-Marie
> The Naughty List - Book One of Elijah Joseph

Savannah Nights
> The Triple Six
> The Night Rangers
> Poltergeist Girl

Chronicles of Nodd
> Fall of Avalon - Verse One

Immortal Love Saga
> My Celtic Luna – Book II

Table of Contents

Best Day Ever

Beltane 2004

My mommy is acting weird. She has been crying all day. It's because of my daddy, but she just keeps saying she will fix it. Everything will be alright. We are dressed in funny costumes. The little black boots on my feet hurt, but I don't complain. I don't want Mommy to cry more. We were supposed to go see Grandma Finley, but something happened, and now we are in this place, and it is way past my bedtime. I have my blanket with me. He's named Specially, and he is a little yellow mesh blanket with silk trim all around. He's so soft and snuggly that I take him everywhere with me. Mommy jokes that there is Hell to pay if someone tries to take him from me.

They never try twice.

I hug him while I watch Mommy. She reads from her big

book of secrets. Her fingers move in the air and there is a scary breeze.

I scoot a little closer to Mommy, scared. It is really dark out here. This part of the park does not have lights like the other parts do.

Mommy is speaking her special magic language.

I try to mumble the words with her, but they are really hard.

She looks like she is in pain.

I don't want Mommy to hurt, so I put Specially over her while I hold the corner.

Mommy doesn't seem to notice me. She is really scaring me.

I don't like it at all. The wind is getting louder and there is a glowing light around the trees in front of us. I blink as the forest changes. It is sunny and bright in the big circle Mommy is making. My eyes widen.

Mommy screams and falls back, taking Specially with her.

"Mommy?" I ask with a small whine. The big sunny hole is forgotten. "Mommy," I say louder. There is a growl behind me and I turn around. My eyes go wide. The sunny, bright hole is gone and standing there is a great big, "PUPPY!" I shriek in delight and throw myself on him. If I knew Mommy was bringing me here to get a puppy, I would not have been so upset. I wrap my tiny arms around the puppy. He is great big and I have to stand on my tiptoes to get my arms around him. He must be scared because he whines and squirms.

I wrap my arms tighter. "Mommy! Mommy! Puppy!" I hold on for dear life. Puppies run away and get lost, and I don't want him to get lost.

He growls at me and I dig my little fingers into his fur, holding firm. "Mommy! He's too big! Help!" He finally knocks me down and rips himself free of me.

I bawl my eyes out.

Mommy isn't moving and Puppy is being mean. "Mommy," I whine between tiny sobs.

Puppy stops stalking and stares at me. Then his ears shift and he looks beyond me. I watch as he gives me a wide berth to circle up to Mommy. His head cants, and he looks down at Mommy.

I get up and I wipe my tears. "Mommy, wake up." I shake her again.

Puppy gives a sniff against me and nuzzles me. Then he leans down and licks Mommy's cheek, nuzzling her.

I'm glad Puppy likes Mommy. I would be really sad if he didn't. Mommy won't let me have pets. She says I'm not big girl enough.

It's like Puppy's licks are magic! Mommy starts to stir.

Puppy sits back on his hind legs, and I lean against him, petting him. "Mommy, please can we keep him? He is so nice! He licked you," I start to plead with Mommy, who is making an awful noise as she sits up. Blood is coming out of her nose. I get scared again, and whimper. I really want Specially now, but Mommy is squishing him under her butt.

When she looks at me, then at Puppy, she screams and yanks me away from Puppy to put me behind her.

"Ow! Hey!"

"Run, Lily." My mommy is being weird, and she hurt my arm when she yanked me.

She moves to her feet slowly, facing Puppy with her arms out.

I don't understand what she is doing until I see her making the magic face again.

"NO!" I shriek and I fling myself back onto Puppy, "No, Mommy! No!" I'm crying hard and loud.

Puppy makes a grunting noise as I collide into him, but

doesn't fall over, or do anything else. Then Puppy does something really weird. He isn't Puppy anymore! He pats me and his words are nice, but they are gibberish. He talks really funny! Like the Swedish chef on the Muppets, only with a growly voice.

Mommy jerks me again and puts me behind her.

I peek around her skirts.

Puppy stands up to his full height and looks down at her. He is HUGE, definitely taller than my daddy.

I cling to the long skirt Mommy is wearing and yank up Specially now that he's free from her butt.

Mommy is now talking in the funny language, too. My mommy knows everything. I wish I knew what they were saying.

He replies. The only word that sounds like a name is Viggo.

He inhales a bit and gives her a grin before he says a bunch of things to her. He comes closer and Mommy backs up, moving us. She is really scared. I can tell.

Mommy brandishes a finger at him, and she clings to me tighter.

He holds his hands up and moves forward slowly as he talks, motioning to me and saying, "Puppy."

It's the only word I understand between them.

Then my mommy looks down at me, and he closes the distance between them, pulling Mommy close. She lets out a yelp, but his hand is on her chin, and they are about to play kissy face when he turns her head side to side before saying a weird word.

He sniffs her and then I realize he does not have any clothes on.

"Puppy! Your pee-pee is showing!" I erupt into giggling.

This makes Mommy look at me, then back to Puppy, and

her hand flies to my eyes. The next thing I know, Specially is yanked from my hands.

I start screaming and fighting with Mommy. "No! Give him back! He's mine! MINE!" I shriek at Mommy.

"Lily," she says in the Mommy voice.

"No! Specially is mine! Mine! Give him back!" I throw myself to the ground crying harder and make a loud scene in this dark part of the park.

I hear Puppy's strange language, but I don't care, it's my Specially and she has to give him back.

I hear Mommy's voice as I'm wailing and crying on the ground. I don't understand them again, but they are both watching me as I scream and holler.

Puppy growls even though he looks like a person.

Mommy's voice sounds really upset.

I don't care. I'm going to scream myself hoarse until they give me Specially back.

Puppy's voice sounds concerned.

Mommy rests her hands on her hips, which means she is not going to give me Specially back.

I wail louder. Then Specially is being dropped on me and Puppy is lying on the ground next to me again. I stop wailing and cling to Specially with my little fists as I look from Puppy to Mommy.

He wags his tail and leans in to lick my cheeks.

It makes me giggle, then hiccup.

Mommy throws her hands up in the air.

I move closer to Puppy and he nuzzles me. It makes me feel better.

Mommy picks up her book and then turns to face us again. "Get up, Lily. Come on," she takes my free hand.

Puppy follows along, his tail wagging behind him.

The walk back to our little apartment is long and I'm

sleepy by the time we get there. Mommy picked me up after I decided I was too tired to walk, and I'm nestled against her shoulder. I fight really hard not to go to sleep and to make sure Puppy follows us all the way home. I lose the battle about halfway there as Mommy is warm.

This was the best day ever!

No You Don't, Mister!

Morrigan is frustrated and drained. She had expected to open the portal to Victorian era New York and find Silar's brother. He could stop Silar from what he's planning. The worst-case scenario would be that Lily and she got stuck in the past. Silar would never find her there.

She gets the door to her apartment open and lets the wolf go first. She closes the door with her foot and drops the book on the dining room table as she carries Lily into the bedroom. Morrigan gets Lily stripped down to her bloomers and undershirt. She leaves Lily's little pudgy body nestled to Specially. More stuffed animals than one could count surround her.

Lily curls contentedly into the covers, murmuring something about Puppy.

Viggo, who has transformed back into human form,

watches the ritual with fascination. He cares little about being naked as the girl is asleep. He grins when Morrigan turns bright red and silently ushers him out of the room, pulling the door closed behind her. Her nails dig into his arm, and he feels the little sparks of connection between them, just like he did when he licked her in the park.

This angel of a woman is scrambling his mind.

He knows he should be concerned. He is in a strange place with all these structures and scents. There is little nature here. The power radiating off her beautiful form intrigues him as well. She does not smell of the devil. She smells of Earth and Fire. Even in those ridiculous garments, she is shapely, and all he wants to do at this moment is claim her as his mate.

"What the hell is wrong with you? What if she saw you again? Pervert," Morrigan hisses at Viggo when they are across the apartment in her room. She coughs and tries to maintain her anger. Morrigan made the mistake of giving him an appraising look, and she was not disappointed.

"Pups see nakedness, Mate. I would not touch your offspring. I am not a monster." He steps forward, trying to close the gap between them.

Morrigan dances back, putting the bed between them.

"Would you put some fucking clothes on?!" She snarls at him.

He gets a wolfish grin then. "Do you have clothes that will fit me? You brought me here, Mate. I was hunting. My clothes are where I left them." He holds his hands up, trying to show he means no harm, and then he brings his hands down to cross in front of his manhood. "Better? What is this place you have brought me to?"

Morrigan is rubbing her forehead. She had studied that incantation for a year. She knew it by heart. Lily and she should be in 1821. How did this go so wrong? When he puts his hands down in front of him, she blinks, then laughs. She laughs at the absurdity of a naked man trying to make her comfortable by covering his raging hard on.

Morrigan could not help but notice his failure to completely do so. She also had to admit to herself that she is aroused by his confidence. His hungry eyes take her in like he could devour every inch of her, and it makes her cheeks flush. With a groan, she turns her back to him and rummages in her dresser. When she comes back with a pair of shorts, she murmurs a few words and they transform into boxers. "Put these on," she closes the gap to hand him the boxers.

"So, you are a witch," he grins at her again.

"I am. I'm Morrigan Finley, daughter of Catarina Finley. Member of the Ember Tree coven. What year are you from?" Morrigan watches him look at the boxers in question.

He lets his fingers brush hers on purpose.

She feels it again. It's a terrifying and powerful feeling, like she could do anything when he touches her. It radiates from her fingers down to between her legs, making her throb. This brings the blush right back to her cheeks. She absolutely was not going to sleep with this strange werewolf just because he oozes sex appeal and dominance.

"I am in my thirty-third year," He chuckles when she startles at realizing the two of them have sat on the edge of the bed together. He inhales again, drawing in her intoxicating scent. It is taking all his restraint to not claim her. If they were near the pack, he would have already claimed her by now, regardless of her point of view on the matter. Viggo is not a dumb pup, though. He is the Beta to his elder brother and knows better than to cross a witch. Witches are revered beings that are gifts from Freya. They bring her blessings to the clan. Mani, the moon god, must be rewarding him to give him such a precious mate.

"I didn't mean you, I meant what year was it when you went to hunt," Morrigan sounds exasperated and tries to scoot away from him.

He casually scoots closer with a mischievous smirk on his face. He knew well what she was asking. He enjoys seeing her flustered like this. It's adorable. He leans in close, "Oh, so that is what you wished to know. In that case," his voice a sultry growl near her, "you must give me something for the answer."

"What?" Morrigan gasps and leans away from him, trapped at the edge of the bed. "No. Nuh uh," she waggles her finger at him. "I'm not giving you anything."

"Suit yourself, Morrigan Finley." With that, he eases himself onto the bed fully, lying on his back and tucking his hands behind his head. Viggo had not bothered to put on the boxers. He also cannot wipe that arrogant smirk off his face. He knows women want him. Fenrir knows how many of the free maids his brother and Luna have thrown at him in their desperate attempt to tame him.

"Fine. What do you want?" Morrigan tries not to look back at him, laying on her bed where he is attempting to trick her into mounting him.

"An honest answer to a question of mine," he casually responds.

"Okay," Morrigan replies in irritation.

"It is the year 1281 by the Christian calendar. Do they even still use that method? Or did all those heathens die off?" He rolls his eyes.

"What? Oh. Yeah. Christians are everywhere. Kind of like cockroaches," Morrigan muses. "What is your question?"

Viggo clears his throat, which makes Morrigan turn to face him, and he waggles his eyebrows at her. The wolfish grin on his face says he knows exactly what his body looks like and then he briefly looks to his manhood, makes it bob for her again and then meets her gaze, bringing all his smolder to bear on her.

"Oh, no you don't!" Morrigan whips up off the bed. "This is my bed. You sleep on the floor, or on the couch, in the other room. I'm not having sex with you! My daughter is in the next room! Pervert."

"What? You would be such a poor host to your mate? She's asleep." He pouts at her, letting his manhood bob.

Morrigan throws a pillow right onto his manhood. "Nope. Not happening. Not again. I've been married, pal, and he wants to kill me."

This makes Viggo spring right up off the bed. "Where is he? I will solve this problem. No one harms my-," All the playfulness has left his demeanor, but he cannot finish his sentence out loud. Morrigan has her fingers pinched in the air, having thrown a silence hex on him.

"No. You're not listening. No more talking until you do. I'm no one's mate. You are not going to go kill anyone. And you are going to sleep on the couch, clothed. Got it?" Her eyes blaze as she looks at him. He grins and grimaces, then finally just shrugs. She releases him at that point.

"As you wish, mate," he picks up the boxers and slides them on. Then, with abnormal speed he draws her right into him, kissing her hard. Morrigan loses herself in the kiss. Until his hands roam down to cup her ass. Then she steps back and slaps him. The ringing sound of her hand connecting with his cheek makes him laugh.

"Bad, Puppy," she tries to sound angry, but is blushing and smiling. Viggo grins and winks at her as he struts from the room. He definitely postures for her as she shuts the door on him. Morrigan sinks down the door and looks to the ceiling. "What have I gotten myself into?"

Who's Afraid of a Little Magic?

When I woke up, I was still in the stupid poofy pants and in my bed. I yawn and rub my face, then I wander into the bathroom.

Mommy says good witches always go potty, wash their face, and brush their teeth.

That's what I do. I can't wait to find Puppy and pet him again. He has soft fur. I grab Specially and I make my way into our living room.

On the floor is Puppy in person form. Mommy gave him shorts. He looks so sleepy that I don't wake him. I get the remote, sit on the floor in front of him, and turn on the TV to find cartoons.

Puppy makes a growly noise in his sleep.

So I pet him. His beard is scratchy. Then I lay back on him, using him for a pillow, and pull Specially over us. I like watching cartoons like this and my eyes drift close. Next thing I know I'm cold because Puppy is moving away from me. "No," I pout and roll over to cling to him.

His words sound super funny as he tries to escape.

"I don't understand you. You talk weird."

I open my eyes and look at him.

His head is canted, and he is chuckling.

I don't think he understands me either. I sit up quickly and I look at him. I make sure Mommy isn't in the room and look at him again. I'm not as strong as Mommy, so I have to touch people when I use magic on them. I reach over and touch his forehead.

He gets a weird look that makes me think he is going to make fun of me. Then I repeat the words I heard Mommy say last night. I'm slower and speak clearly to make sure I get it right.

"Say something, Puppy," I ask him.

"First, my name is not Puppy, it is Viggo." He chuckles.

I furrow my brow. "No! Viggo's dumb. Puppy." I cross my arms.

This makes him laugh a hard, belly laugh, like I told him a joke.

"You are definitely your mother's offspring, pup." He ruffles my hair.

"Wait! It worked! I understand you!"

"Well, I at least now understand the words coming from your mouth, though I fear I may not comprehend them." He smiles at me.

I leap at him, hugging him tight. "I'm so glad Mommy gave you to me! Don't ever leave. I'll get you a collar and leash. We'll go to the park. Play fetch." I'm squeezing him so tight and I can't wait.

"You will, will you?" Mommy's voice comes from the door.

"You'll even clean up his doo-doo when he goes at the park? Will you sit with him when he gets fixed?"

I don't know what fixed is, but I nod enthusiastically.

"No one is touching my... doo-doo," as Puppy pulls my arms from him and sets me aside to stand.

I look between him and Mommy, who is in one of her big t-shirts. "Well, except maybe your Mother," Puppy says as he waggles his brows.

Mommy chokes and coughs, then laughs. "It does not mean what you think it does," she says. Then I see her face darken. "Wait. How does she understand you?"

I look nervous and stand behind Puppy.

"Morrigan Finley, surely you know your own offspring is a witch?" He crosses his arms.

"I do, but this little witch should not know that spell," Mommy's eyes narrow as she looks at me.

"I 'membered it since last night." I offer proudly.

"What did I tell you about using magic without Mommy?" Now she's crossing her arms and looking at me like I'm going to get a spanking.

"But I wanted to know what he said," I whine.

"Come now, Mate," he tries to help.

Mommy does her mean trick and silences him, her fingers in the air.

I look up at Puppy who now looks very mad. I don't think he's used to being shushed. "I don't like it either."

"Lily," Mommy's voice snaps at me. "Do not do magic without me. You could have hurt him, or yourself. You don't want to be a dark witch, do you?"

I sulk and crinkle my nose.

"No. I'm sorry." I whine.

Mommy then releases Puppy from her hex.

"I'm proud of you for doing it right. Now let's get you

some breakfast. Raisins or Marshmallows?" Mommy beeps my nose, then moves to the kitchen.

Puppy looks down at me, still with the angry face, then back to Mommy.

I gently pet his side. "She always does it. It's cheating. It's not fair when Mommy makes me stop talking."

He grunts in agreement.

Mommy makes me cereal and leaves me at the table as she drags Puppy back to her room and closes the door.

I try to listen to them from the table, but my crunchy cereal is too loud. I just hope Mommy doesn't make Puppy leave.

******

Two Years Later

"What, in Odin's name, is this torture device?" Viggo groans and fidgets with his necktie.

I giggle and climb into a chair to get up to his level. I get a hold of it and loosen it a bit. "It's a necktie. Boys wear them when it's important," I smile at him.

"I would rather wear your dress, pup," he groans again.

"I'm sure we could arrange a dress for you," Mommy teases. She is wearing her skinny skirt and pretty blouse. She steps up to Viggo and gives him a weird smile. Then she reaches up to tighten the tie I loosened. "I did not think it was possible for you to look more handsome."

This brings a big grin to Viggo's face and I roll my eyes. "I'm right here!"

A few weeks ago, I got in trouble. Viggo and I practiced magic. Without Mommy. He told me I couldn't hurt him and that it would be our secret. At first it was fun stuff, like making his hair pink for a few minutes. Then I got Mommy's book. When he asked me if I had Mommy's permission to read the book, I lied to him and said yes.

I looked through the pages and decided I wanted to try the spell with pretty vines. I put the small ivy plant on the floor in between us, and he promised me it would be okay. He is super strong and is a werewolf. I have never seen him hurt. I read the spell as carefully as I could, making sure to sound out the big words.

Saying the Latin words and performing the ritual needed makes the plant respond to me. I don't fully understand Latin yet, and I did not know what kind of spell it was, only that it had pretty flowers in the picture. I watched in horror as the plant springs to life and vines grow up around Viggo.

The more he tried to break free the tighter they wrapped around him. His claws tore through the ivy, and it split apart, growing more strands, and getting tighter around him. His face turned red and veins bulged as he struggled against it.

When I finally screamed for Mommy, Viggo was turning blue and gasping for air.

Mommy was furious with me. She banished me to my bedroom and made all my toys march out into the living room. I couldn't even see if Viggo was alright.

Ever since the accident, Mommy and Viggo have been playing a lot of kissy face. Mommy made us both promise not to do magic without her again.

Viggo is such a grown-up. He won't even do it in secret anymore.

"When are we leaving?" I cross my arms in a pout as I watch the two of them grin at each other. I like Viggo. He's my Puppy, but he has been acting like he's my daddy, and he's not. Daddy is a warlock, not a puppy!

"Right now, come here, Lily," Mommy helps me off the chair and takes my hand.

Viggo looks confused when we move to Mommy's altar

and not the door.

"What's the matter? Big Bad Wolf afraid of a little magic?" Mommy winks at him.

I giggle.

Viggo rolls his eyes and comes forward, snaking his arm around Mommy's waist. "I fear nothing, Mate." He growls it out. It means he is scared.

She told me we are going to see Grandma Finley, so Viggo can ask for her hand. I don't know why she would give up her hand. It seems gross, and Viggo doesn't eat humans. He says they are gamey, whatever that means.

As soon as he touches Mommy, she gives me a wink and opens the portal. I hold on to her hand and then feel the whoosh of magic around us. I close my eyes from the whooshy air. When I open them again, we are standing outside of Grandma's home.

Something is wrong. Grandma is always out in her garden when we come to visit. I look at the garden, and it is overgrown. There are weeds everywhere. A good witch never lets her garden go unattended. I frown, but I follow Mommy and Viggo to the house. We walk up the big steps under the horseshoe.

"There's my little flower! Lily Finley, look how big you are!"

I turn to look at Grandma and frown. "Why are you a ghost, Grandma?" I feel like crying.

Wisdom and Warning

"Oh, flower, don't you cry," Grandma pulls me into her arms and she feels real.

This confuses me. I can tell she is a ghost. Ghosts are trapped inside. They can't roam free unless they were killed outside. I hiccup and look up at her. "But you're a ghost, Grandma," my lip quivers.

Viggo snaps his head towards Mommy and Grandma beeps my nose.

"Lily, remember when I told you that witches have the place they live and the home we come from?"

Grandma's voice is gentle and makes me feel better, so I nod.

"Well, it was time for me to return to the home we come from. I'm needed there."

I frown and shake my head. "No. I need you here." I stomp

my foot.

Viggo coughs to hide his laugh.

Mommy gives me the Mommy look.

"That you do, but not yet. I will be here when you need me and the home we come from when you don't. Deal?"

I scrunch up my face to see if she is playing a trick on me. Mommy says Grandma Finley is sly like a fox.

Mommy has tears in her eyes and it makes me sad all over again.

"You promise?" I try not to bawl my eyes out like a baby.

"I will always be there for you, Lily. I promise. Now, why don't you go play with my dollies? They are awfully lonely."

I look at all the grown-ups standing on Grandma's porch then bolt into the house and up the stairs. I love playing with the dollies. They teach me magic.

"You should follow her. Make sure she doesn't find the grimoires." Grandma's voice carries up the stairs.

Mommy comes and sits with me as the dollies begin their lesson.

******

"Follow me, wolf," Catarina says to Viggo. "We have much to discuss before I give you my blessing."

"How did you-," Viggo stops himself with that question. Morrigan had mentioned that her mother was a seer. He follows the woman, who looks as real as he is, into a parlor. The door closes behind him, and this room is heavy with magic. It makes his wolf uneasy. The beast within him itches to release himself against Viggo's will. He has not experienced that sensation since he was a pup, learning to sync with his wolf's soul.

He pulls the chair out for the woman. He would not call

her old, as she does not look any older than Morrigan, which is unsettling, but her eyes hold eons of knowledge when he looks into them. He obediently sits when Catarina motions for him to do so. His eyes never leave hers, and he feels ill-at-ease being alone with her.

"Oh, wolf, you're safe in here." Catarina's eyes are full of mischief. "I cannot perform much more than parlor tricks in this time. I need to say what I need to say to you. You won't understand, but you need to remember it. When the time comes, you need to keep Morrigan from stopping Lily. You will know when you need to do this. You promise me that, and you have my blessing." Catarina knows well he will not understand. It is the curse of Cassandra's line, so instead she leaves it as vague nothings and hopes the boy is smart enough to figure it out.

Viggo sits up and frowns. "You know as well as I, seer, that Morrigan Finley is an unstoppable force. What makes you think she will listen to me when the time comes?"

"Every good wolf knows how to distract their mate." Catarina's eyes twinkle. "Now, promise me, or I will send you whence you came."

Viggo's eyes widen in surprise, and he shifts in his seat as she flings her hands up to create what looks like a portal. On the other side, it is nightfall and forest as far as the eye can see. He's skeptical as she had just told him she could only do parlor tricks. "Seer, I am your daughter's mate. I will be with her, blessing or no. Do not threaten me again. Mani and Freya put us together, not even your magic can tear us apart." He snarls at Catarina.

"Good! You do have a spine! Just remember, you promised!" She then gets up and leaves him in the now quiet parlor, the portal gone from sight.

He doesn't like being manipulated and emits a low growl.

Catarina makes her way up the stairs and stops in the doorway to watch Morrigan with Lily.

Fear swirls around Morrigan's aura like a dark cloud.

"You should go comfort your mate, Morrigan. He has had quite the afternoon. I will watch my flower."

I look up to see Grandma smiling in the doorway, but I can tell she wants to have a big girl talk. Her arms are crossed and she's giving a fake smile. I look at Mommy who frowns at Grandma and then sighs.

She gets up and leaves us in the dolly room.

"Good, now that she's gone!" Grandma comes and sits with me, making the dollies do cooler things.

My eyes are fixated on the dollies, hanging on every word they say. I squirm a little as Grandma runs her fingers through my fiery red hair.

"Lily, you will be a powerful witch. Your children will be strong and magical. Remember that acts done with a pure heart and for love will always triumph. No matter how bleak it might be."

I turn to look at Grandma and she's crying. "Oh, Grandma!" I fling myself into her arms and hug her tight. She told me once that my hugs made everything better. I don't know how long we hug, but it feels like forever. I hold on to Grandma as long as she will let me.

She finally eases me back. "This will be the last you see me in this time. Remember all I have taught you and be a good girl. Happiness will find you in the end." She brushes my hair out of my face and she kisses my forehead.

Then Grandma is gone.

The dollies fall limp and I look around the room. The dust in the air visible in the setting sun's light. I look around again and am overwhelmed with sadness. I trudge down the stairs to find Viggo and Mommy waiting.

"Did you have a good time with Grandma?" Mommy tries to sound happy, but there is sadness in her eyes.

Viggo looks angry, and he keeps moving like he is guarding us.

I come over and I pet him. "It's okay, Puppy Viggo. Grandma wouldn't let anything bad happen to us. She's the most powerful witch in the universe!"

Viggo looks down at me, and then he squats down and smiles. "Lily, as your mother's only kin, I would be the happiest wolf in the world if you gave me permission to marry her."

Mommy's trying not to laugh while looking worried at the same time.

I look at Viggo and scrunch up my face. How can he marry Mommy if she is married to Daddy? I bite against my lip and fidget with my dress. This is a big question and I like Puppy Viggo. But that means he would be Mommy's Puppy, not my Puppy. I don't like that, but I want Mommy happy too, and he makes her laugh. "Will you still go to the park with me? And watch cartoons? And help me learn my spells?"

He smiles more and nods. "Of course I will. You will be my pup. I will do anything to keep you happy and safe."

"I'm not a pup! I'm a witch!" I protest.

"Yes, but you are my pup. It's way cooler than a witch." He winks to show he is teasing me.

"Yeah, okay. But no stupid rules! Or I take it back." I brandish my finger at him like Mommy does when she is arguing with him.

He wraps me into a tight hug and whirls me around, which makes me squeal in delight. He then pulls Mommy in close and kisses her a lot.

"EWW! I'm right here! No kissy face when holding me!" I make gag noises like I'm barfing.

Viggo doesn't let me go. Instead, he kisses my forehead and keeps us both close to him.

Mommy nestles close to Viggo and then we are moving through the whooshy air again. When I open my eyes, we are back in the apartment. It's really late at night and I lean against Viggo. He's warm.

"I will put her to bed, then we can celebrate," he whispers.

"I can't wait," Mommy says in her wispy voice.

"Thank you, Lily," he whispers against my cheek when we get into my bedroom. I keep pretending to be asleep because it's too much work to wake up.

"Did you think you could hide forever, Morrigan? She is my daughter. You have no right to keep her from me." The man's voice sounds familiar, but I was really little when Mommy said we had to be away from Daddy.

"Daddy?" I perk up in Viggo's arms and look from him to the door.

"Do not leave this room, Lily." Viggo's voice is a warning growl.

I know better than to disobey, but that doesn't mean I can't run to the doorway and watch when Viggo sets me down.

He steps into the living room behind Mommy, blocking my view of the man at the door.

"You are not welcome here, Warlock. I suggest you be gone before it becomes an issue. You are upsetting my mate." Viggo's voice sounds super mean and scary.

Worst Day Ever

"I see," the man says.

I cannot see who is talking. There is a lot of space between my room and the front door. I scurry to the couch and crouch down. The shoes on the man at the door are shiny and he is wearing gray grown-up pants. His voice sounds nice. I really want to see what he looks like.

"Silar," Mommy says. She sounds scared.

I want to run and hug her, but Viggo is making Mommy get behind him. He is the best guard Puppy ever.

"Morrigan," the man's voice sounds sad, "why would you do this? We made vows. Took oaths. Your blood is my blood."

I bite my lip because Mommy told me blood magic is the scariest of magic, white or black. If she promised Daddy, she should keep her promises.

"Don't you dare try that bullshit with me," Mommy shouts at the man. "You lied to me. You tricked me into getting pregnant for that prophecy. You had no intention of spending forever with us. You intended to use me as a vessel and your own fucking daughter as-," then Mommy stops talking.

At first, I think Daddy used her quiet hex on her. There is a shimmer at the door which means something bad tried to get in. My eyes go wide and I'm scared. My daddy couldn't be bad. Who is this man?

"You tried to ward me out," the man snarls. "That is not how you treat a guest."

The shimmering flickers out and the man steps forward into our apartment.

Viggo keeps making Mommy back up. He is still in front of her.

I don't know what to do. Mommy is scared, Viggo is growling, and the man who is bad is now in our living room. It's then I get the idea to be the hero. I make sure no one is looking at me and I scurry back into my room. to fish my little ivy plant off the windowsill. I pet it gently and then I run back to the door.

They have moved to the couch and are all sitting. I can't hear what they are saying, which means Mommy put a silence bubble up. Their lips are moving, but no sound is in the room.

I feel like I'm going to throw up, but I have to be brave for Mommy and Puppy Viggo. I peek over the edge of the couch, and I see the man is closest to me, but he is facing Mommy. I blow out and then I quickly whisper the Latin words for the trap spell.

Mommy told me to forget it, but I always remember the spells I learn. I watch as my little ivy plant snakes and curls, then is viciously wrapping around the gray grown-up pants. It squeezes and turns, but then something is wrong.

His hand flicks it away like a fly and suddenly my ivy is jumping off him and wrapping around me.

I scream in panic, thrashing to try and rip my ivy off. It's getting tighter and tighter. It hurts so much. I scream again and beg for Puppy Viggo to save me.

All the adults now shouting and there is a loud thud.

It's getting really hard to breathe.

Mommy's voice shrieks through the air and my ivy plant explodes in tiny sparks of flame, leaving me on the floor.

Next thing I know, Mommy is rocking me and holding me close. "Oh Lily. You brave fool. What were you thinking?" Mommy's petting me.

I cling to her. I peek out from her holding me and I get to see the bad man.

He looks scared and angry.

Puppy Viggo steps between us again.

"Just what have you been teaching her, Morrigan? Had I realized what a danger you were, I would have protected her better from you," the bad man says.

"She is your fucking daughter, Silar. I didn't teach her this. She snuck and learned it behind my back," Mommy growls.

"So, you are saying you are both incompetent and cannot keep track of your own daughter. What an important set of facts to let the judge know," the man crosses his arms and Viggo growls above us.

"You would send your own kin to burn at the stake?" Puppy Viggo snarls.

"No, I'm simply reclaiming my daughter from mutts like you," the man snaps back.

"NO!" I shriek and then try to fling myself onto Viggo's leg. Pain and Mommy's arms keep me from reaching him. "Not my Puppy!" I cry again.

The bad man sighs and narrows his eyes at us. His hand

glows. He was going to hurt Puppy Viggo. "Now that I know where you live, expect to hear from my lawyer." He then squats down and looks at me. "Soon, my darling, we will spend much more time together. I am looking forward to it." He reaches to touch my cheek and I bite at him. He clenches his jaw and then stands up, straightening his jacket. He gives Mommy a dirty look. "I see you have been allowing the mutt to teach her manners. This will be an easier matter than I thought. See you in court, dear wife." He leaves.

******

He really was Daddy and the judge that Viggo feared would burn us was just a scary old man that told Mommy that she was wrong for keeping me from Daddy. The first time I had to go with him, I took Specially. Even though I had not carried Specially for a while now, I needed all of Specially's powers.

Daddy didn't hurt me. He gave me a sad face when I told him he scared me and told me that Mommy sometimes gets confused because of all the magic she uses. He promised me he would help me with magic, and that I would never want for anything.

Mommy and Viggo did not like it and more than once I saw Viggo pacing around outside of Daddy's home in his wolf form.

I asked Daddy if Puppy Viggo could go with us in wolf form, and he refused. I reminded him he said I would not want for anything.

He agreed and then took me to the pound.

I was confused until I saw the puppies. I walked up and down the rows of cages. It makes me sad that they are all in cages. No wonder they are all so unhappy. Puppies need to run and feel the dirt. Viggo told me so.

We pass cage after cage, all with cute puppies in them. Their tails wag and they whine for my attention. I don't stop until we are standing in front of a big cage. Inside is a massive black dog. He growls and snarls. The pudgy lady with the clipboard tells Daddy he is on his last week and that he is not friendly at all.

"Puppy!" I point at him, looking at Daddy.

"Lily, maybe we should look at other puppies. Ones you can hold?" Daddy tries to sound gentle, but I was not budging.

"This is my puppy." I turn and stick my hand in the cage.

The dog barks and snarls at my hand, shifting his weight and trying to scare me. I'm not afraid of him. He is scared because he has been here a long time. "It's okay. I won't hurt you. Do you want scritches?" I make the scritchy hand at him.

"Little girl, get your hand out of the cage. He will bite you." The pudgy woman sounds really scared.

"Silence woman," I hear Daddy say and he is watching me.

The puppy growls and gets closer. Then he licks my hand.

I giggle because it tickles.

He comes forward fully and rubs himself against my hand.

I giggle again and scritch him all over. "Yup! He's the one. His name is…," I scrunch up my face in thought. The dog chuffs and I giggle again, "Really? That's your name?" He licks my hand. "His name is Nick."

"Nick?" The pudgy lady blinks. "No, honey. His name is Killer."

Nick whines, then chuffs again.

"No. That was what the bad man he ran away from called him. He isn't a killer. He's my puppy!" I challenge her.

"That settles it, we will take Nick," Daddy says. He reaches down to pet Nick.

Nick snarls at him.

Daddy leans down and narrows his eyes at Nick. "You bite me, and you will not like the consequences, dog."

This makes Nick whine. It took forever to get the pudgy lady to agree, but Nick walks alongside me to go to Daddy's house.

Visits with Daddy were the best. Every weekend I got to do all sorts of magic things. I learned new charms and spells. I learned how to tap into elemental magic. My daddy told me he came from a long line of royal warlocks. He taught me history, and about Mommy's coven, too. They are a special coven, descended from old gods. I told Mommy and Viggo all about it. I even told them about Nick.

Everything was perfect.

For four years, we lived in this nice pattern. I loved my life. I was getting used to everything. I was excited that Dad wanted me to learn more secret spells. He told me that as his daughter it was my responsibility to protect all the witches and warlocks in New York. He told me the story of his brother, who died at the hands of an evil warlock. Dad was in Boston at the time and unable to protect him. I promised him I would never let anyone die if I could protect them.

******

December 31, 2011

"Don't give me that look, Nick. You know I need to practice. Dad said so. Then we can go to my birthday party." I pout at him.

He whines low and tucks his tail. He doesn't like the spells my dad has me learning anymore. He doesn't even let Dad in the room without a growl while staying at my side. Nick has never liked Dad, but he always sticks close to me.

We both look at Sarah who is sitting on the bed in front of us. She is a witch in my dad's coven. She was really cool until a few days ago. That's when she started doing everything Dad told her to do.

She has the hots for Dad, and that's why she's being weird. "It's just a sleep spell. See? I say the words, I draw the symbol, she goes to sleep, then with a swipe to break the rune she wakes back up. Easy peasy."

Nick growls at me, and he walks over to Sarah. He puts his head in her hand, which makes me pause. Nick never lets anyone else touch him. It's weird.

She sits there quietly and her fingers pet him, but she looks like she is far away.

"Sarah, are you sure you're cool with this?" I ask for confirmation, as Nick is making me feel weird about practicing now.

"Yes, Lily," she replies in a dreamy, soft voice.

I look at Nick and he growls again, coming back over. He noses the spell book in my hands.

"I have read it a hundred times, Nick," I whine.

Nick looks sad then. His head droops and he rests his head on my thigh as I sit cross-legged on the floor.

I have a bad feeling about the whole thing, but I can hear my dad in my head scolding me for not doing as he asked. I really didn't want to miss my birthday party. Thunder booms outside and it makes me jump. "Okay, let's just get this over with. We'll put her to sleep, wake her up, and go to the party. I'll sneak you treats."

His tail wags slowly, but he doesn't lift his head.

I chant the spell. Enunciation is key, and I hit each syllable with perfection. The wind howls its warning, but I ignore it. I need to concentrate. I watch Sarah's eyes as she looks at me. I see tears forming and it causes me to pause before I stutter in the spell. Why is she crying over a sleep spell? My brow furrows, but I finish the spell like Dad wanted me to.

Sarah falls limp. It looks like she is asleep.

Nick leaps onto the bed. He never does that. He lays down next to Sarah and rests his head on her chest.

Thunderclaps rattles the walls, and the wind howls a banshee's wail. It's a cry of death. I draw the symbol with a shaky hand, and I stand up to confirm I put Sarah to sleep. I step forward and Sarah's breathing slow and steady. Her cheeks are flush with sleep. I look at Nick, who is acting weird. His tongue is lax out the side of his mouth. His chest isn't moving. Why is Nick not breathing?

"Nick?" I ask, worry in my voice.

No response.

"Nick." I cry louder and tears are forming in my eyes. I reach down and touch him. Nothing. No heartbeat, no warmth, no response to my touch. "Nick!" I shriek. I wrap my arm around the massive dog, and I fling my hand in the air before me. Mom had taught me to open a portal if I ever needed to come home fast. She said that if I ever felt unsafe, to come right home. I drag Nick into the portal.

We are pulled through the whoosh of time and space. My heart races. There's screaming. Then there is pain, so much pain. There is a crack, and I think lightning has struck my portal.

Nick falls limp on the floor of my bedroom. I collide with the rail of the fire escape outside my window and scream. I try to open the window to my room, and it throws me back against the rail. I scream again. I cry for Mom, for Viggo.

Both run into my room.

Viggo looks down at the dead dog on the floor in shock.

Mom looks at me on the fire escape as I try to get in again and am thrown back a third time. It is hard enough it makes me fall over the rail. Fear wells inside of me.

Viggo, in his wolf form, flying through the air to get to me.

I close my eyes and reach out for him, flailing. I feel fur, then I feel his arms around me as we hit the ground with me on top of him.

He sputters and coughs.

I can tell he is in pain, but he doesn't let me go.

"I got you, pup," his voice is raspy and strained, but his grip is firm around me. Tears are clinging to his lashes.

I'm sobbing. "Nick's dead. I killed Nick. I don't know how to fix it. I cast a sleep spell. Why is Nick dead? Mommy needs to undo it. Please." I'm beside myself when I look up to see my mom running toward us.

I try to reach for her, but Viggo's holding my arms down. "Mommy," I sob.

"It will be okay, Lily. I promise," mom assures me as she touches me.

I cry out in pain, and I the dark spots fill my vision. It's raining hard. As I fight going unconscious, my mother casts a spell. The words are faint and distant, but I feel like my very soul is being ripped from me.

Viggo coos softly to me. He promises he will protect me.

The dark shroud of unconsciousness envelopes me, and my last thoughts are about how today was supposed to be my special day. Instead, Viggo was hurt, Daddy's going to be furious, Mom's upset, and Nick is gone.

This is absolutely, without a doubt, the worst day ever.

homecoming

Viggo comes swaggering into the village with Morrigan a few steps behind him. He carries Lily over his shoulder, as if she's a sack of feed.

Her limp form hasn't moved since her mother warded her in New York.

Morrigan used a different spell to take them to whence he came.

His clothes were neatly folded and waiting for him where he left them. His eyes hold a twinkle, and his confidence is high. His brother will be relieved he has finally settled, and Luna will stop trying to thrust her forsaken she-wolves on him. He cannot help but smirk at the sight of Luna's face as they stroll into the village and to the common house. He leans closer to Morrigan and kisses her on the temple. "It will be alright." He murmurs.

"If not, they will all be toads," Morrigan quips, but her heart is heavy and she fears for Lily.

Lily's magic is strong, and Silar showed her so much more than Morrigan had imagined. The taint of the killing spell still hangs heavily on her. With time, the taint of dark magic would fade, but the emotional scar her daughter would hold is not something Morrigan could erase.

Morrigan wants nothing more than to find a warm and soft bed to curl into and sleep. She had abused so much magic in the past few hours that every step adds weight to her guilty conscience. The only solution she could see to protect Lily was to cut her off from her magic. Morrigan had done it in haste. She regrets the painful shattering of Lily's being, but if it saved her from a life of dark magic, then she would do it again in a heartbeat.

"Brother! What is this? You go hunting for supper and come back an old man with a," the Alpha's eyes turn and settle on Morrigan, a snarl on his lip, "witch."

Silence fills the common room.

Viggo gently lays Lily on the floor before stepping between his brother and his mate.

"And a devil witch," Luna growls as she moves to stand before Viggo.

His eyes dart from one to the other and he squares his shoulders, his hands loose at his sides. He is ready for a fight to protect Morrigan and Lily.

The common room grows tense and quiet when the Alpha descends from his raised table to face his brother. Viggo had told Morrigan he was younger by five years to the Alpha.

She looks between the two men and rolls her eyes at their posturing. What worries her is that Viggo now looks older than his brother. Her frown deepens as she realizes it has been seven years for Viggo, and only a few hours for his brother.

The Alpha looks aggressive as he approaches and Viggo's muscles twitch in anticipation.

From her position, she could see the bruising he took saving Lily's life when she fell from their apartment. He must have been in terrible pain the entire way back to his village. As tired as she was, she did not think when she reached her hand out to touch Viggo and heal his wounds.

Delicate fingers rest on his warm back, and he sucks in air through his teeth. The Alpha looks from his brother to the stunning woman next to him. He takes in her porcelain skin, her vibrant eyes, and hair that is dark with the tint of red. A slow inhale told him she is a Celt and powerful. His brows raise when her mouth moves, and then Viggo grunts and exhales. "She uses magic in the open."

"I do," Morrigan answers for herself.

Viggo stifles a chuckle.

His brother narrows his eyes at Viggo. "You let your woman speak for you?" He grunts and raises a brow.

"Mate," Viggo corrects his brother, and he turns then to pull Morrigan's collar aside. The three stars and crescent moon shine silver against her skin where he marked her.

There is an audible gasp in the common house.

Morrigan holds her breath. She silently prays to the Mother that Viggo will keep his promise to love and protect them.

The Alpha's laugh cuts through the air, and he clamps a hand on Viggo's shoulder.

"Come! My stud brother has found himself his mate! This is cause for celebration!" He pulls Viggo to him, as he guides him up to his table.

"What about the devil witch?" Luna's voice cuts over the new merriment.

"She is my pup," Viggo growls. "Brother, get your woman

in line."

The Alpha looks between Viggo and Luna. He holds his hand up to silence his mate, still looking at Viggo. "You have been hiding this mate for quite a while to have a pup that old." His tone turns accusatory.

"She is the pup of my mate, and I gave my word I would treat her as my own. Lily is not a devil's witch. If she is not welcome into the pack with me and my mate, then we shall take our leave after rest. They are mine and I expect them to be welcome as such," Viggo's eyes move to Luna and stare at her, intending to show his unspoken threat should she treat Lily unkindly.

Alpha erupts into laughter again. He has never seen his brother so serious, nor care for anyone enough to put his life on the line for them. Were he any other member of the pack, he would be dead for the implied threat to Luna.

"Rolf, take the girl to Viggo's room. Come Viggo, and Mate," Alpha says through his laughter. His mirth at the word mate marked in his tone, "let's-,"

"Morrigan. My name is Morrigan Ivarsen, daughter of Catarina Finley of the Ember Tree coven." She comes alongside Viggo and laces her fingers in his.

He smiles and kisses her temple with such tenderness that his brother smiles.

Alpha likes this woman, in spite of her talking out of turn today. She makes his brother act right. What makes him worry, though, is the strange clothing she is wearing. Where did his brother find a woman dressed in her shift with a daughter a season or two from mating herself.

Rolf makes his way forward without a word. He has not taken his eyes off of the unconscious girl on the floor. Viggo called her Lily and pup, but she is no wolf. The taint of death is surrounding her like a dark cloud, but there is something else about her that is innocent and pure. The magic that swirls around her is enough to cause anyone to take pause in approaching her, but Rolf cannot look away. He cannot stop himself from coming forward to touch her. Even with the gasp from Luna behind him, he squats and curls her into his arms.

Lily is no delicate flower. At twelve years old, she takes after her father's line and is tall, standing at five feet nine inches. Her shoulders are broad and she still holds the pudge of childhood. She and Rolf are the same size at present, even with her being four years his junior.

With a grunt, he gets to his feet, and he has to use the strength of his wolf to carry her from the room. His eyes stay fixated on her unconscious form.

She has porcelain skin, fiery red hair that hangs in an unraveling braid as they walk. Her breathing is steady and slow. Her cheeks flush from slumber. Her perfect dark pink lips are drawn into a pensive frown.

He wants nothing more than to pull her close and nuzzle her. Her scent, beyond the hint of death, smells sweet like mead, with the hint of wood smoke. His arms tremble with the effort of carrying her dead weight, and he is forced to set her on the furs that are Viggo's bed. Rolf dares to then lean closer and draw in her scent. He did not dare kiss her sweet lips or do anything unseemly that might make this magical moment end for him.

He knows in his heart she belongs to him. He has the overwhelming urge to protect her, to cherish her, and to make her his. His Luna will never approve, even if they are fated. She hates witches. He thinks she is too young to mate, anyway. The strange garments she wears, the odd scents smothering hers, and the overwhelming scent of death that envelopes the girl is enough to make him keep the knowledge of what she is to him to himself. He decides he will inquire with his uncle how old she is in the morning, and if she is still a pup he will wait. He leans forward then, to kiss her forehead and murmur a silent prayer to Freya to watch over her.

I hear mumbling in Viggo's language, but I don't understand it. Everything hurts and I'm hollow. I also feel like I'm going to vomit. The last thing I remember is Viggo catching me when I fell and then Mom touching my forehead. The smell surrounding me is comforting, a mix of pine and grapes. Then lips are on my forehead and my eyes fly open. It's not Viggo, or my mom. The boy staring back at me has the most piercing blue eyes.

Who is he? Where am I?

I scream.

My hand curls into a fist, like Viggo had shown me, and I swing it as hard as I can into his face. "Get off me!" I shriek at him. I then remember Nick. "No!" I wail, thinking that Mom and Viggo have sent me away for killing Nick. Where is my dad? Will he come save me? Why is this strange boy staring at me the same way Viggo stares at Mom? It's that weird smile Viggo always gives her, even when she's being mean to him.

VII

Not In Kansas Anymore

The strange boy holds his hands up to show me he gives up.

I keep my fists balled as I back myself into the corner. My eyes dart for any way out of this strange place. It smells awful here, stuffy, and old.

He moves and I growl at him to show how ferocious I'm. Viggo and Nick said that growling usually makes people hesitate.

Only, he stops and looks at me, and for a fleeting moment I believe it has worked. That's when he bowls over laughing. His voice sounds sweet to my ears, only I hear gibberish. He keeps laughing, which I take as him making fun of me.

I have to get out of here, so I do what any good witch would do, I fling my hands forward to send him tumbling and shout, "Redigo!" It means get back in Latin.

Nothing happens.

I look down at my hands in confusion as there was no glow, no connection to the Earth, nothing.

This gives the strange boy the opportunity to get closer and he pulls me against him.

I shriek and squirm to free myself, but he is really strong. "Let me go!" I push against his chest.

He says something that sounds soothing but is still speaking in a language I don't understand.

I punch him in the groin.

He lets out a yelp and releases me.

As soon as he lets go and doubles over, I run for it. I get out the door and let out a strangled squeak as I'm now in a room full of strange people dressed like cavemen. I don't think they own shirts.

There is a massive fire pit blazing in the center of the room.

I look left and right for a door, anything to get out of here before anyone notices me. My heart pounds in my chest. I have to get back to New York and my family. Maybe they have saved Nick. I let out another anguished cry at the thought of Nick and barrel for the door to my right. I slam into something akin to a wall and yelp as we go tumbling.

He looks as stunned as I that we are falling to the ground.

I scream at him wildly, hoping to scare him as I scramble off him to run.

Before I can get fully away, I feel myself being lifted off the ground by my shirt. His deep voice rumbles in gibberish as he shakes me at the crowd of cavemen.

I'm in full-on panic mode. It is to be carried back in or lose a shirt. I shoot my hands straight up in the air and drop to the ground with a thud. I look up to see the shocked face of my would-be captor then scramble to my feet and run. I don't look back. I just run as fast as my chucks will carry me. It doesn't matter that it's late in the evening in January and freezing cold out. I keep running. I run until my lungs feel like they are on fire, my nose and cheeks burn with my tears, and I can't shake the shivering cold I feel. I drop to my knees and sob.

I have one arm wrapped around myself as I rock and cry while I keep flinging out the other hand to call the portal spell to Mom's apartment. Not even a hint of magic comes to me, and it's making me cry harder. Then I feel soft fur leaning against my back. I freeze. Slowly, I turn my gaze to see what is touching me and am met with the piercing blue eyes of a wolf.

I scream and fling myself forward, hoping it won't eat me.

Its paw clamps down on my ankle.

"Please don't eat me!" I wail. "I just want to go home!" I ball up, to protect myself, and start shivering from the freezing cold.

The beast lets out a huff and then I feel the warm wet tongue lick my cheek.

"See, I don't taste good!"

The massive white wolf lays on me. It is hard to breathe but it is really warm. I have to admit the fur is soft and the weight on me makes me feel safer out here. Several minutes pass while I sniffle and cry underneath it, but I can't move.

Occasionally, the wolf leans down and nuzzles me.

He's trying to comfort me. I can't take it anymore and I squirm, "Get off me, you're heavy," I whine and squirm. The white wolf eases up but doesn't fully get off me. The shimmer of light as the wolf transforms into the strange boy causes my eyes to go wide. "I've been banished to werewolves?" Why would Mom and Viggo do this?

"Lily," the strange boy says as he points at me, but the rest of his sentence is lost on me.

"You know my name?" I gasp in question. "I don't understand you. Why can't I understand you?" I reach up to touch his forehead and say the spell for comprehension.

The strange boy gets a nervous look on his face as he watches me. Then he gets a goofy look on his face as he talks, but I still don't understand him.

I frown. "It doesn't work," and my lip quivers as I threaten to bawl again. "What's happened to my magic?"

"Lily," his voice is gentle as he says my name again and I whip my head up to look at him. He smiles and then talks to me in gibberish.

"I don't understand you," I slow-shout at him.

He furrows his brow at me and stops talking. He holds up a single finger. I nod, as if to confirm I understand he is saying wait. Then he stands and holds his hand out to me.

I look up to take his hand and get an eyeful of his glorious nakedness. My cheeks turn as red as a tomato, and I force myself to look at his face.

He looks confused for a moment, then looks down to where I was looking, then back at my face. A smirk forms on his lips, and I swear he makes it bounce as if to ask, 'Do you like what you see?'

I turn redder, if that's possible, and erupt into giggles as I look away. Before I can steal another glance, I feel the cold wet nose against my cheek.

He, in his wolf form, nudges me toward the way he came from.

I shake my head no.

He gives a whine and I let out an exasperated breath. He sits and motions with his head again.

I realize he is treating me like Nick did, and it makes me cry again. A sharp pain stabs me in the chest when I think about Nick.

He whines and then comes closer to nuzzle me.

"I'm sorry. I lost my dog. I didn't mean to hurt anyone. I was just practicing and Nick... Oh, Nick. He's gone!" The harder I cry the more he tries to lick my tears away until I'm squealing in a mix of frustration and laughter.

He wags his tail at me.

"LILY!" Viggo's voice in the distance causes me to whip my head up.

"Viggo!" I gasp.

The white wolf wags his tail and tries to nudge me in that direction.

"Lily! Say something so I know you're alright." Viggo calls again, getting closer.

The wolf next to me lets out a howl, and it makes me jump.

"I'm here! Puppy Viggo! I'm here!" I push to my feet and instantly regret it, as it's cold and I'm no longer encircled in the white wolf's warmth. As if the howl propelled Viggo forward, he appeared in the clearing. He looks frantic and angry all at once. He snarls and pulls me right behind him to put himself between me and the white wolf.

"No! Don't hurt him. He kept me warm." I defend him.

"And what else did he do with you, Lily? Where is your shirt?" Viggo growls at me, then switches to address the white wolf in his language.

The white wolf whines up at Viggo and tucks his tail.

"Why can't I understand you anymore?" I pout at Viggo's back.

This was enough to make Viggo pause and turn to look at me. "What did you say?" Viggo's face is drawn into a frown as he switches back to English.

"I can't understand you anymore. Something bad has

happened, Viggo. I can't use magic. Where are we? Where is Mom? Where is Dad? Did you save Nick?" I rapid-fire questions at Viggo.

The strange boy transforms and grumbles behind Viggo.

Whatever the strange boy said made Viggo go stiff, his eyes wide as he looks down at me.

Witches and Wolves

"What? What is it? We didn't do anything. Puppy Viggo! I don't even know his name! Why are you looking at me like that?" I talk more when I get nervous. Viggo is acting weird and I look him over. He's dressed in renaissance fair clothing and looks like he could easily swing an axe or sword, versus the chill stepdad that eats Lucky Charms with me.

He inhales deeply, which tells me he is trying to pick up the scents on me. "His name is Rolf. He is my nephew." Viggo then turns his back to me and looks at the boy he named Rolf.

I'm not sure why Viggo sounds like something is really wrong. Is Rolf bad? He has been nice to me so far. I creep closer to peek around Viggo but stay near him.

He switches back to his own language.

"Do not tell Luna. It will not go well. Your father has not fully accepted my mate and her pup."

I struggle, trying to figure out what they are saying as Viggo jerks his head toward me.

"That is not fair, Uncle. She is my mate. I deserve the blessings of Mani and Freya. Not even my father can deny me that." Rolf looks angry and sad all at once when he replies to Viggo.

"Puppy Viggo, don't be mean to him. He was nice to me. He was keeping me warm since that other guy stole my shirt." I sulk a little, and my teeth chatter more, forcing me to hug my arms around myself.

Viggo, without looking at me, shrugs out of his furs and hands them to me.

I quickly burrito myself in them before they lose all their warmth.

"I am not being mean," he says in English. "He is the son of the Alpha. He will have responsibilities and duties to the clan. He cannot be distracted by anything, and Luna will not take kindly to him playing with you. I am trying to protect you both." He then looks at Rolf and growls something at him in his language.

Rolf sulks. His face draws into a frown and I instantly feel guilty. I must have done something terrible for him to look so glum.

"Fine," Rolf whines. He then turns abruptly and shifts as he runs off from the clearing.

I don't need to understand what they are saying to see that Rolf didn't like it.

Viggo then turns to me and takes me by the forearm as he leads me back in the direction I ran from.

My legs are tired and I feel like a frozen pudding pop as we reach the building I ran out of. I light up though, as my mom is pacing with my shirt in her hand. "Mom!" I run forward and fling myself into her open arms.

She envelopes me into a tight hug and kisses my forehead.

Viggo comes up and smiles at Mom.

"She was not far. Rolf was protecting her." He says it in English. *"We have a small problem,"* he says in his language and I narrow my eyes.

"Hey, no gibberish. I can't understand it." I whine up at them.

My mother thrusts my shirt into my hands and I pull it on, grateful to not be in just a bra and leggings. I get a better look at my mom.

She is dressed in weird clothes, too. A simple dress that laces, and a belt to hold it in place. I frown and look away from both of them. Not caring that they are still arguing in Viggo's language.

I had been in such a hurry to run away I hadn't bothered to look at everything.

The man I plowed into approaches with a broad grin. *"I see you found your pup, Beta Viggo."* He smiles at me, *"What is your name, pup?"*

"He wants to know your name," Viggo says to me in English.

I give Mom a look before answering, to make sure it is okay. "I am Lily Finley, daughter of Morrigan Ivarsen, member of the Ember Tree coven."

The man's face holds some bemusement. *"You speak in a strange tongue,* Lily Finley. *What is your clan name?"*

Viggo answers for me. *"Ivarsen. She is my pup,"* he growls.

Did he just tell this guy I was his kid? He is not my dad.

"Come Lily, we need to get you different clothes and you must speak with Alpha before anything else happens." My mom puts a hand on my shoulder and guides me back into the building.

A few minutes later I'm stripping out of my clothes, bra and panties included, and changing into the clothes laid on the bed I woke up on. The first piece of clothing is a night-gown looking thing. It's soft and smells good, not like the stinky detergent we use at home. Then the other dress that goes over it. A long-braided cord of leather wraps around my waist tying the apron of a dress in place over the nightgown dress. I'm then given stockings. They are heavy and made of wool. They look scratchy, but I find comfort in the soft warmth as Mom helps me pull them on and tie little cords just below my knees to keep them up.

She sets a pair of leather shoes on the ground.

"I want to wear my chucks," I pout.

"You can't. We have to get rid of everything from our time, Lily." Mom's voice is soft and sounds sad.

"WHAT?!" I explode in preteen angst. "What do you mean I can't keep any of it? I have to dress like this. No. Nuh-uh. I want to go home. I want Nick. I want Daddy." I fling myself onto the furs in dramatic fashion.

"Lily," Mom sounds like she is about to cry. I have never heard her like that.

"No! I hate it here. You can't make me stay! I want to go home! I want Nick! I want Daddy!"

"Nick is dead," Mom whispers it out just loud enough for me to hear it.

"Nick's dead?! Why didn't you save him?!" I sob into my arm, and I feel her hand on my back to comfort me. "No. I don't believe you! You just left him there. You did this! Did you steal my magic too? Just like Daddy said you would. He said you were unstable and turned dark. Is that why you brought me here? So, he can't protect me?" I fling all the hate and vitriol I can at my mom.

"Lily Marigold Finley," my mother bellows at me in such a terrifying tone it makes all my dramatics stop.

My eyes widen as I look at her and for the first time, I can only see anger staring back at me. No wisps of the ley lines that always encircle her, no hints of nature, just angry eyes blazing right into my soul.

I bite my lower lip in fear.

"You want to know why we cannot go back?" My mom's voice is low and menacing. It makes me shy away from her. Tears cling to my lashes, and my mother stands to her full height, her jaw clenching as she does not voice whatever dark thought crossed her mind.

"Your father," said through gritted teeth, "tricked you into casting a killing spell, Lily. He tried to taint your soul with black magic. Nick saved your soul by taking the dark magic in your place. There is no saving the life of the martyr. All magic has a price. He paid the price with his own soul to prevent yours from being marred forever."

My mother's words spew like venom at me. I shake my head no in disbelief.

"And while the taint from Nick's death still lingers, you are warded from using your magic. You cannot use it, and any spells you have cast are over. This is your home now. I suggest you learn to love it, because there is no going back, my precious daughter. Now get your shoes on and follow me. Viggo's brother wants to speak with you." My mother turns and slams the door behind her.

I don't move at first. I wanted to curl up and go back to sleep. Mom had never been mean to me on a level like this. She had never said anything bad about Daddy before. She just said they could not agree on how to use magic and no longer loved each other. I look down at my hands. Had I done this? Was it all my fault when I cast that spell? It was an accident. It was a sleep spell. Tears roll down my cheeks as I stare at my hands. My best friend was dead and now my magic is gone.

Mom doesn't lie. She tells the truth as it is needed and only how it is needed.

My Dad was so nice to me. He taught me all these cool things. He told me he would keep me safe, and that it was critical for me to harness my full potential. He told me that my birth was foretold by prophecy, born at the turn of the millennium to bridge the gap of disharmony in magic.

I stood then and trudged out of the room in silence. My hair wisps like flames as I walk, fraying out of the braid, but I don't care. I look at the floor, trying to hide all the tears that won't stop. My twelfth birthday is turning out to be the worst ever.

Mom and Viggo say nothing to me as they escort me to another room. This room is large and warm. The fire crackles off to the side and Alpha, as they call him, is sitting casually in a chair. His brows raise as the three of us enter. *"I said I wanted to speak with her alone,"* this man growls at Viggo. I don't look up. I hug myself and try to stop the silent tears.

"Stand up straight, Lily," Mom whispers to me. "Don't let them see you afraid. Be brave, my sweet flower." Her tone is soft and all the angry words she flung at me minutes ago are gone. She steps forward, *"Alpha, I need to perform magic on you for you to understand and talk with her. She does not know your tongue."*

Whatever she says to him makes the imposing man raise his brows in fear. His response is a mere grunt. It's then I notice how much he looks like Viggo, when Viggo shows his fear of magic. I lift my gaze enough to see Alpha nod, then he gets this weird smirk as Mom steps between his legs to touch his forehead.

Viggo lets out a menacing growl.

"Calm down, brother. As beautiful as your witch is, I have no desire to bed her," the other man says.

I giggle at Viggo's snort in response.

When Mom steps away from Alpha, he looks up at her in question and she motions to me.

"Do you understand me, pup?"

My eyes light up and I look at my mom.

"Good, now the two of you get out." His voice sounds heavy and bossy to me.

Much to my surprise both of them leave without question.

"Sit down, pup."

"Lily. My name is Lily, not pup." I sit in the chair across from him and put my hands in my lap. Sitting up as straight as I can to not show fear to him. The longer he takes to say anything else, the more nervous I get. My shoulders start to droop. I start to fidget. I bite my lip and I look all around, not wanting to see his piercing gaze. It's like he was looking right into my soul.

"Look at me, Lily. I have some serious questions for you. Answer me truthfully. If you lie to me, you will not like the consequences." His voice sounds gentle, but the threat causes my chest to tighten in fear.

"Yes, sir." I swallow hard and I look right at him and hope he doesn't think I'm a liar.

"Are you a witch?" he asks.

"Yes. I'm a member of the Ember Tree coven."

"Tell me what happened that makes Hel kiss your essence." He leans back in his chair and rests his head on his chin.

At first, I don't respond. What is he talking about? Then I say, "Nobody's kissed me. Ew."

This makes him laugh, and he shakes his head. "You stink of death. The Goddess Hel has put her essence all around you. Do you not follow the Gods?"

"Huh? Gods? The only God anyone talks about in New York is the weirdo one that killed his son and everyone but the animals on the boat." I give him a weird look.

"Tell me what brought you here," he clarifies.

"My dad taught me a new sleep spell. We practiced it three times. All three times Michael went to sleep and then woke right back up. Daddy told me to take the spell and go practice it on Sarah. That it would be easier on her cause she was already tired from getting my birthday party ready. Then Nick was weird. He didn't want me to practice. He even tried to shred the spell up with his paws, but Daddy's spells have a ward on them, so they won't get destroyed. That may have been my fault. It's why we don't drink Kool-Aid near the grimoires. Sarah was being weird, too. I got her permission, and then I did the spell. She went right to sleep. Only… then… then Nick touched her and Nick…" I burst into tears again, bringing my hands to my face.

"It's alright, Lily. Take a deep breath. You must have loved this Nick very much. He does not blame you." Alpha's voice is gentle and grumbly. It reminds me of a bear, and it's just like Viggo's voice when he is trying to make me feel better. "Can you still perform magic?" I droop again and shake my head no. "Look at me when you answer," he reminds me.

I look up, "No, sir. Mom warded me and told me I could not have it back until the taint was gone." This makes both of his brows rise. His glance shifts to the door and then back to me. I look scared. "Please don't get mad at Mom. If she did it, she had a good reason. My mom is one of the most powerful white witches in all of New York."

He chuckles at me. "You are a sweet pup, Lily. I am concerned with how much power your mother wields. What happens when she gets mad? Will she unleash your dark magic on my pack?"

My eyes go wide, "D… Dark Magic? Oh no! I don't practice Dark Magic. I'm a white witch. I'm a member of the Ember

Tree coven. It is banishment and being stripped of all power forever for witches who turn dark."

"And you said your mother has taken your magic?" He raises a brow at me.

"She warded me. Wards are protection, not punishment," I recite to him. "I feel sick to my stomach to think I killed Nick. He was my best friend, and he protected me from everything when I was at my dad's house. If I could go back and undo what I have done, I would. I would have listened to Nick when he acted weird." I hiccup a little, and I find some comfort in my own words.

Mom had only warded me. She hadn't banished my magic. It means it will still grow with me, and I will someday be able to use it again.

I wipe the tears from my cheeks and look at Alpha again, "My grandma would say, what has been cast has been cast. To undo it now would destroy who I'm meant to be. So, I guess, I have to accept my fate and hope that nothing happens to us here." I suck against my lower lip again and look at him.

His brows raise as I'm talking. Adults always get these scrunched up faces when they think about decisions. He doesn't say anything for some time, and I'm worried he is going to do something bad. Then he sighs and slouches in his chair. He looks just like Viggo when I force him to watch cartoons with me. "My son is taken with you." He grins then. "I see why. You are a lovely young woman. Healthy, strong, and tall. I have ever seen a woman as tall as you. How old are you, Lily?"

My cheeks turn pink in shyness. I don't like how he is talking to me. "I'm twelve and boys are gross. Tell your son he better stay away from me or I will sock him." I brandish a fist.

Alpha laughs a hard belly laugh that is loud, and I can't

help but smile at his mirth. "Oh, sweet girl," he says as he wipes tears from his eyes. "I see why he is taken with you." He sits up again and bellows, "You can come back in."

Seconds later, Viggo and Mom are with me.

Alpha stands and comes to face Viggo. "You take responsibility for their actions, brother?"

"I do," Viggo says without hesitation and looks at me, giving me a wink.

"One step out of line or any hint of dark magic and I will kill them both." His voice is threatening. "They will take the oath at the next moon. Whatever strange place this New York is, I do not want to hear of it from anyone else in the pack. They have come from the Isles, and you rescued them from Hagor's clan."

"Yes, brother." Viggo says. He grins as he leads us out of the room.

Teach Me

I hate it here. I have been sitting on this log for at least an hour as my mother struggles with the fire in front of us. I keep the furs I have stolen from Viggo wrapped around me and my knees pulled up without offering to help. My eyes are daggers as they stare at her. My toes are frozen and I'm hungry.

It's just before dawn, and every morning since we got here, my mother has insisted we come to this clearing with its fire pit as she tries to commune with nature. She makes me come, even though I can't feel the magic anymore. She does her stupid silence trick whenever I start to protest.

Like clockwork, Rolf appears with a goofy smile on his face and two bowls of hot oats mixed with honey and berries. It's different from oatmeal back home, but it tastes good and keeps me warm.

As hard as I try to hate everything here, I don't hate Rolf.

We have said little other than our names to each other, and I have learned that he calls me his little flower. I have to admit it makes the butterflies in my stomach flutter. He is older, and probably has a girlfriend, but his pretty blue eyes are always kind when they look at me. I can't help but smile back at him.

Today he gives me a broad grin. As soon as I have finished my warm breakfast, he sets the bowls aside. "Come," he says and motions for me to follow him.

"Come," I say in reply and take a step toward him.

He nods enthusiastically and takes my hand, dragging me off into the woods.

I have to clasp my other hand tight to keep the fur around me as he pulls me further away from the clearing. I turn my gaze back to see if my mother is staring angrily at us.

She has not moved from her spot, and there is a smile on her face. It is like she has a secret I don't know. I'm forced to look back at Rolf as he drags me deeper into the forest.

He leads me along for what feels like an eternity.

Little puffs of steam erupt into the cold morning air as I huff along behind him.

"Rolf," I whine after several minutes. He stops and looks at me with concern. I know he is checking me over for any injuries, but I shake my head and hold up a single finger. "I need a minute," I say in English.

"I need a minute," he parrots me, but he doesn't understand what I said.

My mother was stubborn and as part of my punishment she is forcing me to learn the language naturally.

Viggo stuck up for me and said she should learn it, too.

She didn't remove her spell from herself.

"I love how your hair shines in the sun," Rolf says to me. He has that dopey look again.

He speaks in his tongue on purpose because he knows I

will sock him again, like I did when Viggo translated for me before. Then he steps closer. Too close.

Blushing bright red, I fidget and bite my lower lip. I swear I just heard him growl, but not in a scary way. It's a slow and comforting sound, like a sweet rumble from his chest.

We do not need words for that.

"Pretty," he says in English.

I giggle then and put my hand on his chest. Even though we are the same size, I feel small and delicate before him. His shoulders are broader, and he definitely has more muscles. I don't understand the feelings I have right now. Maybe it's because he is the only one who is nice to me besides Viggo and Mom.

Rolf's mom hates me and because she does, so do all the other women.

They spit at the ground when I walk by. They mutter things I don't understand, but I'm not dumb. I have an excellent memory, and I have been meaning to ask Rolf what things mean.

"Teach me," I say, and he nods.

We established this broken way of asking for him to translate.

"Hel's whore." I repeat the phrase to him. Whatever it was I said is bad.

Rolf's face transforms into pure fury. His eyes shift to an inky black and I see his fangs elongate as white fur starts to sprout on his skin.

"Who?"

I bite my lip, not wanting to get anyone in trouble. It would only make them hate me more. I suddenly don't want to know what they said, and I shake my head no.

"Lily," his voice is still animalistic in its growl. "Tell me." He demands.

He scares me with the way he fluctuates between wolf and man.

"No." I shake my head again. "Show me," I say in English, pointing to my eyes. Then I motion my hand around to change the subject back to whatever he dragged me out here for.

His eyes narrow and several deep breaths later, he is back to just the boy again. He then takes my hand and his thumb trails along the back of it. I smile and we begin forward again. It isn't long before we are in a tiny opening of some thick bushes and we are squatting down. Rolf takes his furs off and leaves them next to me.

I raise a brow at him and then cover my eyes as he is taking his clothes off. Why is he getting naked? My mom is going to kill him! She made it painfully clear to Alpha and everyone else that I could not mate until my taint had been expunged and that would take until my eighteenth year.

Rolf looked devastated at the news that I was not considered an available match for another six years.

Viggo tattled that Rolf had whined and wailed about how all the girls in the pack are well on to their second child by that age.

I roll my eyes behind my hand and turn to walk back when I see why he is getting naked, and it has nothing to do with me. My eyes widen and my heart pounds in my chest when I lower my hand and I see the beautiful doe just off the path.

"RUN, Bambi's mom! Run!" I burst through the bushes and wave my hands like a crazy person, but it works. I spook the doe into turning and fleeing without a second thought. I did not, however, see the buck off to the side who is now chuffing and hoofing the ground. I feel like I'm moving in water as I hear the angry noises. My eyes meet the buck's.

His antlers curve into the sky with the malicious promise

of death. He bounds forward, dropping his head, intent on impaling me to protect his doe.

I scream and turn to run, tripping over my furs and skirt. My eyes close tight and I bring my hands over my head, hoping I survive the injuries, and Rolf can get me to my mother.

Nothing happens to me.

My ears ring and I feel like vomiting. Every muscle in my body has clenched. I open my eyes right at the moment Rolf snarls and sinks his fangs into the buck's throat.

He had transformed into his wolf. His beautiful white fur is splattered in blood. His head tears up and he flings the gore aside.

The buck crumples immediately and twitches. The magnificent beast's eyes lose the sheen of life as he stares blankly at me. Steam rises from the pool of blood as it leaves his throat.

"Lily. Look." Rolf's voice pierces my ringing fog.

I cannot look away from the stunned look of the buck.

Rolf's fingers take my chin and turn them to face him. His chin and front are covered in blood.

I vomit. This makes me blush and tears form in my eyes. Great, I'm gross and puking in front of the prettiest boy I have ever met. I groan as I spit to clear my mouth.

"Lily," his voice is thick with concern.

"I'm fine. I… I… You killed Bambi's Dad." I'm speaking in English, and not clearly.

Rolf huffs like he always does when he's frustrated at the lack of understanding me.

I point to the deer and cry harder.

His face has nothing but confusion on it. It's then I remember he's naked, squatting in front me. "ROLF!" I squeal and turn a dark crimson. I cover my eyes and push him back.

His laugh is rich and booming as he moves away from me.

"Clothes," he says in English.

I know he means dressed and I uncover my eyes.

He is only half dressed, but he has scooped up the buck to fling it over his shoulders. He motions to his furs and shirt on the ground. I get up and gather his things, and we make the trek back to the village.

When we step into the square where several of Rolf's friends, his father, and Viggo are chatting. Rolf gives me a wolfish grin.

I know that grin. He's about to do something that's going to get a lot of attention. He enjoys bringing attention to the two of us.

Mom and the other women take pause in their argument over a garden plot to look at us.

I hate having all eyes on us and I shake my head no at him.

His grin gets bigger. He drops the buck on the ground at my feet, taking a knee before me, with his head bowed. "I present you my kill, my flower."

There is an audible gasp.

I don't know what he said, or what he is doing. I look from him to Alpha, to Viggo, and finally to the murderous gaze of Luna.

"He has gifted you his kill, Lily," Viggo says.

My heart hammers in my chest and I don't know what to do, or how to act. Why would he give me something so gross?

"You accept, or reject, it. It is a sign that he chooses you, Lily. He wants everyone to know he will provide for you."

The hate-filled gazes of the surrounding women, and the curious anticipation of everyone burns through me like a wildfire. I nod my head. I don't know the words used to accept verbally.

His breathing is labored and I can tell he fears what I might say or do. He cannot hear my brain rattle as I nod like a fool in front of him. His head snaps up and his blue eyes meet mine when I touch him.

I'm furious with him for embarrassing me like this. I also feel like the whole universe is right with him showing everyone he would do this for me. I don't want to hurt my only friend in this place. I nod again and try to put a smile on my face.

Luna storms toward us and my eyes widen.

Rolf is up in an instant and turns to face her, putting himself between us.

"No!" She barks at him. "You will not do this with Hel's-."

Rolf and Viggo sound like twin engines rumbling in anger as growls rip from their throats.

My mother gasps and covers her mouth.

"Anyone who calls my Lily Hel's whore again will answer to me." Rolf's voice carries across the village.

I'm filled with a sense of dread, like I just gained the best gift ever and lost it within seconds.

By the Pale Moonlight

From the moment Rolf dropped that deer at my feet I could feel the hate rolling off of Luna. I don't understand why she hates me so much. I'm just a kid and she is a queen, or something. I don't want to be here either. If she could send me home, I would go in a heartbeat.

Viggo saves me from her wrath. He steps forward and scoops up the buck onto his shoulders. "Come, Lily. I will show you how to accept Rolf's gift." His voice is gentle and there's amusement in his eyes.

I follow, and we make our way to the butchering area. It's gross. Blood and bits of guts mixed with flies makes me gag. "You want me to do what?" I stare at him wide-eyed with the knife in my hand, mortified I'm being forced to butcher a deer. I cry the entire time. By the time we were done, I'm covered in blood, guts, and who knows what. My arms hurt from tearing through flesh and ripping skin apart.

Viggo tries to comfort me by reminding me that this is the only way to get food here. That they don't kill for sport, and it's a great honor that Rolf laid his kill at my feet.

It doesn't help.

"Lily pup, Rolf believes you are his mate." He takes the knife from me as I stare numbly at the butchered deer. Then he turns me toward the river to wash the gore off the two of us.

"What? I'm a kid. I can't be a mate. Gross. Is it like when you got all weird with Mom? Is he going to pee on my leg or something?"

Viggo laughs hard and shakes his head as we approach the river. "Oh, Lily pup. You are a funny girl. It means that he believes the Gods Mani and Freya, have paired your souls together. He will wait until you are ready since your mother tricked them into thinking you will be tainted until you are eighteen." He winks at me.

"Oh. That explains all that. I thought she was crazy when she said it. Wards usually wear off pretty quick."

Viggo veers to the left and guides me down a path along the river until we come to a little pool with an area where we can walk into the water. The women come down here periodically to do laundry and to bathe.

"Go on, I will keep watch to make sure you have privacy." I eye the water and then him. It'll be freezing cold. I step out of my shoes and stockings, not wanting to get them wet, then I slip the leather apron off. He takes it from me and holds it as he turns his back. I don't remove the underdress as I wade into the water. I ring and rub the dress as I start to shiver in the water, my teeth chattering and my skin taking on a bluish tinge.

"Viggo! She'll get hypothermia. Honestly, do you even bother to

think about the fact she is not a wolf?" My mother chastises him.

"How else do you expect her to clean herself, Morrigan? She is covered in viscera." Viggo sounds defensive.

I try to ignore them as I scrub harder, but my clothes won't come clean.

"Get out of the water, Lily. By the Mother, I swear if Luna doesn't kill you, Viggo will." She sighs as I come out of the water looking like a drowned leaf. She gives Viggo a dark look and then she steps forward. She touches my forehead and I feel pain as the magic smacks against the ward on my person.

There is a haze of steam rising from my clothes and the surrounding air heats enough to flush my cheeks. Bloody droplets waft into the air, like a child had run around me with a demented bubble wand. When they float far enough away, they fall to the ground in little splats.

While my dress has been cleaned and dried, the magic can't actually touch me. The aching hole in my chest makes me whimper.

Mom steps around me and helps me undo my braid and ring out my hair, then braid it again.

I still shiver and hug myself as I watch her move to the over tunic of my dress and repeat the process, drawing out the blood and leaving it clean. I slip it back on and tie it in place, followed by my stockings and shoes.

Mom looks at me with a sad smile, but she pulls me into a tight hug and drapes her furs over me as we walk back up to the common house.

Shortly after, Mom and Viggo are summoned to Alpha's room.

Rolf appears after I'm by myself and motions for me to follow him. His fingers lace into mine as he drags me through the common house until we are tucked near his father's room.

There's a lot of shouting and growling going on in the room. I can't even pretend to understand what they're saying. It's too muffled, and they were talking too fast.

Rolf grimaces while he keeps his pretty blue eyes locked on me. "Come." He takes my hand again and leads me away again. He drapes his furs around my shoulders when we step outside.

It's snowing and I hold my hand up, letting the delicate snowflakes kiss my palm and melt away.

Rolf smiles as he leads me into the woods. His hand never leaves mine, and he strolls casually with no furs on, showing off how he is not affected by the weather.

Viggo had spent the afternoon explaining Rolf's behavior to me, and now I'm a little scared. I like Rolf. He's the only one who has been nice to me since I woke up in this weird place. I can't even imagine what it means to be someone's mate. I haven't even been kissed. I don't count Steve Baker in kindergarten. That was gross, and he only did it to get a gummy worm from Nathan Kese.

I'm lost in my thoughts as I follow Rolf, realizing too late that I have no idea how to get back if he leaves me here. I frown at the thought and miss my cell phone. Stupid time travel.

"Lily." The way Rolf says my name makes me smile as I face him.

We are in a small clearing cast in the silvery light of the moon.

"Rolf," I say with a smile.

He chuckles and pulls me closer.

I bite against my lower lip and then release it.

He is too close, but he smells so good. His eyes trail down to my lips, and his free hand comes up to cup my cheek.

I stiffen and my eyes go wide. I know that look. Viggo gets

that look when he looks at Mom. It's the wolfy, 'I'm going to do gross things to you when Lily's not looking' look. I hold my breath and close my eyes tight. I don't know what to do here. I want him to kiss me, and the idea of his tongue in my mouth is gross at the same time.

His lips tenderly press against mine. They are soft and taste of mead. I relax and his lips press firmer. His tongue never touches me, thank the Mother. I pout when he pulls away. Why am I pouting? It was my first kiss. It's wonderful! All the tiny little explosions are radiating down my body. I feel warm all over and I want him to do it again.

When I finally dare to open my eyes, he is smiling at me. Not smirking but smiling. It's the most beautiful thing I have ever seen.

"Mine," he says in English.

Of course, he has to ruin it. What does that even mean, mine? He doesn't own me. I roll my eyes and push him back a little. "Free," I point at myself and say it with venom.

"Mine," he says with a growl and a hurt look on his face.

This confuses me. Why is he hurt? He is the one being a stupid, pigheaded, gross, good kissing boy.

"Free," I shout at him. "Not slave," I stomp my foot.

He looks even more confused then. "No. Not a slave. Mate." He points to his chest, where his heart is.

I narrow my eyes at him and then sigh, realizing where the disconnect is.

He frowns.

I don't understand all these feelings welling inside of me, but this is the moment I believe I'm going to watch him walk away forever.

When he lets go of my hand and turns to walk away, his shoulders are slumped and I panic.

"Wait, don't go," I frantically move forward to take his

hand, trip over these stupid skirts, sending me right into his arms. The momentum is enough to send us to the ground. I end up on top of him.

He gives me a lopsided grin, wrapping his arms around me.

The butterflies kick into overdrive. I want him to keep holding me and never let go. I sigh heavily and let myself relax into him, resting my head on his chest.

The soft growl that emits from him says he likes this.

My cheeks flush pink and I know I should get off of him, but I want to stay right here in his arms. He confuses me and makes me feel pretty.

"Teach me," he says after several minutes and then he is easing me off of him, so I'm laying on his furs on the ground next to him. He rolls up onto his side and I nod. He turns a faint shade of pink. He takes my hand and puts it on his chest, where his heart is.

"Heart?" I ask. He shakes his head no and lets out a huff. Then he puts his hand on my chest. If I didn't know Rolf, I would have punched him square in the jaw. His hand rests above my budding breasts while his other hand kept mine on his. I scrunch my face up and think about what Viggo told me about mates earlier.

He hadn't told me about the word in their language, and I forgot to ask him. He's typically good about teaching me words.

"Viggo and Morrigan are mates. Like husband and wife?" I sigh and I hate my mom all over again for not charming Rolf with understanding. I then get an idea. I wriggle my hand free of his and then I jab him in the chest. *Mine,* I say in his language.

He nods enthusiastically.

Comprehension washes over me. He is asking to be my

boyfriend, not my master.

"Mine," he repeats the jab to my chest, and I gasp at how much it hurts.

"Boyfriend," I jab him in the chest.

"Boyfriend," he jabs me and it makes me laugh. I shake my head no.

"Girlfriend," I point at myself. "Boyfriend," I point to him. "Mates." I motion between us.

"Mates," he says in English. Then he repeats, *"Mates,"* in his language. He motions between us.

"Mates," I reply in his language, and nod in confirmation.

He pulls me into another kiss, his lips firm against mine and demanding. Then he does the grossest thing ever. He slips his tongue into my mouth.

And I like it. I even try to touch his tongue with mine.

When we break apart from the kiss, we are flush-cheeked and breathing hard.

I never want this moment to end. I try to memorize how the snowflakes sprinkle into his dark hair, and the way he smiles at me.

He pulls his necklace over his head and slips it over mine. The pendant with his family's crest hangs heavy between my breasts and he stands, helping me up. *"Lily, I will always be yours. I will forever protect you. Provide for you. Not even the Gods could keep me from loving you."*

I don't know what he said, but I strive to remember every word. It sounds beautiful and I will repeat it to Viggo later. "Rolf," I murmur, not sure what to say, or do.

He leans up and kisses my forehead.

We head back and are greeted by Viggo and Alpha. They look furious and I shy a little.

Rolf puts his arm around me and eases me closer. "Safe," he whispers in my ear when we get close.

He looks between us, inhales, and then smirks. "Give Rolf back his furs and get to bed. Your mother is looking for you."

I don't argue as I slip Rolf's furs from my shoulders and hand it to him. His fingers brush against mine and I blush before trotting into the house around Viggo and Alpha. I linger just inside the door and I watch Rolf's face.

Whatever the two men say to him makes him look as though he has been kicked in his junk. Then fury washes over him. He growls up at Alpha.

I hold my breath and for the first time in my life I hear Alpha sound like a monster. His words are harsh and commanding. It makes me want to pee myself at how scary he sounds.

Rolf buckles. He does the weird thing where his head lowers and he turns to show his neck to Alpha. It crushes me to see him look like that.

Whatever has happened is because of me. I'm beginning to think I'm a curse and I should just run away for good.

Absence Makes the Heart Grow Fonder

The next morning, I stood next to Viggo and Mom, watching the warriors ship off to who knows where.

Rolf among them.

Luna and Alpha kept him from talking to us before they shipped off, but Rolf and I had a secret language. It has been the only way to truly communicate with each other.

He pointed to his chest and mouthed the word *"Mine"*.

I blushed and repeated the action, and that seemed to be enough.

Our secret promise reaffirmed, and his sad blue eyes bloom into a smile.

I couldn't wait for him to get back. I had not realized he would be gone for two years.

Two years of long torture.

Luna took a shine to me, but not in any way I wanted. She

took it upon herself to become my teacher.

Nothing I did was right. My mending was crooked and needed to be fixed. My ability to spin yarn, horrible. Then she caught me writing. Given it was with a stick in ashes, and it was me signing my name with Rolf's in English.

She brought down her wrath upon me.

It became consensus that I was touched by Hel, and that the goddess was cursing the entire village with my presence. I could not write around them anymore. When I tried to join the conversation, I was ignored, or spit at. Talk about the grossest thing ever. I can only take so much of this abuse.

Mom told me to stand up to Luna, but to show respect, as she is the leader. She said the others would see the truth and would treat me better.

My mom is a horrible, selfish, liar.

For six months, I kept my head down and listened. My memory is excellent, and I repeated phrases back to Viggo, who told me what they were.

When he wouldn't, I knew they were about me.

Most of the conversations circled around the hushed whispers of me being of mating age, in spite of my mother's best efforts to keep them at bay.

My being 'unmated' became a problem when two boys tried to corner me at the wading pool.

I broke one's nose and was pummeling the other one when Viggo pulled me off of them.

We were all hauled before Alpha and they blamed me, telling Alpha I had cast a spell on them.

This made everyone terrified, gasping and retreating.

Alpha stood before us and his eyes narrowed at the boy who spoke next to me.

I shook like a leaf. What would happen if he believed them? I hadn't used magic. I had used my fists. I looked at

Viggo, then to Mom.

Mom had been crying and Viggo looked on with a frown.

Then Alpha stood before me. "Look at me Lily Viggodatter." I lifted my gaze. "Tell me what happened."

"I was at the pool, trying to wash the berry stain off of my hands. They tried to touch me, so I hit them. I would do it again."

Alpha's gaze was hard and focused on my chest.

My hand came up and covered the pendant; afraid he would take it away from me. I normally kept it hidden under my clothes, but the tussle had dislodged it.

He steps closer and inhales.

I had taken the blood oath at the full moon after Rolf left and in my mind I heard, "Do not let Luna see my son's gift." He lifted my chin then to meet his gaze and looked right into my eyes. "Are you capable of using magic, Lily?"

"No, Alpha. My ward remains." It sounded formal, but I have learned they talk in a much more formal fashion, so I have tried to adapt to it.

What happened next made me feel better about my place in this pack.

"Lily is spoken for. Her mate is off raiding and has agreed to wait until her magic has returned to her to claim her. To move on this girl is to insult me."

His command rang throughout the room and they all submit. I even turn my neck to him.

Viggo and Mom relax.

The two boys were punished by Viggo, as he is my father and has the right in their eyes. It only makes things worse.

Anything good for me makes Luna hate me more.

I snapped on my fourteenth birthday.

Luna and her evil circle of hens were picking and picking at me. They had not realized I had long since understood them as they talked. The funny thing about being immersed in a place where they only speak their language, you learn it fast. Not to mention, languages and I get along well. I mean, I learned enough Latin to cast spells before I started kindergarten.

I was struggling with the mending, as I was daydreaming about Rolf coming in and rescuing me from them.

Luna slapped it out of my hands and caused the mud to splatter all over it. "Clumsy oaf," she growls at me. "Filthy fire hair and freckles. Even your face bears the mark of Hel."

I shifted my weight forward to get up and get my mending. I don't move to avoid her, and my size is enough to knock her on her butt, causing mud to splatter on her and the evil circle of hens.

"You attacked me!" Luna shrieked.

"It was an accident," I couldn't hide the smug look on my face. "I was trying to save my mending."

Luna was on her feet, and she slapped me before I realized what was happening.

I had never been struck in the face before. My eyes widen as the growl from behind me suggests that someone did not approve of Luna striking me. I swallow hard, and I fear if I turned around, I would find Viggo's angry look. Whoever was unhappy behind me held authority and the other women all turned their necks in submission.

"Perhaps you should be a better teacher, Luna. If you spent half as much time teaching her our ways, as you do punishing her for existing, she might be less clumsy. Lily is sorry for knocking you down. Apologize." Alpha's voice was thick. He was not using command, but he had publicly stood for me against Luna.

I cringe inwardly.

He was not making me any friends by sticking up for me.

"I'm sorry, Luna. I did not mean to knock you down," I lie and attempt to sound pitiful. I try to look like I'm sincere.

Luna snorts at me. She had not bought my apology, but she was forced to accept it with Alpha standing behind me. She merely turns and storms off. The evil hens soon followed her, leaving me with Alpha. When I turned around, his arms were crossed and his brow raised. His jaw twitched and I couldn't tell if he wanted to eat me or laugh.

"Come. You will not work with them again. I have need of you elsewhere." He turned and his shoulders shake a bit. Was he laughing?

We moved to the opposite end of the village to the forge, and I looked on in confusion.

He moved me beyond to the old woman's hut. "Ingrid, I brought you the help you asked for," his voice sounded like he was laughing.

I'm trying not to gag at the smell in this hut. But all the pieces of leather work were amazing. I trailed my fingers over the intricate patterns and the way they looked so modern.

"Hmph. I do not need help." The old woman snapped. "You brought me the fire-haired pup to appease your wife. She finally crossed the line and stood up for herself?" The old woman looked right at me, and I turned as red as my hair.

"Ingrid," Alpha sounded frustrated. "You said you had more work than you could handle. I bring you a fresh young pair of hands to help. Teach her what you know. I would be in your debt."

Ingrid snorted at Alpha and nodded. "Fine. I'll keep your pup's mate safe from Hagor's bitch sister."

The frustrated growl that came from Alpha confused me, but he was smiling.

I missed something. The fact someone else called me a mate made me wonder if Rolf and I were known to everyone.

I loved working with Ingrid. She worked me hard, treated me fairly, and listened to me. We talked about the pack, about their way of life, and about the Gods.

Her stories and warnings were fascinating. She hated Luna. When I asked her why she told me what had happened.

I thought Luna was Rolf's birth mother. She was a political marriage made after the true Luna was killed in an attack by the native people.

For a year, I grew and shined under Ingrid's protection. Whoever Ingrid is to the pack, everyone respects her. Everyone but Luna and her evil hens.

Luna tried to come into Ingrid's hut one time and found herself face to face with a vicious and angry Ingrid. I had never seen Luna show fear until she stood face to face with Ingrid. She scurried out of the hut without completing whatever task she had in mind.

Two days later, the horn blared. One of the raiding parties had returned.

I leapt from my tree stump of a seat, letting the gloves I had been working on fall in my place. My feet carried me as fast as they could down to the docks. I teetered like a small child about to be unleashed on a candy store.

The ship glided along the water and the men shuffled about on the deck.

It has been two years. Would he still feel the same? Would he recognize me?

I had lost all the baby fat and while I still held some curve. I looked more like a woman than a teenager, even if I'm only fourteen. My heart races and I clutch his pendant tight. I barely noticed others starting to gather at the docks as well. I felt a hand on my shoulder and look to see Viggo. There is a small smile on his face, but I know he is holding my shoulder to prevent me from doing something that would incur Luna's wrath.

Other women rush their men, and happy reunions are all around. It is then I see him. I swear he has gotten bigger. Was he always that big? His hair is longer and pulled back. There is a beard forming on his face.

Our eyes meet.

I bite my lip and then I tap my heart to mouth the word, *"Mine"*.

"Mine," his voice growls in my head.

To have and To hold

My smile could not be erased from my face. Rolf and I were swept into the duties of unloading the boats, but every time I looked up, I caught him looking at me.

His gaze bounced from amused to something I didn't understand, but it made me blush every time he looked at me like that.

I clung to the rail of the boat more than once in helping unload to keep from being dumped into the water.

Once all the supplies and spoils were unloaded, the clan prepared for a welcome home feast. Bonfires were built, food prepared, and the barrels of mead rolled out.

I had been working all day with Ingrid and am smudge covered. Not to mention the hard work of unloading the boats, left beads of sweat running down my back as I made my way into the woods.

I learned to not bathe with the other women. It always ended in some sort of squabble, or one of them accusing me of something. Instead, I followed the little stream until I found another pool, all on my own. I peel out of my clothes and fold them. I wind my hair up and pin it with the delicate bone sticks I made under Ingrid's guidance.

They're weapons, and if my mother had allowed it, I would carry a pouch of poison to dip them in. It is a sore point between the two of us.

She will not let me near any of her herbs, or anything magic related. She claims she shuns me from learning magic to protect me. When she does ask me to help her, it is always for something physical and gross.

Viggo says she is protecting me as well, but I believe neither of them.

I slip into the pool of water and sigh. The water is cool and feels wonderful against my flushed skin and sore muscles. I reach for the sliver of soap my mother made. It smells like strawberries and I lather it up in my hands before I begin to work it over my dirty face and arms.

Two years had done wonders to my figure. I'm not any taller than I was when he left, but at five feet nine inches, I'm still hands taller than all the women here, and some men. There is nowhere near as much food here as at home and for two years I have gotten more exercise than I did my entire pre-Viking life.

As I work the soap down my arms and torso, I admire myself, wondering if Rolf would like how I look now. I have the high Irish cheekbones of my mother's family, and the catlike shape to my eyes.

Ingrid says my smile holds mischief, and my eyes a secret. Rolf's eyes look like hers, and I wonder what his mother looked like. Ingrid had told me stories of her time as Luna and how she teased her Ivar mercilessly about naming his son Ivar as well.

I hum as I splash water on my face, then lower myself to rinse the soap from my body. My thoughts carried me far away. I don't hear a person approaching until I hear the branch snap.

I whip my head toward the source and hug myself on instinct. I didn't want whoever dared to invade my private spring to see my naked body.

"Who's there?" I hissed out the words in the old language.

Another twig snaps and then the piercing blue eyes are a few feet from me, his white fur looks like a dandelion at the end of its life. His tail wags as his gaze trails down my form and he steps closer.

"Oh, no you don't." I point at him. "You will not get one step closer, Rolf Ivarsen, or I will castrate you myself."

He whines and then wags his tail, lowering his body and commando crawling toward the edge.

"What if someone sees us?"

Before I could react further, he shimmered and settled himself into the water only a few feet from me, naked.

My eyes widen and my cheeks burn as red as my hair. Rolf left a sixteen-year-old boy and returned a man. I turned my back to him and tried not to get myself in any further trouble.

"Do not hide from me, Mate." His voice is deeper.

That rumble sends the butterflies right through my stomach and I glance over my shoulder at him.

"I see you still wear my pendant."

"What? Of course I do," The smug look on his face made me narrow my eyes. I harrumph at him and hug myself tighter to not let him see anything. The way he is looking at me makes me blush.

His pupils are dilated and the specks of blue and gray

make him look ethereal. He is scruffy and dirty. The smirk kissing his lips makes me roll my eyes.

"Pig," I tease and move to get out of the water.

His hand whips out and catches my forearm, pulling me across the water and to him with such ease it makes me gasp. We are inches from each other now. "Pig, am I? Does that make you a pig as well?" He inhales and his forehead touches mine.

Lightning zapped down my spine and made my entire body tingle. Heavy and aching for him to touch me more.

"Rolf," I whined.

We could not be caught like this. Luna would have my hide, and her evil circle of hens would happily stitch it into a rug for her.

"Lily Viggodatter, you are my mate. Do not run from me," he made this noise that was a mix of growl and whine.

Viggo warned me that Luna would do something drastic should I reveal our promise to each other.

"I have spent many long nights dreaming of you. Your beauty rivals Freya's. I just want a few minutes to hold you close and breathe you in. I promise to not claim you until you're eighteenth year. I would wait an eternity to claim you, my flower." His arms moved to envelop me and shift me into his lap.

I had never been so close to a boy, let alone naked in his lap. Our eyes meet again and the intensity makes me shy again. There is a battle raging behind those eyes.

I learned that wolves are considered adults at sixteen.

Viggo explained that women develop faster and go into heat at younger than sixteen.

My mother and I were having none of that when Viggo talked about it.

But sitting here, in Rolf's lap, all I can think about is how much I want him to kiss me.

His breathing slows, and I match him. I don't know how much time passed until I heard my mother's voice calling for me in the distance.

Rolf sighed, and he tightened his grip on me. "Don't go, my flower," he whispers.

"I need to. And so do you, Rolf. I'm sure Alpha and Luna would like time with you." I lean in then and I kiss him. It is awkward.

He growls against the kiss, and his hand comes up to cradle my head, his fingers lacing into my loosely pinned hair. He tilts his head a bit and deepens the kiss.

I moan into it. If I give in now, we're both in trouble.

My mother's voice is getting closer.

I splash him, which makes him laugh, and release me.

Quickly pulling myself out of the stream and tugging my under-dress over my head looks like I was doing something naughty.

His eyes on me make my skin flush. I yank on my stockings and overdress before slipping my shoes back on. I pull the pins from my hair and let the braid tumble down my back.

"You look like a flame that breathed itself into a woman. I will die a thousand times waiting for you, Lily," he sighs and gives me a lopsided grin.

"I will see you tonight," I giggle at him. "Try not to die between now and then. I'll be forced to give Uther all my attention."

He growls.

I hurry toward the sound of my mother's voice. I glanced back only once to see he was still watching me.

My spirits soared. Rolf was my only friend. With him back, the world was right again.

A Secret Told

My mother and Viggo were in high spirits.

Alpha finally agreed to allow them to build their own home, no longer requiring us to live in the common house with him and Luna.

Viggo claims it is because Mom healed one of the returned raiders.

Mom said it was because Luna is pregnant again and they needed Viggo's room.

Either way, they were in a good mood for once.

Mom asked me where I had been and I told her I was bathing in the spring.

Viggo gave me a raised brow as he inhaled.

I shifted further from him.

He chuckled. "That spring was quite enjoyable... and private."

I laugh and blush more.

Mom didn't get the joke, but she is looking between us with a suspicious gaze.

I shrug and follow along with them.

The feast itself is grand. Mead flows, and the fires are high. I find myself flush cheeked and tipsy before long. Wolves take a lot more to get drunk, but it is always amusing to them when I partake. I don't care that Sacha, Luna's younger sister, is near Rolf and his friends. I dance around the fire alongside the other young women with my hands in the air. The music played is lively and the drums sing to my soul. It's near Beltane. The thrum of the ley lines under me are strong.

My mother is positively radiant in the fire's glow.

I had wildflowers tucked in my hair. I don't remember when I did it, but I look like a forest nymph dancing around the bonfire we are gathered at.

The adults gathered at Alpha's fire, and he listens to his raiders tell great tales of their adventures.

Sacha sits with her arms crossed and eyes staring daggers into me.

I smile and keep dancing. When I come around the fire again, I collapse down next to Rolf, and he hands me a mug of mead. I giggle, trying to catch my breath.

He looks at me with those hungry eyes again.

His friends are laughing and teasing Rolf. These men that went raiding with him don't seem to care that I'm the girl kissed by Hel herself.

"You should have seen it! There I was, minding my business. Then those two thought they could enjoy a bath with me." I talk fast and light. I had not noticed the darkness that shifted into Rolf's gaze, and how his friends went quiet. "So, I socked them!" I babbled in English, forgetting they don't understand me.

"You did what?" Rolf's words were like venom and he looked angry.

I furrow my brow. "Don't be mad, Rolf. I socked them." I curled my hand into a fist, and I made a punching motion. "I was beating in the one's face when Viggo pulled me off of him. No one touches me without my permission." I hold up my mug, but the rest had fallen quiet and I look from Rolf, to Sacha, then to his friends. Rolf looks murderous. Sacha is smiling like the cat that ate the canary, and Rolf's friends were looking at Rolf as if they were waiting for a command from him.

"Yes, well. That was just one incident where you caused so much trouble, Hel's whore." Sacha sips her mead and my eyes went wide.

"What did you call her?" Rolf whirled and acknowledged Sacha for the first time. His lip curls and his eyes narrowed to slits. If looks could kill, poor Sacha would be toast.

Her eyes go wide as saucers, and his friends are to their feet immediately.

I was too drunk to think rationally, so I did what I do best, get into trouble. I sway up to my feet, and I put myself between Rolf and Sacha.

"She called me Hel's whore. Guess that makes someone we know Hel." I giggle at him, but he does not look amused.

"Lily," his growling my name turns me on.

I shrug. "You cannot hurt her. She is Luna's sister and is here to find her mate. Your father said she is like a daughter to him." I don't move from between them.

Rolf steps closer, crowding me.

I lift my chin in defiance.

His nostrils flare and I can tell he is used to getting his way when he rages like this.

His friends have sat back down and are laughing amongst

themselves to see which of us relents first.

"This is a party for you. Be happy. Do not let her get to you." It's words I have heard a million times from Ingrid when I cried in her hut about how everyone hates me.

"No one disrespects my…" He stops himself.

I frown. His hesitation stung more than I ever thought it would. I definitely was too drunk to handle all these emotions. We had been having such a good time, but there was something akin to betrayal in his hesitation.

"Your what?" Sacha pipes up behind me.

"My friend," he says with all the gusto of his rage gone. His eyes were locked to mine, and he knew. He knew he hurt me far more than being called Hel's whore ever would. "Lily," he reaches to take my hand.

"You should apologize for scaring her. I'm going to dance." I downed my mug and moved out of his reach before he could correct his mistake. I flung myself back into the circles of dancing people, carrying myself away. I danced through the various circles where he could not see the tears in my eyes until I could slip away from the village. No one would stop me, not even the guards at the edge of the village. I imagine Luna told them to let me wander as I will, hoping a native would kill me, or I would get lost and never return.

I ran as fast as my feet would carry me. I knew where I was going and didn't need to be careful. I ran until I found myself outside of the Lenape woman's home. Her fire burned brightly outside, and she fanned the smoke to the sky. When she saw me, she gave a sad smile.

"Why are you crying?" Her voice is gentle.

"It was stupid. I thought he would say it in front of everyone. That he would tell them I belong." The floodgates of my emotions open and I let out a small wail.

"Didn't you say you had to keep it a secret?" She moved

to my side, sitting next to me.

"Yes. But that does not mean he should… I mean… He was about to rip off the head of a stupid girl, and I couldn't let him do that. Then he was mad. At me. He was being weird."

She thumps me upside the head and I yelp.

"Ow! What was that- Ow!"

She thumps me again. I stand in a huff and clench my fists at her.

"Fire girl, you are being a child. If he tells everyone, how are you his secret? Are you not happy he is home and safe? What do you care about the words he calls you?" She whacks me again. It hurts. For a little old woman, she is strong and violent. "Now you go home before you ruin this," she motions to her fire.

I look from her to her fire then back and narrow my eyes. "Okay, Fine." I huff as I turn to head back, now rejected twice.

"Secret love will blossom when you least expect it, fire girl. Do not forsake your wolf for protecting what is his. Wolf spirits do not handle rejection well." Her words call to me over the wind like she is walking with me.

If I weren't the daughter of a witch and warlock, I might have been more creeped out by it. As it is, I wander back toward my village slowly. I drank far too much mead and now my head is starting to hurt and the heavy sleepy feeling of being drunk slows me down. I can smell the burning wood in the distance, telling me I'm close to the village. But try as I might to focus, I'm having a hard time finding my way back. I'm covered in sweat from the exertion and it's late.

I sink down in a small grove. I know where I am, but I just need a minute, and I flop back on the ground to look at the sky. There are millions of stars shining above. I never would see these if we were in New York when we're supposed to be. I breathe heavy and slow, trying not to feel rejected again. What did I care that he did not want to say we're mates out loud? Maybe he was thinking of breaking up with me because I stood up for Sacha. Stupid Sacha. I should have let him yell at her. I don't know why I stood between them. I just felt like he might actually hurt her, and that would be bad, for me.

I close my eyes, trying to think. The ground here is soft and I could hear the revelry not too far away.

His cold wet nose brushed against my cheek and he whined, followed by licking my cheek.

My eyes flew open, and I looked up at Rolf in his wolf form.

He whines again and nuzzles me.

"No," I pout and roll so my back is to him.

"Lily," his voice is behind me. His hand on my shoulder to roll me back. "Look at me, my flower."

"No. I'm not a secret. Am I even really your mate? Or were you just telling me to bed me?" I jerk from him and curl up.

He sighs.

When I look up, he's in wolf form and heading back to the village. He stops and looks over shoulder at me, those eyes burning with a fire I hadn't seen before. He growls at me and jerks his head toward the village.

I furrow my brow and stumble my way back to my feet, following him.

He stalked right to where he left his clothes, transformed in front of me, and changed.

I covered my eyes to peek through my fingers at his rather perfect body.

Once dressed, he took my hand and led me right to the common house.

Alpha and Luna had moved inside with Viggo and Mom

while the rest of the village was still celebrating.

"Alpha, Luna," he starts as he pulls me alongside him in front of them.

"What has she done now?" Luna's voice growls from her perch. "Really, why we let her stay is beyond me. She's a curse on this pack, Ivar."

Rolf lets out a low and menacing growl that makes everyone go silent. He looks between his father and Luna. "Luna, talk about my mate like that again and I will forsake all oaths to you. When Lily is of age, I will claim her properly."

My eyes go wide as Alpha, Viggo, and Luna spring up from their seats.

Viggo scoops me up onto his shoulder, walking away.

It's futile to fight his strength, so I sulk on his shoulder.

Alpha's holding Rolf by the shoulder while his other arm blocks Luna from moving.

Rolf's looking at me and I bring my hand to my chest, mouthing the word "Mine".

Rolf's voice fills my mind, "Mine. Always," even as he turned his head to submit to his father.

Midnight Conspiracy

"Put me down!" I shout for the umpteenth time at Viggo.

He ignores me and keeps walking.

My mother hurries along with us and she is frowning.

"Viggo!" I whine at him and squirm, trying to get down. I know it's useless. I don't even have a good chance at beating him in strength when fully sober.

He marches me all the way to Ingrid's hut before he puts me on the ground.

I rub my stomach and give him the dirtiest of looks. "What are we doing here? Why is everyone angry? Why did you haul me away like Rolf was going to hurt me?"

Viggo paces and looks upset.

The heavy stones of dread fill my stomach.

"Morrigan, you said it was infatuation." His voice is full of anger and fear.

Viggo never gets scared and I hug myself.

"I said that it might be that she was infatuated because he was nice to her when no one else was. You are the one that said mate bonds were unbreakable. Is it really so bad?" My mother took my side and that's never a good thing.

I chew against my lower lip and shift my weight on my feet. My head hurts like little Viking goblins are banging their shields against it and the sensation to vomit creeps up my throat.

"Yes. You know why Sacha is here," he snaps back at Mom, and his growl is enough that we both step back.

My eyes go wide and Viggo learns his mistake too late when my mother steps right up to him and binds him with roots that shoot up out of the ground.

I swallow and step closer to Ingrid's hut.

Viggo snarls and then is breathing hard as he is forced to lean forward and get at Mom's eye level. He bears his teeth in frustration and then the vines tighten. "Morrigan," he growls at her.

"No. You are acting a fool, and I don't trust you won't hurt me. Look at you, Viggo. Your claws are extended, and you snarled at us. You are the asshole that said the mate bond was this all-powerful and undeniable claim. Do you remember your oaths to me, Viggo Ivarsen? Or should I leave you here to take my child home?"

I perked up. Could she take us home? I could not decide if I was angry or excited at the prospect of going home.

Viggo stops moving altogether. His claws retract, and his body goes limp in the vines. It looks like Mom punched him right in the gut.

My stomach decided it liked the idea of puking. I cover my mouth and run around Ingrid's hut to puke behind it. I retched twice and felt terrible.

A gentle hand rests on my back, and another hand brushes my loosely braided hair from my face. "Oh, Lily. How much did you drink?" My mother's voice is a mix of mirth and worry. She pulls us to the nearby tree stumps and brushes my tears from my cheeks.

"I don't know. A lot. Oh, Mom. He promised me we were mates forever. But then he hesitated. He wouldn't tell them at the bonfire. He said I was a friend." I hiccup and try not to cry.

"I'm so stupid. I went to the Lenape woman, and she kicked me out. Said I was being dumb and not to reject him. She's never wrong. So I yelled at him. I told him he was a liar. Then… Then he said it in front of Luna. In front of Alpha," I whisper shout at her as if this were the end of the universe.

"And now you and Viggo are fighting. I'm cursed! I should just leave." My lip quivers as I look at my mother in the moonlight. She is so beautiful and perfect. She fit right in here, and she had Viggo. I have no one. Now, I don't even have Rolf. I couldn't stop myself from crying.

"I want to go home," I whimper as I sink down to my knees and bury my head against her skirts.

She gently pets me. "Lily. You are not cursed." Her voice is soft. "I know it has been hard for you, my darling. I promise it will be alright. Now tell me the truth," she tilts my chin up, so I'm forced to look at her. "Do you believe you are Rolf's fated mate?"

Silence fills the air, and I knew it the moment she asked it. The way I dreamed about him. How my heart raced at how he looked at me. When we touch, sparks run through my body. I knew without a shadow of a doubt that Rolf Ivarsen and I were meant to be together forever.

"Uh huh. But I've ruined everything. I told him he was lying, and that he didn't really believe it."

My mother smiles at me then, which confuses me. Why is she smiling? Did she think this was funny? Was she making fun of me? "Then we just have to get you alone together so he can mark you," she chirps.

I blink at her as if she has grown a second head. Did I hear my mother correctly? "But I'm not old enough?" I whine.

"Since you are my pup, I can give permission, and then it's a matter of doing it. But there is no going back, Lily. Once he marks you, you are his, and he is yours. Are you ready for that?"

Of course, I wasn't ready for that. I'm only fourteen. I get nervous and fidget.

She laughed again.

"I am ready!" I protest too much and she gives me a smile that says she's biting her lip to prevent something from coming out of her mouth that would upset me.

"Alright then. In the morning, when we head to breakfast, I will distract Luna and Sacha. Then you steal him away to your little spring. Tell him to mark you, or to take back his pendant."

I'm dead. This has to be a weird afterlife dream. That I'm lying on the common house floor, bleeding out from Luna's attack and I've conjured this whole conversation to pass peacefully. I can only nod in response.

She helps me up and the pair of us walk back to the common house.

Viggo waits on the steps, and she gives me a hug and a kiss on my temple. "Go to bed, Lily. I need to talk to Viggo."

I don't look at Viggo, as he will know we are up to something. He always figures it out.

The next morning, I woke early and took the time to braid my hair properly. I pull on the clean clothes and find my parents naked in bed. "Ew! Hey! We agreed to have no naked time with me in the room!" I make gag noises.

Viggo chuckles against Mom.

"C'mon. We're going to be late." I tug at my mother.

"What is the rush, Lily?" Viggo cracks an eye open and looks up at me from the furs.

I gulp and shrug. "No reason. Just hungry. Don't want to miss out on the hot food." I'm a terrible liar.

"Go on, Lily. I'm right behind you." My mom groans from her snuggled position against Viggo.

"Mom, you promised," I whine.

Viggo raises a brow and sits up. "Well, if you promised, Morrigan. You should get going," he rips the furs from her.

"Just remember I can turn you into a toad," Mom retorts as she gets up.

Viggo never takes his gaze off me. His eyes are narrowed and his head tilted as if he is trying to figure out what I'm up to.

I purposely don't meet his inquisitive look. I help Mom get ready and pretty much shove her out the door. I can hear Viggo chuckling as it closes behind us.

We rushed to the common room, and when we entered, I knew immediately something was wrong.

It's mostly women and elderly. The raiders, minus the injured, are not in the common house. I look at my mom with a worried gaze and she shrugs a little. She turns to head toward Luna and I turn to get some food.

Sacha hurries toward me, her skirts ruffled with the speed of her movements. "This is your fault," she shrieks at me and slaps me.

It's hard enough it brings tears to my eyes and makes my head whip to the side. I felt the rage rise in me. I had done nothing but be nice to her. I even protected her from Rolf's wrath. I have no idea what she is accusing me of, but I was not going to take this. I growl and move to claw her eyes out. I may only be a human, but I'm bigger and stronger than her. I will at least get a few licks in before I'm pulled off.

My mother moves between us, and her hand is in the air, holding the silencing hex in place.

It took all my willpower to not smirk.

Sacha's face shifts from anger to fear in no time flat. She tried to scream.

My mother's other hand slowly came up with dancing flames on her fingers. It was for show.

I knew the illusion.

Sacha didn't, and she flails and retreats in silence.

"Ivar, are you going to let this witch burn my sister?" Luna's voice is shrill behind me.

Blessings and Curses

I turned and came face to face with Alpha and Luna.

The room had fallen quiet once again with me facing Alpha and Luna with a problem, or a fight. He's going to banish me this time, I know it. He always looks frustrated when he looks at me.

I lift my chin to meet his gaze square on and find him containing a smirk himself.

He shrugs from his seat, "Sacha struck her pup unprovoked. She knows the rules. Being your sister does not excuse her from following our ways. Morrigan has every right to protect her pup. Seeing as her pup protected Sacha from Rolf's wrath last night, I would think she would be more grateful to the girl. Do you not agree, my love?" There's a twinkle in his eyes.

I'm missing something and lower my gaze just enough to

watch without looking disrespectful.

Alpha is taking my side, again, against his Luna. It makes me feel weird that he would stir such trouble, but I'm learning fast that he does not particularly care for Luna. "Morrigan, you have scared the girl enough. Let her go," he commands.

"Of course, Alpha," my mom chirps and waves off her hex.

I knew it couldn't be that easy.

Sacha comes forward, shoving me aside. "She is the reason they are all gone! You promised me we would be mated, sister! Now Rolf has gone on the raid to the Isles! Do you expect me to wait that many more years? I will be too old by then! And this whore of Hel distracted him all last night. What am I supposed to think? Your pack is cursed!" Her voice rises to a ringing octave that makes the others in the room wince.

My mother puts her hand on my shoulder. Her heavy breathing is the only way I know she's angry. She sounds like a dragon ready to snort fire out her nose.

"You would do well to remember whose pack you are in, Sacha Hagordatter. Call my pup a whore again and I will send you home to your father in pieces." Viggo's voice growls through the room with all the power he exudes as beta of this pack.

"You hold no rank here and are a guest of Alpha and Luna." He comes forward, putting himself between Sacha and me.

I have to resist the urge to peek around him and stick out my tongue at her. I leaned enough to see her.

Fear etches her little heart-shaped face and she breathes harder, looking from Viggo to Luna to Alpha.

Alpha lets out a growl. "Enough! I will no longer have this pack ripped apart because of your daughter. Now, I have made my decision. I sent the raiders to claim what is ours from the Isles. When they return, my son will claim his mate. That is final." He slams his fist on the table he sits at, and it cracks under his abuse.

I jump and swallow. "Lily Viggodatter is a member of our pack. She took the blood oath under the full moon. The next person I hear mistreating her will answer to me directly. I don't care about their rank, or station. I am the Alpha of this pack, and this is not how we behave toward our own!"

He purposely looks at Luna, his gaze murderous. "Am I understood?"

My mother's hands tightened on my shoulders, and Viggo squared his shoulders.

Everyone, including myself, turned our heads and exposed our necks in submission.

Even Luna turned her head.

I wanted to puke again. My appetite is gone. I felt like Alpha just made my life worse.

He stormed from the room. I was left confused and worried.

Luna and Sacha are carbon copies of death stares as they watch me.

Laughter comes from the back of the room. "Oh, girl. You push my son too far. You would do well to remember you are a chosen mate, not a fated one. Lily, come. We have work to do." Ingrid's voice is full of confidence and mirth. "You need to clean up the vomit you left outside my hut."

I extract myself to follow her.

My heart felt heavy. Rolf had been sent away because of me. Now I know that he is supposed to be mated to Sacha.

Ingrid tried to assure me that it would not happen. That her son respected the pairs that Mani and Freya made. She reminded me I wore Rolf's pendant, not Sacha. She didn't believe I was cursed, either.

Our work together changed.

Her hands were starting to shake, and she could no longer work the intricate details into the leather. She set me to learning the finer work.

I threw myself into it.

My mother found herself busier than normal due to an unusual number of women pregnant all at once.

Weeks turned into months, and months into years.

Ingrid died shortly after my sixteenth birthday. She made me promise I would continue with the leather working and not give up hope. She blessed my mating to Rolf and told both Alpha and Viggo as much.

We were the only three she allowed in the hut when she passed.

Luna had changed completely toward me after that. She and Sacha included me in their conversations. They helped me learn their ways better. They made sure the others treated me as a beta's daughter should be. They considered me an adult now.

Viggo and Mom had moved into their own home and wanted me to stay with them.

I did sleep there, but I spent nearly all my waking hours with Luna, Sacha, or working leather. I did especially well in bracers.

A few of the men that remained in the pack, and came of age the same time as me, approached me about mating and were defeated when I showed them Rolf's pendant. I did not hide that he claimed me.

Even if they did not believe it to be true, they left me be for fear of what Rolf might do when he returns.

Since my sixteenth birthday, I feel like I'm a shell of a person and my dreams are filled with Rolf.

My mother got pregnant.

Viggo was over the moon. It was all he could talk about, how he was going to have a strong pup.

It hurt more than I thought when he beamed and doted on my mother.

My mother could not perform magic while pregnant. Magic is wild and unpredictable even when there is not an imbalance in the witch. She continued on with her midwife duties, but her healing was limited and careful when needed.

It led to my seventeenth birthday. I spent the night alone, staring at the water, trying to will Rolf home. The wind was whipping and the snow was falling hard. I swear I heard his voice in the wind. I felt the power surge from the ley lines. I called to Rolf again in my mind, and I felt the whisper of magic. Like Specially had been all those years ago,

The comfort of magic was kissing my soul. I did not dare tell my mother.

She gave birth to my brother three days later.

I helped her deliver my brother, and it confirmed what I felt, power building inside of me. It sang to me and I breathed easier, knowing that soon I would be myself again. I couldn't wait.

I moved my things from Viggo and Mom's home. My jealousy was high, and I did not want to risk anything happening to Utred. I was just getting my magic back and hurting him would surely seal my fate. I turned inward and threw myself wholeheartedly into working the leather for the pack members.

If they requested it, I would work it. I became useful and felt I had a purpose, even if I was lonely. Every night for an entire year I waited by the water's edge, looking for the ship on the horizon. I silently prayed to Mani and Freya for Rolf's safe return. I had no idea how far the Isles were from here, but

I was beginning to believe Rolf was never coming home.

As my eighteenth birthday approached, I had given up hope. Rolf was never coming back, and I was not going to live alone in this hut the rest of my days. I would wait until they celebrate at the full moon after my eighteenth birthday, and I would open the portal home.

My mother and Viggo had Utred, they wouldn't miss me.

I had made all the preparations. I worked the spell over in my mind every day, and at night I still lingered by the shore.

The day of my eighteenth birthday Luna entered my hut.

I watched her carefully as she moved from item to item. "Come, Lily. You have worked enough today. We have word the ships are returning today. We should get you ready for tonight." She smiles at me like she knows how excited I would be to know that.

Hope fills me. I eagerly set aside my work and follow her.

Much to my surprise she had a hot bath drawn for me. I sat in the tub as they poured the hot water in, and I gasped. Steam rises into the frigid air.

She scrubbed my skin, and she combed my hair.

It was surreal how nice she was to me. It made me nervous and jumpy.

When she presented me with the gown that had been dyed and was as green as my eyes, I gasped. "It's too much, Luna. I cannot accept this." I murmur in awe of the lavish gift.

"Nonsense. It is your eighteenth year. Rolf is returning. You should have something nice. Think of it as an apology for how I have treated you in the past." Her voice is soft, and it calms me.

Sacha was nowhere to be seen.

I assumed she was in her room, sulking. She and Rolf are the same age, making her twenty-two, and old by their standards. I reluctantly accepted Luna's gift and followed her to the common room after. I felt like a princess in this dress. Not that my clothes had been less than this as I'm the beta's daughter. Despite that, I feel like this is more luxurious than anything I own.

We enter the common room, and I take my place next to Mom and Viggo.

Luna takes her place next to Alpha, and Sacha is walking in on Rolf's arm.

Sacha's beaming from ear to ear.

Rolf's jaw twitches and his body is stiff.

The common room is full of almost every pack member, and Rolf's expression is grim.

I'm seeing red. How dare Sacha touch what's mine! Then doubt fills me.

I reach up and touch my chest, "Mine?"

"Mine," he touches his chest and his voice is in my head.

I relaxed a bit, but I did not like how Sacha was smiling. She came and took her place just behind Alpha and Luna.

Rolf came up the steps, and his father hugged him tightly. Then he turned him to the gathered pack members.

"My son returns successful!" There are howls and cheers. Then Alpha clears his throat. "My son has waited for this day for some time. He has declared he would take his mate today. Luna," Alpha formally offers the attention to her. It is Luna who blesses mates and pairs them.

"Rolf has found his fated mate. She will be the sun to his moon, the tempered hand to his rage. No better pair could be made. Come Rolf. Come Sacha. Let what Mani and Freya have blessed not be cursed by any that cross your path."

I gasp and I go stiff, my eyes on Rolf. This is not happening. He said he was mine. I felt it in my bones. I feel like I'm being stabbed and salt being poured into the wound. My fingers are white as they clutch his pendant.

His eyes are wide in shock and confusion, soon followed by fury. He says nothing at all. He stands there dumbfounded as Sacha comes forward and flings herself against him.

My lip quivers and then Alpha is speaking. "What a joyous union," his voice is flat and lacking the gusto he usually holds when speaking.

I couldn't take it. I had done everything I was supposed to. I had let myself fall in love with him.

Everyone here has betrayed me or abandoned me. I look away from Rolf first.

"Lily," my mother says, but it sounds far away.

I don't look at her. I look at the pendant in my hand, and the magic surges inside me. Strong emotions make magic more powerful. I did not trust myself to not hurt someone. I thankfully did not have to answer to anyone.

The music started and people were cheering and congratulating Rolf and Sacha.

I was going to be sick. I did look up to see Luna looking right at me, her smug smile revealing just how she knew exactly what she had done. My heart felt like it was ripping into a million pieces the longer I stayed here and watched Rolf not honor his oath to me.

I did not make a scene when I left the room.

Once outside, I ran straight to my hut and grabbed my things. I ripped the pendant from my neck, and I held it in my hand. I wanted to throw it away and to forget all about Rolf and all these horrible people, but something stayed my hand.

I swear I could smell Ingrid all around me. It was like her hand closed around mine to keep the pendant in it.

I wail and look to the ceiling of the hut. I could not stop myself from crying. So, I pulled the pendant back up and tied it back around my neck. I would wear it to remind myself to never fall in love again. To never believe a pretty boy when he says all he wants is me.

I knew I was cursed.

Fleeing my hut, I don't look back. I run fast and hard to the clearing where the old spirits gather.

The Lenape woman showed me this place. She said it is where I came from.

I'm breathless and tired when I reach the clearing. It's close to midnight. The power wells inside me. I chant in Latin. Slow and steady, I repeat the spell. I don't dare close my eyes, so I don't lose my chance. I struggle as I sob, feeling more alone than I ever did in the clan.

Would my father even recognize me? Has he forgotten me?

Would my mother and Viggo try to stop me, or even care?

It all swirls in my head when Midnight finally rolls around.

I shout the spell into the sky, pouring all my heart into it and the power ripped open the hole in the ether.

On the other side is Central Park, bright and sunny. It's the middle of the day. I rush forward without a second thought. My body sears with pain as I'm convinced the universe is finally ripping me into the million pieces my heart is already in.

Then it was gone. I was stumbling into a clearing in Central Park. I leaned over, resting my hands on my knees as I gasped for air. Tears still pour down my cheeks as the pain in my chest won't leave me. Like half of me is still back in the past. I force myself to lean up and turn to face the past just on the other side.

My hand lifts to close the portal when, without warning, the massive white wolf with piercing blue eyes knocks me onto the ground.

There is No Place Like Home

I grunt as I hit the ground and then I'm smothered in licks and nuzzles. Rolf is too strong for me to push him off of me and I swear he has turned into a puppy all of a sudden.

I was not having it. He just ripped my heart to shreds and now he wants to kiss and make-up?

"Get off me!" I yell at him.

He doesn't budge, but leans up, panting. His fluffy white tail swishes faster than a hummingbird's wings.

I swear it looks like he's grinning. Can wolves grin?

"I said get off me," I say as I try to sit up and push him back.

He eases back, but not out of my personal bubble. He leans down and takes my skirts into his mouth, tugging me back to the open portal.

"No! I'm not going back."

He immediately drops my skirts. His tail stops wagging, and he droops, giving me a soft whine. Those big blue eyes looking at me with the saddest expression I have ever seen.

"No! Not fair! Not the sad puppy eyes!"

He shifts and closes the space between us again, "What about sad human eyes?" His voice is thick and sultry to my ears. His scent fills me, even though it is the grimy scent of sweat, the sea, and the forest. His arms snake around my waist.

I turn as red as red could be. "Rolf, you're naked," I hissed at him.

"You say that like you have not seen me naked before, my flower." He gives me a wolfish grin.

"You can't be naked here. There are people." I whisper shout at him. Thankfully, we are in a secluded spot, and no one has seen us yet.

"Well, then we should get back before anyone sees us." He tugs against me as he eases back, wanting me to follow him.

"No!" I rip myself from his grasp. "I'm never going back there. Why don't you just run back to your mate," I snap in a bitter tone.

"I ran to my mate. Why would I live without you? If you're staying, I'm staying." He crosses his arms and bobs his head. It makes me think of a genie granting a wish.

"Right. You don't have to lie to me anymore, Rolf. I saw your truth in the common house." Tears well in my eyes and I bring my hand up to pull his pendant off.

He leans forward, getting right in my face. His face is scrunched up in confusion. Without warning, his hand shoots up and laces into my hair as he pulls me the remaining distance and his lips touch mine.

It is the softest kiss I have ever had. The tenderness in the kiss makes me melt against him. The electrical current that runs between us felt like a firework had exploded inside of me.

"Lily, you are my mate. Not Sacha." He wanted to say more, but there was a sound behind us in the forest cloaked in night on the other side of the portal.

Male voices call for the two of us.

He never takes his gaze from me, and his expression turns serious. "It is time to decide, my little flower. Do you banish me to a life of loneliness without you? Or will you take your rightful place at my side?" His fingers are held out for my hand as he stands, giving me a view of everything I have dreamed about for the past few years.

I place my hand in his.

His smile beams like the sun as he pulls me close and turns to the portal.

Viggo appears in the clearing.

Before he can come through, I throw my hand in the air and close the portal.

Viggo's growls fade as the portal snaps shut.

Rolf watches as his life is closed from him and his gaze is stone.

I can't read his expression. The tidal wave of emotions washing over me threaten to drown me in confusion.

His gaze shifts to elated surprise, and he pulls me into a heated kiss. "I knew you could not forsake me," he murmurs between kisses. "And now, no one can stop us," he smirks as he tries to guide us back to the ground. His gaze turned to one of lust.

I slapped him. "No! Bad Rolf."

He blinks in shock. I don't think anyone has ever struck him like this before. "Did you… Just… Huh?" He gets the weirdest look on his face, and then I feel his manhood raging hard against my stomach.

"Filthy pig!" I snort at him and push him. "Turn back into your wolf." I hiss at him as I blush.

"Oh. I did not realize you had such desires." He shifts right into his wolf who still has a raging hard on.

I palm my face. "No! Bad Rolf!" I bap his nose. "This place is different. Wolves are hidden. You cannot just prance around like a naked barbarian."

I sigh when he sits on his hind legs, swishes his tail, and cants his head in question.

"I'll tell you, why not. Because it is different here. People wear clothes. They have jobs. They don't raid anymore. They get married and have kids. They drive cars. They live in buildings, and they don't follow stupid Viking werewolf law."

I don't know when I started pacing in my rant, but I did. When I finally stop ranting, because he has not moved, I look at him.

His tail swishes happily in the grass and his tongue lolls.

Is he laughing at me?

"Oh, you think that's funny," I brandish a finger at him and then I remove the long leather belt that ties my overdress around me.

He sat up straighter and pants, his tail wagging faster.

I smirk at him as I saunter closer. "You like that idea?" I purr. I scritch along the crown of his ears and in a swift motion, I tie the belt around his neck as a make-shift leash.

He chuffs in confusion up at me as I pull it tight enough to use as a leash. His tail stops wagging.

"You want to see this world?" I rest a hand on one hip as I hold his leash in the other.

He shifts back into human form, sitting cross-legged on the ground, still raging hard, and crosses his arms as he gives me the dirtiest of looks. "You would make me a slave?" He sounds hurt and angry at the same time.

I look to the sky and sigh in frustration. "Not a slave. There are rules about animals here."

"I am not an animal, Lily. I am a man." He growls.

"Yes. A very naked man. There are also rules here about wearing clothes. So, unless you can magically make clothing appear, you need to be in wolf form. And to walk around with me in wolf form, you have to be on a leash." I point at his naked body in frustration.

"Well, you are a witch. Just make them. I have seen your mother do it." He counters.

"Yah, well. Why don't you go ask her how to do it? She did not teach me magic for the past six years. Remember?" I stomp my foot.

"If she did not teach you magic, how did you open the portal?"

"I can remember things. My mom taught me a spell to take me home if I ever got in trouble before we went to your pack." I confess.

"Wait. You can remember spells from when you were a child? That is amazing." He lights up, looking at me with a newfound awe.

I exhale sharply. "Just shift back into wolf form."

"I will always have to wear this collar?" He frowns at me and gives the belt a light tug.

"No. It's only until we can find a place to get you clothes. First, we need to know what year we are in. Then we can find a place to stay. Now change back so we can go." I demand.

"As you wish, my flower," he shifts back into wolf form.

We emerge from the little grove onto the walking trail. There is no mistaking Rolf is a wolf next to me. He is also massive compared to what normal wolves look like. As we moved through the park, people were staring at us.

Even though it is New York, Rolf's presence makes them uneasy.

His head lolls back and forth as he takes in the surrounding sights.

We move up the stone steps to the sidewalk where newspaper stands cover the corner.

As cars whiz by, Rolf puts himself between me and them, nearly knocking me over in his efforts to protect me from the metal beasts.

"It's alright," I coo and reach down to pet him like a dog. "They won't harm us." I confirm to him as his head snaps up at me. I ignore his indignant expression and look at a newspaper. I frown as the newspaper reveals I have only been gone for about twelve hours.

It is January 1, 2012.

XVII

Better Than Sliced Bread

This is amazing news.

I smile down at Rolf and then I give him a tug. "Come on. I know where we can go."

People part for us like the seas did for Moses.

Rolf's presence is enough to make even the strongest of police officers take pause as we hurry by. Since he is on a leash, they don't say anything.

I glance at Rolf as we hurry along.

The way his ears helicopter and his hackles stay up, and his warning growl when anyone gets too close shows how anxious he is. He kept bumping into me to stay close.

I felt bad for him. This concrete jungle had to be a complete shock to him.

The longer it took for me to get home, the more I worried I would not remember the way. I give the belt a light tug to stop him when the crosswalk sign says to stop.

He looks up at me in confusion and then the cars move. He gives a low whine, and I did not think about it when I reached down to pet and comfort him. He leans into my hand.

The invisible tug between us is growing stronger. It did not matter how scared I was to run away because he was here. All the heartache and rejection I felt ebbs.

He chose me.

Guilt weighs heavy in my heart that I have trapped him away from everything he knows. I could not risk Viggo coming through and Mom following.

They would drag me back kicking and screaming.

I'm never going back. They hated me there, and I did not belong, just as Rolf does not belong here. The light changes and I move forward with the crowd behind us.

Rolf keeps close.

It wasn't until I saw the building I called home that I felt a sigh of relief. I step up to the door and enter the code to unlock it. Fear rears its ugly head as I gingerly step through the threshold and the ward allows me to pass. Visions of the night Nick died flood me.

Rolf nudges me with his muzzle.

I was frozen and crying, afraid to confront the worst night of my life. "This way," I say as I move to the elevator. I push the button and it dings open.

Rolf jumps and growls. His hackles go up and he bumps back against me, pushing me away from it.

"Rolf," I try not to laugh at him.

The empty elevator lingers for a moment, then the doors slide close.

He bumps me back again.

"Rolf. Look at me," I demand. "It is safe. I promise. There is nothing to hurt us here. See?" I press the button again, and the door whooshes open. I step into the elevator and hold the door open for him.

He growls, not liking it. One paw at a time he eases forward.

"Oh, I see. Big bad Rolf will jump through a massive magical portal across space and time, but is afraid of an elevator?"

He snorts at me and comes the rest of the way into the elevator.

I push the button for my floor and look down at him as the door closes.

He shifts his weight and lowers his center of gravity when the elevator goes into motion. He starts to shimmer, which indicates he is shifting.

"Not yet."

He snorts, remaining in wolf form. The door dings and slides open, making him growl again.

I pet along his ear as I step off the elevator. The walk down the hall is like one of those nightmares where the hallway gets longer and longer. Six years are erased in seconds and my hand trembles as I fish the key out of the hidey hole my mother kept it in.

The door eases open and Rolf trots in first. Now he wants to be the big brave wolf.

I hesitate before I try to pass over the threshold of our apartment. The last time I tried to come home I was thrown off the fire escape. My mother's ward had blocked me from entering because of the taint of dark magic. What would I find here? Would Nick's body still be on my bedroom floor?

Rolf sits inside the apartment, wagging his tail at me. He then barks.

Pulled out of my spiraling revelry, I roll my eyes. "You're funny," figuring he was throwing my teasing back at me. I take a deep breath and hop through the threshold, like I was playing a game of hopscotch. I cry out in happiness when I'm not thrown out, close the door and lean back against it, breathing easier. Now, I just had to pay rent and help Rolf acclimate.

Rolf springs from his spot on the floor to shift into human form and pins me to the door. His mouth is devouring mine in a ravenous kiss. His hands slam against the door, caging me in place, and he presses his body against mine.

I moan into this kiss.

His hands come down to pull my body against his, reminding me of how very naked he is.

I try to push him away. I have not forgiven him for what happened in the common house and my anger clings to me like my dirty clothes.

He didn't fight for me. He stood there and let Sacha hang all over him.

My hands push against his chest again. When he does not relent, I fight dirty. I slide my hands around him and get hold of the belt still acting as a leash, and I tug it hard to force him away from me.

He growls and his eyes narrow as he realizes what I have done. With a quick motion of his hand, he slices my belt to pieces. It was enough to distract him and slip from his clutches.

I have never seen Rolf so angry, and I hope to never see that again. I put my back to him as I move into Mom and Viggo's room.

He stalks after me. "Lily Viggodatter, we are mates. I will have you." His voice is rough and I can't tell if he is demanding or begging.

"I'm not mating with someone who smells of Sacha. You stink and you have not earned my forgiveness for not defending your oaths to me." I move into the bathroom, knowing he will follow, and I turn on the shower.

He starts to say something, and I cut him off, "No. You will use this shower and clean yourself.

This," I pick up the body wash Viggo used, "is to clean your body."

"You pop the top here and squeeze it into your hands. This one is called shampoo. You lather it up into your wet hair and rinse it out. Then you use this one. It's a conditioner. You put it in after you rinse out the shampoo, then leave it for a bit before you rinse it out. Once you are done, you use this."

I shove face scrub into his hands.

"It goes on your face, and you rub it in, then rinse it off. When you get done with all that, you turn off the water like this." I show him how the shower handles turn.

"You then take that and that," I point at Viggo's toothbrush and the toothpaste. "You unscrew the top and put the paste on the brush, then scrub your teeth with it for the entire length of the pup lullaby. When you no longer stink, we will talk about what happens next."

I storm out of the bathroom and pull the door closed behind me. I wanted to stay there and shower with him but knew it would only lead to sex. "Then use the fluffy towel to dry off!" I shout it through the door and before he can reply I walk away.

I move across the apartment to the bathroom that used to be mine and shut the door, followed by locking it. I stare at myself in the mirror after peeling out of my clothes. I'm dirty, my hair is a tangled mess, and my teeth look awful! I don't recognize myself, last I looked in this mirror I was eleven years old. I was pudgy and held the roundness of childhood. I played with dolls and my best friend was a dog.

The woman staring back looked more like my mother than

how I saw myself. I touch my cheek and then look down at myself. My breasts are fuller, but my waist is smaller.

Six years of my life, gone.

My eyes fall on the pendant between my breasts. I bring up my hand and brush my fingers over the stone pendant. Rolf is here, with me. "Mine," I whisper.

In the shower, I scrub and scrub. Everything in here is for a child, not a grown woman. Even my toothbrush was pink. I wanted to stay under this water forever, and enjoy the luxury of indoor plumbing, but I did not want to let Rolf flounder alone too long.

I brushed my teeth and wrapped my hair in my Barbie towel until it had absorbed enough of the water. Then I take my time to comb out my long hair, leaving it loose to dry. I wrapped myself in a larger fluffy towel to exit the bathroom. The stinky laundry detergent makes me smile. I gathered up my old garments and exited the bathroom.

As I approached my bedroom, I stood in the doorway. The room is empty and the sun peeks in, making the dust look like little fairies floating through the air. I stare at the floor where Nick's body had been. Did my mother come back and get rid of his body?

I take a reluctant step forward, then another. I can pick up the faint scent of Nick. Warm air circles me like a hug. It has to be Nick's spirit. Spirits linger where they are needed, and I needed to know he forgave me.

He had martyred himself to save me.

I don't fully understand all of it, but I know he did it for a reason. I was not strong enough to ask him, and then the sensation was gone, leaving me alone in a little girl's room.

I trail my fingers over the white dresser with gold trim. It looked like princess furniture when Mom bought it for me. I open the jewelry box full of charm bracelets and plastic beaded things. It plays Somewhere Over the Rainbow with a tiny ballerina twirling and takes me back to when we lived here before.

I open the drawer and pull out a pair of white cotton panties, and a bra. Oh, how I have missed bras. It fits around without issue, but my breasts are now pressed up and cut in half as they overflow the cup, looking weird and squished. "So much for that idea," I mutter and remove the bra. Maybe I can raid Mom's stuff.

I gulp as the thought of never seeing my mother again hits me. I had not thought of how losing them would make me feel when I ran through the portal. The tears well and I force myself to not cry. I refuse to mope about the family I have lost.

She chose to live in the past with Viggo and my little brother. She chose them over me.

I move down the drawers and pull out a pair of pajama shorts, and matching tank top. I rub my hand over my face looking at the My Little Pony pajamas. "Whatever," I mutter again, and I leave the room.

As I come back into Mom's room, Rolf is sitting on the bed. He looks perplexed, and he is frowning. He is still very naked.

I clear my throat.

When he sees me, the frown disappears and his mouth hangs open. His skin is tanned and his hair is a light brown, almost blond. He has braided it back, revealing the shaved sides of his head. He had shaved them before he came home and the stubble is growing out. His beard is clean and combed.

I can't believe he is only four years older than me.

He looks older with a beard. His shoulders are broad and his muscles ripple as he shifts his weight.

My eyes trail further down his stomach, and I blink as his manhood is raised to salute me. I squeak and force myself to pull my gaze back to his eyes.

He is grinning at me. "Like what you see my flower?" He stands, giving me a full view of his physique.

I cough and blush as I move by him to the dresser. I open the drawer and throw a pair of boxers at him. "Put those on and put that thing away," I motion over my shoulder toward his manhood.

He chuckles behind me and I purposely don't turn around. I move to the closet and slide it open. "These were Viggo's clothes. I hope they fit."

He comes up behind me and he leans in. "You smell like you did the day we met." He audibly inhales and I feel his hand on my hip. "I knew at that moment you were mine." His voice is soft against my ear as I stare at Viggo's clothes.

My heart beats faster and everywhere he is touching me makes goosebumps appear. Butterflies dance in my stomach.

"Now," his lips touch my shoulder, and I turn my head to look at him. "Now, you are a stunning woman. Forgive me, my flower. It has always been you. I did not intend to hurt you when I returned. I had every intention of announcing our bond and marking you before the clan. Luna knew this. It was the only reason I agreed to go on the raid. It was supposed to be your name she called in front of the pack."

His fingers trail down my arms, overloading my brain with sensations. He turns me to face him and tilts my chin up, so our eyes meet. Intense emotions swirl in his gaze like the beginnings of a hurricane. "I told them all. I told them you were my mate. Then I ran after you. I will never break my oath to you, Lily Viggodatter. I am forever yours. If you will have me."

Whatever anger I had been holding onto was gone.

He looks at me with such a need for my forgiveness.

"You are mine, Rolf Ivarsen."

I lean up to kiss him.

Our moment is interrupted and both of us frown. It is as if the Fates are in on the conspiracy to keep us apart. Someone is at our front door banging against it as if their very life depended on us answering it.

Family Reunion

Rolf frowns and holds me tighter, not wanting me to go answer the door.

I lean up and nuzzle him before I escape his embrace again. I hesitate in approaching the door.

The banging gets more urgent. "I know you are here, Lily. Open the door!"

My eyes go wide and fear fills me. The voice on the other side of the door is my father, Silar Windraven.

My mother had said my father was the reason Nick died. She filled my head with all this horrible doubt, and I can't control how fast my heart is beating.

It is enough that Rolf steps between me and the door, his gaze focused on me. "Why are you afraid?"

I feel the power coming from my father and my gut tells me to run, to take Rolf's hand and flee via the fire escape. I blink at him and open my mouth to respond, close it, and open it again. I look like a fish out of water as I struggle to answer.

He shakes me by my forearm, "Focus on my voice," his tone becomes gentle. "Who is that man? I will kill him where he stands if he hurt you. Say the word, my flower, and I will fight for you."

My eyes turned into saucers with how wide they got. I shake my head no. "You… can't do that, Rolf. There are laws now."

His extreme response was enough to trigger my brain to function again.

"He is my father. Listen to me. To him, I have only been with you for twelve hours. When I opened the portal to come home, it brought me back to the time I left.".

His brow furrows as I have slipped back to English in my fear.

I reach up and touch his forehead, murmuring the spell I remembered from my childhood. It should allow him to understand everything now.

"Lily! Who is with you? Let me in! I have been so worried about you! Please, darling, open the door. Daddy will protect you." Silar's voice alters immediately, losing any sense of anger it held before.

Rolf frowns as he looks over his shoulder and then at me again. He turns his back to me and focuses on the door. He touches it with caution and pushes against it. "How do you work this door? Where is the bolt?"

I suppress a giggle at the idea of 'bolting' the door, then reach around him and turn the deadbolt to unlock it. "You turn the doorknob, like this." My hand curls around the handle and turns it slowly to show him.

He then ushers me back, and he turns the knob, allowing

the door to open enough to make himself visible. While Rolf is only twenty-two, he looks older. The hardships of living in 1281 will age even the cleverest of witches and wolves.

I imagine I look older than I am as well. It can't be helped. It didn't matter anyway. The only way to change my appearance was through blood magic, and that is the darkest kind.

"Who the fuck are you? Where is my daughter?" Silar pushes against the door intending to bully his way past Rolf.

I bite against my lower lip as the door rattles but does not otherwise move.

Rolf's posture is arrogant and menacing. He means to intimidate my father. "Who the fuck are you? What do you want with my flower?" Rolf repeats the question back.

I hear him in his native tongue, but my father hears him in English.

Rolf's lip curls with the hint of his animalistic nature and my father stops moving.

I wish I could see his face, or hands. If he intended to attack Rolf with magic, I would have to intervene. The tension is thick and the longer they are silently staring each other down, the more anxious I get.

Neither man will bend to the other.

I buckle first. "I'm here, father. Please don't hurt Rolf. He is important to me."

Rolf's gaze snaps to me and he narrows his eyes.

I had just berated him for not telling the world we were mates and here I was not doing it. I convey without a word I did not want my father to know just yet.

Rolf sighs and he turns his gaze back to Silar. He does not immediately move to let him in, as if he is debating killing him without my consent. Then he steps aside and allows the door to open more.

My father has a raised brow as he steps into the apartment. A small smile forms when there is no ward to thwart him.

My frown deepens at the realization that the thresholds were likely gone because my mother was gone from this time. I would have to learn how to ward if I wanted to keep Rolf safe.

Rolf closes the door and then takes up his position between us again. His arms are crossed and his shoulders are broad enough that I'm sheltered from my father. It is Rolf's instinct to protect and block me from what he perceives as a threat.

I'm sure between my erratic heartbeat, and what he knows of my father from my mother, he is in no mood to let me near the man. I ease closer to Rolf, nestling against him and forcing him to put his arm around me as I watch my father.

Silar's expression morphs into one of disbelief. "Who are you?" He hisses and moves with a speed neither Rolf, nor I expected. He had me by the chin and there is an eerie green glow coming from his hand.

While Rolf may stand the same size as my father, he is definitely the stronger of the two. His snarl rips through the air as he picks Silar up by the throat and shakes him like a rag doll.

The motion forces Silar to let go of me, but now he is putting his hands on Rolf's forearm with the eerie green glow getting brighter.

"Touch my mate again, and I will rip off your arms to beat you with them. Do you understand me, Warlock?" He shakes my father anew and tightens his grip on his wrist.

"Mate?" My father croaks. "My daughter is twelve years old. What have you done to her? Put me down before I kill you, mutt."

Rolf's fingers tighten around Silar's throat and I whine,

putting my hand on his arm.

"Please, Rolf. He is my birth father. He will not harm either of us. Please." I hoped both men would back down. The amount of testosterone filling the air was stifling.

Rolf's lip curls again and he lowers my father to his feet but shoves him back enough to keep the distance between us. I

Silar rubs his neck, then rights his dress shirt and vest. He looks between the two of us and his eyes narrow.

"Lily, explain what is going on here." Silar moves to the chair and sits himself down, motioning to the couch for the two of us.

I roll my eyes as Rolf makes me go around the side opposite my father. But I'm relieved no one is murdering anyone yet. It is then I realize I'm in pajamas that are form fitting for me, and Rolf is only in boxers.

As my father looks between us, I feel as though we had been caught having sex and now, we are getting 'the talk.' Having gone through puberty in a Viking clan full of werewolves, not only did I know all about the birds and the bees, but I also knew so many ways to create pups my father would blush.

When I don't answer right away, a dark look crosses my father's face. "What has your mother done?"

"She… is gone." I chew against my lip. I was on the verge of tears again at the idea of being caught between my parents. I realize something is going on that I don't understand, and it circles around me.

"Nick… died," I whimper. "I killed him. I was practicing my spell, like you said to do on Sarah. Sarah and Nick started acting weird. He touched Sarah, and then he died. Mom told me if I ever needed help to teleport home. So, I tried. I tried to bring Nick here and have her fix it, like she always does. Only,

I couldn't get in. Then she warded me. She took away my magic and made me go with her... to Viggo's family. It's... different. Rolf is Viggo's nephew. When we met, he knew we were mates. He has been my only friend this whole time. Please don't be angry, father." Something told me not to tell him I had traveled back to 1281.

Rolf's hand wraps around mine and squeezes it and his eyes are full of questions.

I had omitted a great deal of details to Silar.

All I talked about was how cool my father was and how much I hated my mother when we were back in his time.

My mother is not a liar. She never has been and so I'm going to at least confront my father about Nick before I make my full judgment on which parent is telling the truth.

My father's expression is drawn into a pensive frown as he watches the two of us. It's too hard for me to read what he is thinking, but he does not like what he is hearing, I know that much. Then he lets out an exasperated breath. His eyes linger on our held hands before he looks up to meet my worried gaze.

"I am sorry Nick is gone, Lily. I know how important to you he was. But you left my house only fifteen hours ago. It doesn't explain how you are a full-grown woman before me. With a mate, no less." He rubs his hand over his face. "Your magic is weak, like it has been suppressed."

"Mom said I was tainted with dark magic, and she warded me to let the taint wear off. She said Nick martyred himself to save me. Is that true? Did I cast a killing curse? You said it was a sleeping spell." I hold my breath after.

Rolf stiffens.

Father Knows Best

"Oh, my darling girl. The moment I felt something was wrong I came looking for you. Something must have happened while you practiced that made the spell go awry. I am so sorry you had to go through that." He sounds sincere.

Rolf's tension does not ebb. He stares at Silar with a frown on his face. Rolf does not like my father. He looks at his cousin the same way. If he were in wolf form, his hackles would be up.

I wish I could compel my father to speak only the truth. I have seen Mom do it before, for Alpha.

It involves a potion and she would never show me how to mix it.

"That does not answer how you have aged so much in fifteen hours." He circles back to the obvious fact I'm no longer twelve. It also seems to agitate him more than anything else I have said..

I give Rolf a questioning look and he shrugs his shoulders. I purposely speak in his native tongue, assuming my father does not know it. "Can we trust him enough to tell him I traveled to the past? He will be furious."

"I do not trust him at all, Lily. There is something wrong about him. My instincts are to keep you from him. I would only trust him with what is necessary." His thumb gently traces along the scar on the back of my left hand. It draws my gaze down to my hands, which are calloused and lightly stained from leather working. I expel a heavy breath and wish I didn't feel like this toward my father.

"Mom did this to me. She caused me to age," I say in English. It isn't a lie and my father's brows raise in surprise.

Rolf's expression remains blank as he watches Silar, which I'm thankful for.

"She did it because she thought it would stop you from doing something to me. She thinks you are a dark Warlock." I put the accusation on the table and wait to see how my father replies. One thing living with the evil circle of hens taught me was to watch a person's body language more than their words. It is not perfect, but I would like to think I could see if he lies about my mother.

He looks defeated and leans forward, looking down at his hands. "I love your mother deeply. But she is, was, a disturbed witch. My coven shunned her magic, between that and having you, she could not handle it. I am so sorry you are put in this horrible position, my darling. Come back with me to Boston. Let me prove to you I am none of the things your mother accused me of. Bring your friend with you. Let me be the father I should have been."

I frown and feel guilty for believing my mother at all. My father looks beside himself and a quick glance at Rolf tells me he believes Silar's answer as well.

"I'm not going to Boston with you. I just got back and I want to be in New York for a while. This is my home. I want to show it to Rolf. Maybe get a job. I don't know. Rolf and I have had no time to develop our bond as he would like." I offer Rolf a smile and he reciprocates. "But I'm not opposed to coming to visit you on the weekends. Or you coming here."

"You're twelve-years-old Lily. Even if your mother aged your body." Silar corners me in my lie of omission.

Rolf tenses again. "It means Lily, unfortunately, that you are still a minor. Since your mother is not here to take care of you, I am legally obligated to take you in and care for you. You do not have a choice in the matter."

Rolf growls and moves to his feet to protest.

Silar stands as well.

"Lily Viggodatter is an adult and makes her own decisions, regardless of your desire to control her."

"Rolf. You fail to understand the gravity of the situation we are in. The laws of the land, and the government, are what prevent me from leaving her alone. Plus, she is my daughter. Just because your uncle named her Viggodatter, it does not take away my claims to her birth. What kind of father would I be if I abandoned her like her mother has?" He vaguely motions in my direction.

This was spiraling out of control. I was not sure what to do. Do I tell the truth? Or do I pretend to be twelve again?

He then turns his gaze to me. "My darling, while it will be unfortunate that you are going to have to relive these six years before you can be considered the adult you are," he puts emphasis on calling out my lies. "I promise to give you what freedom I can while still upholding my moral and legal obligation for you as my daughter. Because the great state of New York views you as having just turned twelve years old."

I knew I had been had and my father was taking me to Boston, regardless of my point of view. "Will you accept Rolf as my mate?" I question him.

Silar gets the same face that Luna got every time Rolf and I were mentioned in the same sentence. He groans as he rubs his hand over his face. "While I understand that you have aged since the last time we saw each other, I am not comfortable accepting you behaving like an adult with a man who is obviously older than you." He looks Rolf up and down as if he is trying to guess his age.

"Then I'm not going. We are only four years apart in age and we have waited four long years to become mates." I cross my arms and take up a defensive position.

"Lily, I understand. Believe me, I do. You have waited four years. As a favor to me, can you wait a few more months as I wrap my head around your being sixteen?" He questions my age.

"I'm eighteen." I sigh and decide to quit holding onto the lie.

"When I returned here, I could not get past the ward. I was on the fire escape and every time I tried to get in, the ward threw me further back. I fell and Viggo caught me to save my life. Then mom stole my magic. She completely warded me off. Next thing I knew we were in 1281, back at his clan's village. For me, it was six years ago. Rolf has been waiting for me for six years. It is not fair to bind me to stupid mortal laws when we both know I'm an adult, and by the laws of Rolf's clan I have been an adult for two years. Either you agree to allow us to mate in one week, or I am not coming with you, and you will have to report me as a missing person."

Rolf has remained silent, at my side. The proud smile on his face tells me he agrees with my terms. He is also doing the thing Viggo does when he wants people to think he is dumb.

He stays quiet.

His expression for the most fleeting of moments is full of an emotion I could not place. Then it was gone, and his stony facade was back in place.

What I wouldn't give to be a mind reader right now.

"Alright, I agree." He says and holds his hand out to shake. "I Silar Windraven, accept your terms, Lily Finley."

I gulp as a witch's promise cannot be unbroken. To do so brings great pain on the one who breaks their word. Our hands connect and there is a binding silver cord that wraps around our wrists, then dissipates, allowing our hands to part. "Great. We also need to go shopping. We have no clothes."

This brings laughter from my father. He reaches into his pants pocket, and Rolf takes a fighting stance in response. Silar holds his hand up and slowly retrieves his wallet. "Here. Take this. It should suffice. You have two days before I expect you home in Boston."

I take his credit card and nod. This may not have been the right choice, but it gave me two days alone with Rolf in New York City.

My father leaves after giving me the card.

"We should not go there, Lily." Rolf's voice is full of concern. "I do not trust that man. Your mother was right to not trust him."

"We have no choice. He's not wrong. All he has to do is call the police and they will make me go. They will put you in jail because they think I'm twelve and it is illegal to mate with a twelve-year-old. I would rather you go with me and protect me than force me to go on my own.".

"What an awful place you live in," Rolf mutters. "I am going to die waiting a whole week more. What is that thing he gave you?"

"It is called a credit card. Instead of carrying coins, it allows me to say I will pay for things later. The stores get their money from the bank, and then the bank gets the money from my father plus a fee for the convenience. So, why don't we show you just how generous my father can be," I wiggle the small piece of black plastic at him with a mischievous glint in my eye.

Clothes Make the Man

Rolf and I have had the longest day, even if it is only a little after two in the afternoon.

I put the black card on the dining room table and I yawn. I can't imagine how tired Rolf must be, having been on a boat, then spent the day socializing, only to travel through time to New York with me.

He gives me a wry grin as he crosses his arms.

"What?" I ask him as I yawn again.

He steps closer to me and draws me into his arms. "You are the fiercest little creature I have ever met, my flower."

His rumbling chuckle makes me smile and his arms are around me to promise to keep me safe.

He sighs and tension radiates from him. "I do not trust that man. There is something about him that makes me feel the need to protect you."

It's my turn to sigh. "Rolf, can we not think about that right now? I'm exhausted from today and really just want to curl up in bed with you holding me. We can worry about my father tomorrow when we go shopping."

I didn't have to tell him twice.

He hoisted me up over his shoulder and stalked toward Mom and Viggo's room. He stops at the door and his nose crinkles. "It stinks of Viggo in here. How do you sleep in this room?"

I giggle. "My room is over there." I point at the other side of the apartment.

He swats my ass, turns on heel, nearly banging my head on the door frame, and stalks into the other bedroom. He drops me down on the twin bed.

I bounce on the springy mattress and prop myself up on my elbows.

Rolf takes a slow turn to survey the room. He furrows his brow at the One Direction poster. Then he runs his hand over the ornate dresser. He looks at the toy box with stickers plastered all over it.

"I have never seen such colors. And who are these boys you have trapped on this wall? What did they do for you to curse them?"

I laugh again.

Rolf furrows his brows at me before he pins me on the bed. "Oh, you think that is funny?" He straddles me and begins tickling me.

"No! Stop," I squirm underneath him. "It's funny! They aren't trapped," I say between gasps.

He keeps tickling and we're wrestling around on the bed not big enough for both of us. Then Rolf is kissing me. It is a hungry kiss. His hands sliding under my tank top and up my sides as his lips coax a soft moan from me.

My skin tingles and I writhe underneath him, my legs parting to invite him in. As tired as I felt, I wanted nothing more than to keep making out with him.

When he finally pauses to catch his breath, our foreheads touch. "I need you," he whispers.

"One week," I murmur back.

"Now," he presses with a whine.

"I gave my word, Rolf. To break it would have dire consequences." I whimper and pepper his face with kisses.

He pulls away from me with a frown. "What do you mean by dire consequences?"

"I mean, my father is bound to honor his promise and I mine. If we break it, it will cause us pain." If I remembered correctly about how those sorts of things worked.

He grimaces more and pushes up off the bed, moving away from me.

"Where are you going?"

"Get some sleep, my flower. If I stay here with you, I will take what is mine." He stalked out of the room and slammed the door behind him. For a guy who had not been here that long, he definitely picked up on things fast.

I sigh in frustration as I fling myself back on the bed. Pulling my pillow over my face, I scream into it.

Rolf comes barreling back into the room, destroying the door as he shoves it right off the hinges. So much for mastering modern technology. "What happened? Who hurt you?" He's over me, throwing the pillow aside and jerking my body as he inspects me.

I blink in disbelief and look from him to the door, then erupt into laughter.

He growls back at me in warning to not mock him.

"I screamed in frustration because I wanted to…" I trail off and my cheeks are dark with my blush.

Rolf's expression shifts elation as he processes what I confessed to.

The sweet smile that fills his face gives me relief.

He rolls off of me and lies on his side next to me. He is strong enough he rolls me away from him and then pulls my body against him with a grunt.

His manhood is poking against me, and I wriggle to get comfortable.

"Keep that up, my flower, and oath or not, I am taking you," he growls against my ear in his deep and sexy voice. "Now lie still and go to sleep."

As tired as I am, I struggle to fall asleep.

Rolf relaxes against me and his breathing levels into a gentle snore. His breath is warm against my neck.

I match my breathing to his and nestle closer to him. I could not believe he was here with me, and Luna could not hurt me anymore. I hope Mom and Viggo are okay and don't get into trouble for what I did.

I woke before Rolf in the wee hours of the morning.

We had rotated around to where he was on his back, and I nestled against him with my leg draped over him. I tilt my head up to take in his face. Peace is painted across it, and I lean up to get a better look. His lashes are long and thick. His beard is brown with specks of red and blond hidden in it. I miss his youthful face without the beard, but he must like it, he has let it grow long. His brown hair has bleached itself from days in the sun. It's long and braided. The braid is fraying loose at the end as he had not tied it off. I swear I'm staring at a God sleeping in my childhood bed.

The smirk that forms on his lips. "You stare loudly, my flower," his voice is thick from sleep and sounds even sexier than his normal tone.

I don't think I'll make it a week at this rate.

"Yeah, well, you snore." I tease him as I get up and dart into the bathroom across the hall before he can try anything.

After several minutes of rummaging through Mom and Viggo's clothes, I had chosen a pair of jeans and a t-shirt.

Rolf chose sweatpants and a t-shirt.

I snatch up the black card and we head out. We make our way to the elevator. Rolf, even in human form, eyes the elevator with suspicion.

I could not stop my laughter. "It is called an elevator. It is a box on cables that raises and lowers when you push the button."

"Who raises and lowers it?" He cautiously steps in with me when the doors whoosh open. "They must be quite strong."

"It's mechanical and works without a person. You will find that a great many things work without a human here."

"Witchcraft, then." He mutters.

"No," I laugh. "Well, yes. Though now they call it science. A person put all the parts together and made sure it worked before they put it in place. Taxi!" I shout as I raise my hand.

The yellow cab stops in front of us and Rolf tries to put me behind him.

"This has replaced horses. A carriage." I pull the door open and get in, motioning for him to follow. I give the cab driver the name of the store I want to go to.

Rolf is all tension and snarling lip the entire ride.

I don't blame him, as cab drivers in New York are worse than the biggest berserker wolves.

I didn't think about Rolf not understanding he had to be modest until we were standing in the suit shop and I suggested he try something on.

He reached for his pants and started to push them down when I gasped and my hands grabbed hold of his pants to stop him. It brought us close together and in my haste I touched somewhere I shouldn't. He gave me a grunt and then a smirk to suggest he was going to take me right here on the sales floor when I squealed again and the clerk cleared his throat.

"Perhaps you would like a changing room, sir?" The clerk looks like we smell bad.

I didn't care about his snooty attitude as I took Rolf by the hand and led him to the dressing room offered. I hang up the options I have on the peg and turn to see Rolf grinning.

"Nice of them to give us private quarters," he wriggles his brows as he steps closer.

"You, sir, are incorrigible. Try on the clothes to make sure they fit. Keep the ones you want and leave the ones you don't. Come back out clothed in your original clothes." I duck under his reaching arm and pull the door closed behind me.

The clerk nods in appreciation when I return alone to the sales floor.

Energy Burn

Rolf and I spend the day shopping, eating, and enjoying each other's company. He tells me stories of his journey to the Isles.

I think he's talking about Ireland, or somewhere in the UK, based on how he mocks their speech in his stories, but the names for them aren't anything I recognize. I was all smiles when he praised me for teaching him English, as it allowed him to somewhat understand the people he raided.

We discover he loves soda and pizza.

However, I will not make the mistake of letting him drink so much in a single sitting ever again. Over the next few hours, he was the most hyperactive puppy I had ever met.

We wandered shop after shop, spending money like it grows on trees.

He has not relaxed one second of our time out shopping.

He crowds me and keeps a hand on me, no matter how odd it looks. He can't help but stare at people and how they act. How women, in particular, are far more forward.

I cut our shopping short.

"Central Park," I say to the cab driver as we slide in with all our bags. We whiz and duck through traffic until the cab stops at the entrance.

Rolf looks at me with a curious gaze.

We meander down the stone steps into the park and keep walking toward the tree line. It takes a good five minutes to find the clearing we appeared in. I glance around to see if anyone can see us and I turn to face Rolf.

"Strip." I command.

Rolf's eyes light up and he eagerly pulls his shirt off over his head, followed by kicking off the shoes and thrusting down the pants. His erection is raging hard as he stalks toward me.

"No! I mean. Yes. But not here. By Freya, that thing is huge! You need to burn off that energy. You are too hyper." I motion my hand vaguely around him. I can't pull my gaze away from his bobbing erection.

"I know the perfect way to burn off energy, my flower." He continues stalking toward me.

I use our bags as shields and giggle as I back up.

"Oh, Rolf. I want to. I do." I quiver with anticipation at him ravaging me in broad daylight in this little meadow of Central Park. "I meant for you to shift and run about in the trees here. I know how much you love nature and I have kept you cooped up in a strange building all day."

He stops moving. Then he gives me a small frown. He flinches, like I smacked him.

I stop my retreat and my voice gets softer. "We have to leave for Boston tonight, and I'm scared. I would rather you get all the tension out of your system before we go, so you can protect me. When we get home, I promise we can spend time together properly."

His eyes look at me with a wary gaze.

The bond between us tightens, like a rubber band threatening to snap. The Lenape woman had warned me to not reject him. I swallow hard, hoping he forgives me and understands.

Rolf shifts into his wolf form as he runs into the wooded area.

"Don't get caught by anyone!" I shout after him.

I gathered up his clothes and folded them as I sat down to wait. I didn't know enough about either the mate bond, or the promise, to make a good decision about how to handle both. The hurt in Rolf's expression when I denied him again made me feel like I was a horrible person. My father had no right in making me wait longer, but I fear what he might do if I break my word. I fret and shift my weight as I wait for Rolf to return.

It felt like an eternity waiting for him. Then I was filled with dread. What if I had not closed the portal properly, and he found it? What if he went back and chose to leave me here, alone? What if I had dreamed the whole thing and wake up in my hut back at the village, without him? What if someone saw him and reported him running loose in the park, causing some cop to shoot him? What if he changed in front of people and got into trouble? I looked in the direction he ran off and then to the sky. I was not used to looking at a watch for the time, and by the way the pinks and smoggy haze filled the air, I could tell we had been here for at least two hours.

It was not safe to stay in the park after dark. At least, that was what my mother had told me when I was younger. I gather the bags up and I get to my feet. My anxiety and fear that he is going to reject me increases the longer he's gone. I don't know where this came from, or why I suddenly felt like I might lose Rolf. I look to the sky again.

"Please don't take him from me," I pleaded to Mani and Freya.

I close my eyes and take deep breaths. My hands are white knuckled as they hold the shopping bags. I strain my ears to listen for him and hear nothing. I open my eyes again to take another look around. I did not want to abandon this spot, as he would come back to it if he was coming back. I felt as though someone were watching me. I take a slow turn in the clearing to see if I can make out any person, or wolf.

When I see nothing, I sigh. I cannot shake the sensation of being watched. The longer Rolf is gone, the more anxious I become. I did not realize how insecure I was without him near until I was standing in this clearing, praying to the Gods, he had not abandoned me.

"Rolf," I whisper to myself.

"I am here, Lily," his voice is gentle behind me, and I whirl around to look at him. He looks agitated, and he is covered in sweat. He pulls on his clothes. His gaze moves from me to behind me, then to other locations around us. He steps closer to me after he is dressed, and he brings his arm around my waist. While he looks calm, as soon as my head rests against his chest, I feel his heart hammering in it.

"We need to leave this place now. There is something dangerous here," he speaks softly against my forehead before he kisses it. "I would never abandon you," he adds.

"How did you…" I look up in astonishment.

"We are fated mates, my flower. I can glean your thoughts. I felt your distress and came right back. I was on the other side of the park. I am sorry for scaring you. Whatever that bitter potion you gave me made me feel like I could run to the moon and back. I should drink it often." He rubs soothing circles on my lower back.

I still feel the odd sense of being watched. I know Rolf will protect me, so I'm less afraid in his arms.

"Let us go home, Lily."

I nod, and we wander from the clearing.

His arm is around me, keeping me close to him. His skin is like fire, and I feel the fire seeping into me, making me want to tear my clothes off.

The nagging feeling of being watched follows us all the way back to the street where I hail a cab. We are whisked home in minutes, and once we are away from the park, I'm only left with the burning feeling Rolf's touch gave me. I knew young female wolves went into heat when their mates were near and they had not finished the bond, but I'm not a wolf. Surely, I couldn't go into heat.

We made our way up to the apartment. As we approached, we saw the door standing open.

I stop moving and hold my fingers to my lips to silence Rolf.

He motions for me to stay and when he takes his hand from my back.

It takes all my resolve to not whimper.

He stalks toward the door, and it amazes me how silent he is. He leans against the wall next to the door and places his palm on it to push it further open. His brow furrows at whatever he sees in the apartment and it's killing me to not know. He holds up his other hand to stop me before I can move.

He lunges forward.

His clothes flutter to the floor in tatters as his white wolf appears. Then there is growling coming from the apartment.

I'm riveted to the spot. I could do nothing about a physical threat. If the threat were magical, I would like to think I could do something. I jerk into motion and come rushing into the apartment. I'm not going to leave Rolf to face danger alone.

When I step into the room, it's empty. There is no furniture, no damaged door, nothing. It was as if someone came in and moved all our things out of the apartment while we were shopping. I frown and look for Rolf.

He stands a few feet in front of me holding still, but his hackles are up.

My eyes follow the line of sight he holds and find a young man cowering in the corner.

His hand is shielding him from the massive white beast. "P-P-Please don't eat me. He sent me to collect you, Miss Windraven."

"Viggodatter." I corrected him.

"Y-Y-Your familiar," he whines and points at Rolf.

"That is my mate, not my familiar." I corrected him again.

Rolf growls louder and lunges forward to scare him, but I see his tail wagging. He is being a jerk right now.

"Though, I'm tempted to turn him into a toad for continuing to frighten you. Who are you? Where are all our things? Why are you in my apartment?" I wanted the boy to fear me.

But Rolf brushed against me in his effort to put himself between us. It sent that electrical current through me and caused another reaction. My body felt like I had been set on fire, and I dropped to my knees with the amount of power surging inside of me.

Rolf was in front of me and had not seen me.

The boy had and his fearful gaze turned comical looking in the amount of panic painted on it. "What's wrong with her?" He points at me. His face was holding a mixture of disgust, along with the panic of the sudden feverish flush of my skin causing me to buckle right before his eyes.

I dropped to my hands as well, losing all the bags I was carrying. The last thing I see is Rolf's arms coming around me. His naked chest felt so good against my cheek before I passed out. The ringing of Rolf crying my name is the last thing I hear.

In the heat of the Night

I was at my spring near the clan. It's warm out and my clothes are piled on the ground. I ease into the ice-cold water with a gasp, and I hear the rustle of movement near me. In a flash, I covered myself, unsure of who was approaching my little sanctuary.

He appears in wolf form, his piercing blue eyes laser-focused on me. He changes and prowls toward me like the Alpha he was born to be. We don't say a word to each other as he lowers himself into the cool spring. His earthy and natural scents fill my senses.

My arousal grows as I bring my arms up to rest on his shoulders.

His gaze smolders, conjuring the fire burning through my body.

I need only one thing... Rolf. My lips press to his and my calloused hands glide down from his shoulders along his hairy chest. My nails drag along his skin, feeling the way goosebumps rise to the touch.

He growls against my lips and slams me back against the rock wall. His rough hands pulled my wrists above my head.

"Mine," he growls in my ear.

"Mine," I echo.

His one hand holds me arched in front of him while the other freely roams down my ivory skin. His tanned skin is a stark contrast against the soft and tender flesh of my breast. He squeezes and pinches the nipple, forcing it to be taught.

I whimper and wriggle against him, not to free myself, but to beg for more. I want him, all of him, and he is torturing me.

"Lily," he murmurs.

His knee presses between my legs and I eagerly part for him, bringing them up to wrap around his waist. His erection rubs along my thigh as he lets go of my wrists to grab my ass and force my legs to part even further.

Another moan escapes my lips and I'm going to be consumed by this wanton fire if he doesn't claim me.

"Lily," Rolf calls me again. He sounds as if he were on the other side of the world and not pressed against me, threatening to steal my innocence. He growls and thrusts with all his might.

My eyes fling open, and I'm soaked with sweat. I pant, and the unsatisfied ache grows exponentially. I'm lying on my back in a plush bed with the softest sheets I have ever felt, even though they are drenched in my sweat. I breathe hard, staring at the ceiling. Everything is on fire as I yearn for Rolf's touch. Closing my eyes, I focus on my breathing.

When the ache does not relent, I bite my lower lip and slide my left hand down my sweat soaked body. My fingers slide under the cotton panties and along the springy curls until I press down between the folds of my womanhood. I'm wetter than I have ever felt during those lonely nights in the hut. My clit throbs under my fingers and as I press against the nub in a steady motion my legs lax on the bed, opening me to a butterfly-like position. I turn my head and gasp as I feel the pressure build. I needed Rolf. I close my eyes tighter as I imagine him strolling into the room and claiming me like the Viking raider he is.

"Keep this little show up, my flower, and you will get your wish." His voice is husky and thick a few feet away.

I freeze, my skin turning as red as a cherry, and my eyes fly open to meet the lust-filled gaze of Rolf watching me. He is sitting in a chair near the bed I am in. I know I should be embarrassed and cover myself, but all I could think about was him taking me. I give a coy smile and tilt my head to get a better look at him.

"Is that a promise?" My voice is sultry.

I resume rubbing my clit, changing the motion to force my hand further into my panties and allowing my finger to press from my clit to slide into me, then back. I kept my gaze on him and moaned as I tormented myself. I could see him shift in his seat, his fingers white knuckling the arm rests. A low and promising growl emits from him.

"Rolf," I murmur.

I watch as he raises to his feet and takes a halting step toward me. The bulge in his pants is unmistakable. He does not have a shirt on, and his muscles are twitching as he restrains himself.

"Please," I beg and I roll my hips in time with my finger.

"I need you," I pant at him.

He comes closer. His primal nature makes him look like a predator closing in on his prey. I watch him climb onto the bed and position himself over me. His scent sends me into a frenzy as I stroke my fingers faster, whimpering up at him.

"Lily," he breathes out, "your scent is…"

I reach up with my free hand, pulling him into a wanton kiss before he could finish the thought. I didn't want to hear his sweet nothings. I wanted him inside of me now.

He frees my hand from between us, guiding both hands above my head. His fingers lace into mine and his body is crouched over me.

Our tongues battle for dominance in the sloppy and eager kiss. Everywhere he touches me it is like he erupted a volcano of pleasure. I'm seeing stars with how wonderful it feels. I ache more for him.

"Rolf," I begged again.

He moans in the kiss, and his body tenses against me. His fingers lace tighter in mine and his kisses trail along my jaw, down my neck, and to the soft spot where my neck meets with my shoulder. Then he pauses. His breathing is ragged and I whine at the sudden stop. Without a word, he pushes off the bed, leaving a chilling vacancy where his inferno had just been.

My body burns brighter and I whine in protest.

He stalks out of the room, slamming the door behind him.

This brings tears to my eyes. What had I done wrong? The dull ache is a painful need now, and I'm confused. Then I feel horribly embarrassed. I sit up and pull the sheets to cover myself. Was I not pretty enough? Was he changing his mind about wanting me for a mate? Did he think I was too easy? Tears roll down my cheeks as the wanton feelings give way to the insecurities. The horrible feeling that maybe Luna and Sacha were right about me all along. That I was Hel's Whore, and now Rolf has to run from me to resist whatever spell I have put him under.

I turned and put my feet on the cold hardwood floor. Now that I'm not in a lusty haze, I see that I'm in my bedroom at my father's home. I stare at the large dog bed next to mine for Nick and guilt wells again. I wipe my tears on my forearm and push off the bed. I have no idea how long I have been asleep. My things, including the things I bought the other day are neatly stored in this room.

Nothing of Rolf's was in this room.

My shoulders slouch as I feel that niggle of doubt again. He does not even want to be in my room with me. Had he asked my father to send him back? But he had looked at me with a burning need, I know I saw it.

"Awe, there is my darling," my father's voice fills the air. "What is it, Lily? Did something happen? Has that mutt hurt you?" He envelopes me in his arms in a fatherly hug.

Shame burns across my cheeks. Not even two minutes ago I was trying to seduce my mate and here I am hugging my father. "No. Nothing happened," I hiccup against him. "That's the problem. I'm afraid he doesn't want me anymore."

"Oh? Lily, you would not break your promise to me, would you?" His voice is gentle, but I could hear the undertone.

"No, father," though we almost had. "But he left angry. I upset him, and he doesn't want to be here anymore." I sniffled against him. I wanted to be a stronger woman. I didn't like feeling like I wasn't good enough for Rolf. I deserve love like everyone else. I feel the invisible tether of our souls in the bond. So why do I feel like Rolf hates me? Or is he growing tired of me? Had I waited too long to complete the bond?

"Shh. Come now. We'll talk to the boy. First, you need a shower. You have been asleep for two days. Then we will discuss what needs to happen next." He brushes my coppery hair from my face and kisses my forehead as he guides me toward my bathroom. "I will have the staff prepare a meal for you. It should be ready in thirty minutes. I will see you in the dining room."

I nod absently and then enter the bathroom. Wiping my

face with my hands, I try to focus on getting cleaned up. The burning feeling has all but subsided, but the odd feeling of being watched fills me again. It's coupled with a burning rage and has my nerves on edge. I check every inch of the bathroom for any kind of talisman, or trinket, anything that might give off the dark energy I'm feeling. With nothing revealed, I lock the bathroom door to make sure I will remain alone.

Oh hell No

We gathered in the dining room for the meal my father had prepared.

Rolf appeared and looked as though he had been for a run. His body is sweaty, and his hair holds little bits of leaves.

I offer a light smile and motion to his hair.

He gives me a lopsided grin and flicks the bits from his hair in an easy motion.

We meet at the table my father is waiting at. I turn my attention to my father, who looks like a king on his throne at the head of the table.

He raises a brow at me and then looks to Rolf. As the two of us sit down, my father shakes his head.

I tuck my damp hair behind my ears and I feel twelve-years-old again with the way my father is acting.

Rolf and I look at each other again and he touches his chest in our special sign to show that we belong to each other.

My face lights up and I touch my fingers to my chest in response.

His expression is stoic and unreadable.

I have seen him like this only a few times before. It usually meant he did not like something. I don't feel like I can talk openly to Rolf in front of my father. There's something in the way the two of them interact that puts me on edge.

"I have arranged for you to finish your schooling," my father begins. "We will get you assessed and pick up your education where needed. I will resume your magical learning in addition to your education. It is a travesty that you have been denied your abilities. What was your mother thinking?"

"She was protecting her pup," Rolf growls between bites.

"From what? Lily was in no danger. Accidents happen. Had Lily not panicked, we could have done something for that poor dog." My father waves his hand dismissively.

I blink and pause mid-bite at this interchange.

Rolf is staring at my father, but Silar is ignoring him.

I finish the bite and remain quiet.

"If you were better at instructing her, you would not have had a child practicing magic unsupervised. From what Morrigan explained, the spell used was not a spell a child should have been learning." Rolf shifts in his seat and his lip curls in response.

"Morrigan is a disturbed witch that has abused her magic, put her daughter in danger, and prevented her from growing properly. What would you know of how witches and warlocks progress? I would be surprised that you know anything other than rutting and fighting, mutt." My father casually picks up a glass of wine and sips it as he watches Rolf.

I hold my breath and watch Rolf as well.

He shifts in his seat and his jaw clenches. He flicks a look to me, then back to Silar. He sits up straighter, sets his fork down, and drums his fingers on the table before he responds. "I know that your daughter was traumatized and her mother felt the urge to flee far enough that you could not find them. Between raids and rutting, I was sure she begged my father to protect her and her pup… from you. Now, why would a woman go through such lengths to keep your only pup from you over an accident?" He looks from my father to me again and I feel like a deer in headlights.

I had spent the last six years of my life hating my mother for taking me away from everything, and here was Rolf defending her. I had not been privy to the conversation Mom and Viggo had with Alpha. He always spoke to me alone in those first days.

"Yes, well, none of that matters anymore. Lily is home, where she belongs, and we will right the wrongs and get her where she needs to be. Lily, I would love to introduce you into the coven proper. You are a Windraven, and if you choose, you could take your place in the Ember Tree coven. Even your mate could understand the importance of belonging." My father's voice never rises.

I'm not dumb, and the tension between my father and mate sets my nerves on edge. I lay my fork down after a few bites, no longer able to eat with how anxious I am. "Rolf can join me at school?" I look hopeful while changing the subject from my mother's choices. I didn't want to be separated from Rolf for hours on end with a bunch of other kids I'm older than. "Won't it be awkward with us both being adults?"

My father chuckles and shakes his head no. "Lily, you will have a tutor. I would not want to explain your odd appearance to the school. As for," he looks at Rolf and his face scrunches in disdain, "the boy, I am not sure the mutt is capable of learning."

"That is enough!" I slam my hand on the table and frown. "He is my mate. We were fated to be together by Mani and Freya. I will not sit here while you belittle him. You will afford him every opportunity you afford me. If you cannot respect him, then we will leave, laws or not." I cross my arms and try to give him the sternest look I can muster.

Both men grow quiet.

My father's face draws into an angry frown.

Rolf's face draws into a broad grin.

"Very well," my father grumbles. "I will arrange a tutor for Rolf as well."

I smile at Rolf, feeling like I had won the battle when I see his expression has formed into a pensive frown.

"Why do we need schooling? We are adults." He is looking at me, but his question is to my father, and is a challenge.

I'm confused by this challenge. Rolf always seemed to enjoy learning my language before. Why wouldn't he want to learn all the other things?

"We will learn to read and write. About history. Science, and math. When I was in school before, I got to read wonderful stories, and learned so many things." I'm animated and talking with my hands as I explain.

"What would we need all that for, my flower? When my father passes, I will assume the clan and will raid the old lands. What will this schooling teach me that I do not already know?" He leans back, feeling smug and smiling at me.

"I see," my voice gets low, "and where do I fit into all of this raiding and plundering?"

My father shifts and rests his chin in his hand as he gets a smirk.

Rolf is oblivious to the danger he has walked into as he

continues. "You will keep our clan in order, guiding the pack, and raising our pups, of course."

"What clan? What pack? Just where do you intend to do all this raiding? There is no raiding now," I retort, the anger rising within me.

Rolf stands then and leans forward, putting his hands on the table, his anger rising as well. He narrows his eyes and his body shifts to become intimidating. "When you are done running away and come take your place by my side at home. Our pack will need us, and I will not forsake my oaths to my father."

My chest rises and falls with fear and anger. "I see. So, all I am to you is a breeder, good for warming your bed in a place where everyone hates me while you get to run off to Gods know where with all your friends. Doing who knows what with any girl you find more worthy than me. Well, then I should just send you back now, so you can mate with Sacha. I'm sure she would make the perfect mate for you. Roll right over and show you her belly like the bitch she is. Do you plan to keep me hidden in your grandmother's hut too?" I throw down my napkin on the table.

"You are my mate, Lily Viggodatter. Your place is by my side. In my home. Leading my pack. You are mine and you will act like it. You should not trust him. Your mother did not. Viggo did not. He did not protect you before. What makes you think he will protect you now?" Rolf has never raised his voice at me in anger. He is shouting now and the menacing growl in his voice threatens to undo my resolve.

"NO!" I scream at him. "I'm not going back to that horrible place. There is nothing for me there. NOTHING. They hate me. They would have cast me out were it not for this!" I rip his pendant from around my neck and brandish it at him. "They think I was born of Hel and sent to curse them. Just how much do you think they would follow me, Rolf? Huh? How many will fight to protect Hel's Whore and her pups while you are off having fun with your friends? Maybe Mani and Freya got it wrong." Tears rolled down my cheeks. "You don't want me, anyway. I'm not even a wolf."

It was too much for me. All I could see was how he looked at me. As if I were a monster and not what he thought at all. I was sure he hated me like everyone else in his clan. I couldn't take it. He was the only reason I suffered all of their abuse. I throw the pendant down onto the table and run from the room, ignoring him calling my name.

When I get back to my room, I slam the door shut and lock it. I didn't want to deal with my father, or with Rolf. Both men felt like they could decide my fate for me. I fling myself on the bed and scream into my pillow before I curl up and hug it.

Teacher's Pet

Banging on my door causes me to bolt awake.

I had cried myself to sleep, hiding from them. It stings that Rolf did not come and tell me I'm wrong about everything I have said. I feel miserable and the doubt that fills me about him even still being here makes me frown.

The banging continues until I answer it. When I fling it open, my father stands with his arms crossed. I roll my eyes at him and leave the door open to storm to the dresser. Once my clothing is retrieved from its hiding place, I stomp into the bathroom and close the door to change. It only takes a few minutes, and I come back out with my hair in a messy braid down my back.

I follow my father down the long hallway. The longer we walk the more agitated I get. "Did he ask to leave?" I finally ask. Fear wells and the sense of dread makes me feel like there are stones in my stomach.

He stops abruptly and turns to face me. His left eye is swollen, and the purple bruising made him look monstrous. His angry expression levels on my shocked one and he snorts. "Your mutt," he hisses out as he closes the distance between us, "is already waiting in the library for you. He has made it quite clear he is not leaving without you and when I refused to let him into your room last night, he attacked me, Lily." He turns on heel and continues down the hallway.

We enter the library and near the window stands a man and a woman. The woman has a gentle face and her blond curls are pulled up in a high ponytail. She has a sundress with a cardigan on, and little ballerina flats that complement the colors in her dress.

The man is handsome, with wavy black hair, and olive skin.

Rolf leans against another window, staring out it. His arms are crossed and his jaw is clenched. His hair is neatly braided down his back, and he looks out of place in his dress shirt and slacks.

My father approaches the two people I guess are our tutors, and I make my way to Rolf.

I'm still angry with him. He has made it clear he expects me to be his breeder, and I made it clear I was not leaving this time again. The closer I get to him, the worse I feel about how we left last night. I'm terrified that when his gaze turns to me it will be filled with anger and hate. I shift my braid and play with the end as I look down. I wish I could hear his thoughts.

He keeps his arms crossed.

The longer the silence lingers between us, the more I think he doesn't want to talk to me. I don't know what is wrong with me. I was never this insecure about Rolf before. The urge to cry is growing. I huff a heavy breath to prevent it.

He shifts and his hand comes to my face, curling his fingers under my chin. It forces my gaze to meet his. "Do not ever lower your head in shame, my flower. You are mine. You have nothing to be ashamed of." He leans forward and kisses my forehead, then eases back.

I fling myself against him, and he wraps his arms around me. "Did you attack my father?" I whisper it against his chest and I hear the low growl escape him.

"I did not attack him. We had a conversation about what we thought should happen between us, and he insulted you. His bruised face is a reminder that no one insults my mate." He shifts us around as he reaches into his pocket and retrieves my pendant. "You left this on the table."

He gives me a wry grin as he separates us to slide the pendant over my head again. I wanted to address the conversation we had the previous night at dinner, but not with all these people around us. We will have to find some private time later.

I was easing forward to kiss him when a throat cleared behind me.

We turn to face the noise.

My father is standing with his arms crossed, looking murderous. His expression immediately shifts to a gentler one when he looks at me. "Lily, this is Henry Sparrow. He will be your tutor for your traditional education. I expect you to behave." He motions for me to come over to him and he leaves the two of us to show the woman to Rolf.

My eyes focus on the woman as she approaches Rolf. "This is your tutor, mutt." Silar's tone is short. "Address her as Miss Bryant. I trust you can keep your paws to yourself better than you do with my daughter." He doesn't linger and goes to the door. I was still staring at Miss Bryant when my father mumbled something about lunch. I don't fully understand the level of jealousy welling in me, but I don't want Rolf to spend the day with this woman. He's supposed to be spending the day with me while we learn new things.

"Come with me, Miss Windraven." Henry put his hand on my shoulder and before I could step away, Rolf growls across the room. The man immediately takes his hand off my shoulder. "No touching, got it."

I was so caught up in watching Rolf and this woman in my jealousy I didn't hear him call me Windraven. Rolf and I look at each other and I blush as he rubs his hand over his face. I turned my back to them with great effort and followed Mr. Sparrow to the table we were going to be working at.

"Wait, you are the little boy I will teach today? But... But..."

"Is that a problem Miss Bryant? My flower insists I must learn her book learning. If you are not capable, perhaps we should ask Silar to let you out of your duties and I will learn from the birdman." Rolf looks irritated when I look over my shoulder.

"No. No. I just, well, I'm a kindergarten teacher. I was told you needed to start your education at the beginning. That you needed the foundations."

Rolf's eyes narrow, and he says nothing for several seconds. I cannot help but smile at this playing out. Then I see him chuff out and shrug. The two of them get closer and voices lower to where I can't hear them. Then they begin to walk away, which makes me frown. The whole point of my insisting he learn, was to spend time with me. Now he is spending time with a completely different woman.

Mr. Sparrow raps on the table with his pencil and it pulls my attention away from Rolf and Miss Bryant. He sets a test booklet in front of me, and hands me the pencil. "You have three hours to complete the exam. This will allow me to see where we need to focus your learning and where you are sufficient. Time starts now," he says as he reaches for the timer.

The exam had hundreds of questions across multiple subjects. I barely finished by the time we stopped for lunch.

Rolf and Miss Bryant had completely disappeared. They did not even appear at lunch. They were probably off in the woods and he was making sweet promises to her.

I frown as I hold the pendant he returned to me. I tried to shake this tiny green monster whispering in my head all the awful things that Rolf and Miss Bryant are doing right now. I did not see my father at lunch either. He was probably overseeing business for the coven, so I sulked in my seat with Mr. Sparrow sitting across from me.

I spent the afternoon with my father. He came to collect me, leaving Mr. Sparrow to look over my answers. My father's mood had brightened since he departed this morning. He leads me into his office and I have memories of my younger self walking in with Nick by my side. I didn't realize how intimidating this office felt until I was standing here without Nick. I wish Rolf were here and try not to pout at the idea he is probably having much more fun without me.

My father thrust a Latin dictionary into my hands, along with a pen and a journal. "We will work on your Latin today. I expect you to be through most of that before dinner." He points to the journal in my hand.

I had never been so happy for dinner in my life.

I take the items back to my room, and I freshen up before appearing in the kitchen. My father was leaving for business in New York, so no formal meal. I slip into the entryway and see the plump older man bouncing happily to music coming from his CD Player on the shelf. He is prepping food for the next day and motions to the waiting plate of sandwiches and juice.

I laugh. "I'm not a kid anymore. I do drink other things now."

His grunt of a reply was enough to keep me from rejecting the juice pouches further. I turn with my feast and am stopped dead by the wall of a man in front of me.

"Rolf, I could have dropped dinner!" I whine up at him. I take him in and he looks as though he had been subjected to torture. "What happened?"

"She has me singing some horrible song. A B F G Minnow Q. It is complete nonsense. Your father mocks me." His eyes flash with anger, and then his anger turns to me as I laugh.

"Do you mean A B C D E F G-?" I sing the alphabet song, but he covers my mouth before I can continue.

"You know this monstrosity? How?" His eyes narrow at me.

I wait patiently for him to remove his hand so I can speak. When he does not remove it, I lick it. I wanted to diffuse the tension we both feel. I can smell her perfume and my eyes narrow up at him. When he moves his hand away, I snort. "Did she teach it to you while in your lap? It's how you learn the letters of the English alphabet. Though it's taught to us when we are little. Most kids can sing the whole thing before they start school."

"People here torture their children with songs of nonsense?" He takes the sandwiches from me, allowing me to carry the juice pouches.

"Yes. How do you teach your language to children?" I notice how he does not answer the question about Miss Bryant as we walk out of the kitchen. I lead us back to my room and he happily joins me.

"Not with nonsensical songs," he retorts. "Or strangely colored books. She told me I should have you read it to me to help me get started." He brings up his other hand and brandishes the little orange book.

I have to bite my lip hard to keep the guffawing laughter from escaping me. "I see. Well, it is quite a tricky book. I mean, Green Eggs and Ham trips up even well-versed people."

Rolf's expression is dark when he realizes I'm teasing him.

It makes me feel bad and I nuzzle him gently in apology. "I will be happy to help you with it," I say in a softer tone.

He eyes me suspiciously, but we get settled at the sitting table in my room and enjoy the sandwiches with juice pouches.

Afterwards, I have him join me on the bed and I gather up his homework.

His brows raise in surprise when I sit in his lap. "Now, I'm going to point at the word as I say it. I will read it in English first, then in Norse." His nod is my only confirmation. I did not miss him sliding his arms around me.

I needed his touch and being nestled into his lap with his scent flooding me, made me relax. I wriggle and squirm to get comfortable, and he chuckles behind me. "Keep that up, my flower, and we will get very far."

"I know," I chirp as I open the book. "Now pay attention," I try to sound stern, but giggle as I begin to read the book to him.

XXV

Take Me Over

"Why are the eggs green?" Rolf grumbles at me. "Who is this, Sam? Who trapped these demons on this page? You let children read this? Do you teach them how to ensorcell these creatures? Is this why you read it the way you do?"

I erupt into giggling and struggle to read further. Rolf's questions are serious and I don't want to mock his lack of education, but it is hilarious he believes these creatures were real beings on any level. We have been working through the book for about thirty minutes when he started with the onslaught. Now, I'm holding the book closed and laughing in his lap.

"Are you mocking me?" He growls a little, there's laughter in his voice. He then sends me into the air, upending me until I'm pinned beneath him and the book is long forgotten. His fingers deftly brush over my sides and stomach, making me squeal and squirm underneath him. He straddles me.

As I fight one hand away, another finds its way to a spot to tickle me. It leaves me breathless in my laughter underneath him.

He wastes no time in devouring me with ravenous kisses. His touch is like fire again.

Need burns through me like a volcanic eruption. I moan and I give up the defense of my ticklish stomach to wrap my arms around him.

His kisses trail along my jaw and he nuzzles me before he kisses against the crook of my neck and it feels like fireworks explode down my spine. His skilled hands have snuck under my shirt, brushing up my skin until he can push it up over my head, only allowing me to lift to lose it before he leans down and draws one of my nipples into his mouth.

I want more. I want him to keep touching me, and this blazing inferno to consume us. "Rolf," I say his name in a needy whine. My anger at him vanquished. He could ask me to ride with him in a handbasket to hell and I would.

He chuckles as he relinquishes the first nipple, and his scratchy beard tickles across my chest as he draws the other nipple between his teeth.

My fingers run through his hair and I try to pull him up to me to kiss him again.

Rolf denies me.

I feel the cool air of the room as he pulls away from me entirely. I frown and sit up as I see him standing a few feet away, looking at me. His hands are loose at his sides and he has a raging hard-on.

"What is it?" I ask with a shaky voice. "Why did you stop?" I reach for my shirt and the insecure feeling of being ugly whispers in my mind. "Am I so awful you do not truly want to mate with me?" The room feels heavy with doubt now. I'm convinced he is looking at me like a monster again, so I turn from him to not see it.

"What? Lily. No." He paces like the wolf he is and runs his fingers through his hair. Then he stops and raises his hand with three fingers displayed. "Three more days," he growls. "Three more days! Not a second longer." He turns and flees from the room, like his life depended on it.

I was left, mouth open, staring at the retreating sight of my Viking. I pull my shirt on. It is as if the tiny, green goblin was waiting for him to leave. She is in my head reminding me he smelled of Miss Bryant, and he is the one to always pull away. I try to tell her to get lost, but her voice gets louder. She reminds me he wants me for breeding while he runs off to do whatever he wants. My eyes narrow and I throw myself into trying to learn the Latin my father assigned me.

That night, my dreams were filled with Rolf. It starts with us arguing. It escalates to him tying my hands to the bedpost and claiming me from behind with no tenderness, or lovemaking. It's primal and violent as his hands palm my hips and he thrusts into me from behind. I wake panting and wet. My entire body hums with energy. All I can think about is how much I want my dream to turn into reality as I stare at my bedroom door in the dark.

The next morning, I see Rolf returning from his morning run. He is only dressed in sweatpants, and I follow him as he makes his way to his room. Before he could slip into his room, I catch him and I shove him against the door. My eyes meet his and then I see his gaze shift. He is aroused and I have not even done anything to him. I kiss him hard, and my hands grip his waistband.

I wasn't thinking, all I could process was that I was on fire and I needed him to touch me to make it stop or make it worse. I don't care which, and I kiss his bare chest as my fingers hook onto the waist of his pants.

Rolf's hands are planted against the door and his breathing is hard. He struggles to not respond, but I feel his erection against my stomach. His eyes never leave mine as I continue kissing down his stomach, his pants now pooling around his ankles.

I was winging this. I had never taken a man into my mouth and Rolf is huge. What would I even do with that thing in my mouth? I didn't care. I wanted to drive him crazy and have him claim me like he did in my dream.

I lick my lips and then part them as I draw his head in and I swear his eyes bulge from his head.

"By Odin," his voice cracks and his manhood twitches. One hand comes down and he laces his fingers right into my hair, pulling me forward.

I gag, and my mouth tightens around his throbbing shaft.

He swells and presses to the back of my mouth.

I gag again, trying to draw a sharp breath through my nose.

His pupils are dilated with lust and his breathing hard.

Tears cling to my lashes as I struggle to accommodate him. I try to ease my head back.

His hand tightens in my hair. Then he whines.

I chuckle and push against his hand more to give myself a reprieve. I draw him back in and I bring my hand up to his thighs. I felt awkward.

But he bucks his hips forward, trying to push himself deeper in. His eyes close and he leans his head back against the door. He must like what I'm doing.

I feel the dull ache building between my legs. I bob my head faster, trying not to think about what I'm doing, and going with what makes Rolf make the best noises.

Then he pulls back and away, a loud pop sound happens as he frees his cock from my mouth. He had opened the door and pulled himself away from me into his room.

I stand to follow when he slams the door closed.

"Rolf!" I whine.

"I... will see you... in the library," he calls from behind the door.

The library was a disaster. I was frustrated from my failed attempt at seducing him and it was making the jealous green goblin grow in my head. I'm convinced he is denying me entirely because of Miss Bryant. I stare daggers at her when he enters the library.

He had showered and was fully dressed now. He approaches me first and then I see it. I was calmer until he came close. All I could think about was him again. I moved forward, and I kissed him. His hands slid down, and he wrapped me into his arms as he kissed me. I felt him pick me up enough to back me to the table I will learn at in a few minutes.

Miss Bryant and Mr. Sparrow gawk at us as we ignore them.

"My flower," he moans between kisses.

I bring my legs up and wrap them around him.

He peels himself free and turns me around to press me against the desk, pinning me. He presses tight against my body for a fleeting moment before he rips himself from me. "I... I will go outside to study today." He sounds pained and then he was gone.

I whimper. Why is he doing this to me?

Mr. Sparrow caught my arm before I could chase after him. He looked uncomfortable, but he was not letting me get out of lessons. Not that I paid attention at all. I did not see Rolf the rest of the day.

He avoided meals and skipped studying with me. It was like he was avoiding me. When he was nowhere near me, I felt murderous and jealous. The moment he got near me it all dissipated and I returned to the nymphomaniac.

The next morning, I woke from the wet dream of Rolf claiming me like a beast to see him hovering over me in the dark. His breathing is hard, and his body tense. He does not say a word.

My heart immediately starts jackhammering in my chest.

He yanked the covers off me and climbed onto the bed. His hand gripped an ankle, and he tugged my legs apart, kneeling between them.

I part for him.

His fingers grip onto my panties and he tears them from me, tossing them aside.

I can't breathe from excitement and fear.

He leans forward and his rough fingers stroke along the soft ginger-colored curls.

I moan.

This brings a grin to his face as he stares down at me. His fingers work faster over my clit.

I swear he is setting me on fire.

He shifts his hand and uses his thumb to rub my swollen clit and I feel two fingers press into me.

I gasp as it feels like he spreads me too far open. My moans turn into pleading whimpers.

He rocks his fingers in and out of me with great control.

I don't care. He is touching me, and I want more. I want him inside me. I shamelessly rock my hips and tighten around his fingers, milking them. I writhe and whine in my begging for him to claim me. Closing my eyes, I bite against my lip as I feel the pressure build and then the tidal wave of sensations overtakes me. My legs clamp tight on his hand and I quiver with the slightest movement. My orgasm rushes over me and any coherent thought I had is gone.

Rolf slows his fingers down until he fully withdraws them from inside me. He leans up, and he kisses me on the forehead before he moves away from the bed.

I open my eyes to see what he is doing. His arousal is front and center. "Don't go," I whisper.

"I cannot stay in here, Lily." His voice thick with arousal and desperation.

"Why not? We are mates. Please don't reject me." I whimper in fear.

He draws in a sharp breath and he takes another step away from me. His back is to me. "Lily, you reek of dark magic. You smell like the day I met you. Someone is doing something to you. Even as my mate, you should not go into heat. You are not a wolf. I fear if I claim you before the seventh day you agreed to wait, something bad will happen to you. I cannot let that happen." Without allowing me to respond, Rolf shifted into his wolf and fled out the door he had left open.

I'm stunned. His words cut me to the core. It makes me feel dirty from having his touch. The room felt like a winter storm had settled in when I finally swung my feet over the edge of the bed. It took several minutes to get up and close the door. That Rolf thought someone was doing this to me, and that I did not want him of my accord made me question everything. It wasn't long before I had succumbed to the goblin in my head that told me all the horrible things Rolf had not said out loud and cried myself to sleep.

Oaths and Curses

Rolf had had enough of Miss Bryant and her insistence on remaining too close to him. He had told her, more than once, he was spoken for, and did not appreciate her behavior.

The woman would agree to his boundary, then he would find her right in his bubble again. She also was teaching him nonsense. Compared to what Lily was learning, it was complete gibberish. He's convinced it's Silar's doing to insult him and keep him from being near Lily. He loves Lily, but their time here is temporary. He has duties at home, and Lily is his mate. He would remain by her side, but their conversation about when that would be is not over.

Since they have come to this time, they have been in danger. He can sense it. Silar has such a dark presence about him, that it makes Rolf wonder how Lily cannot see it. Her father is not telling them everything. Every conversation that he has had with the man has left Rolf feeling violent and confused. Rolf is the son of the Alpha in their clan. He is accustomed to getting his way and putting the fear of the Gods in those that would cross him. Here, he felt like nothing. Like he was more a pet than a lover to Lily.

This would change once her vow was satisfied.

His current problem was violating Lily's trust further. He knew he hurt her when he left the previous night. He could feel all the pain and anguish he caused his beautiful mate. He has never been good with words with her. He could give orders, raid villages, and plunder loot, but the moment he gets in front of the one person in the world he would do anything for he turns into a bumbling idiot. He knew that she would be with Mr. Sparrow until dinner, and that gave him plenty of time to search her room now that he had ditched that insufferable Bryant woman.

What made him hesitate is that he was going to do it without permission.

He could feel the rage welling inside him at being denied his mate. The mate bond is strong, but it will not force a pair together. Whatever is happening to them, is taking all reason from the both of them. When he gets anywhere near her scent, he is thrown into a maddening need to mate with her and to claim her as his own. He had promised himself he would make it special for her. That he would take her to the spring she found and would have her under the full moon. It haunted his dreams every night on that long boat ride to the Isles. Only to have Luna try to destroy it for him. He would have words with his father when they returned.

Luna will never hurt Lily again.

He rolls his shoulders as he stands in front of her room, preparing for a battle. With a quick glance to guarantee he is not seen, he steps into her bedroom and locks the door behind him. Her bed is half made, clothes are strewn about, and her scent is everywhere. His manhood stiffens at just the scent of her. He'll be running for hours to work it out of his system at this rate. This is not the first time Rolf had invaded someone's chambers for an object without intent to murder them. He strips from his clothing and folds it, setting it in a chair at her sitting table, and shifts into his wolf form.

His snout lifts into the air, and he sniffs. Then he moves, following the scent. He was not looking for the sweet scent of his mate that is driving him to madness, but the rotten scent of death and destruction. The sulfur smell of Hel's wasteland. He moves around the room, as if following the trail. Back and forth, into the bathroom, and back until he is looking at her dresser topped with jewelry boxes and trinkets.

The air shimmers as he shifts back into human form and looks over the items on the dresser. None of them made his blood run cold when his hand brushed over them. He is not magical, but he knows Hel's magic. The witches in the Isles and the natives in the forest where he is from use it. He stops at a small box sitting open and the little plastic card Lily had used the day they acquired all of their clothes is nestled on a bed of pink velvet. As soon as his fingers touch it, he feels the surge of energy and the unending desire to consume Lily. The lava of desire burns through him like nothing he has felt before.

Her father handed her this card after their oaths were exchanged.

His eyes narrow and he looks down at the little plastic square in his hand. Her father had tried to curse her into breaking her oath. The card vibrated in his hand and he was panting with need, his dick painfully hard. His thoughts are muddling and focusing on needing Lily. He grits his teeth and brings his other hand up, now holding the plastic in both hands. He had never seen a talisman like this, but he knew how to deal with talismans. His fingers tighten on the card and in seconds it is snapped in two.

The pieces fall to the floor as a dark cloud of smoke hisses between his hands.

His body stiffens, and he stares at the card pieces on the floor. All the rage, and doubt that had been clouding him, making him want to constantly touch Lily was gone. He felt as though a large weight had been lifted off his shoulders. He squats down, picking up the pieces of the card. He would talk with Lily about this later tonight, after he confronts Silar. They were leaving this place. It was no longer safe here, and he gave his word he would always protect her. When he stands, he turns to retrieve his clothing and stops in his tracks.

A young woman with mousy brown hair and sad eyes stares at him. He inhales and scents death on her.

A low growl escapes his lips.

She holds her hands up but does not say a word.

He growls louder, and he approaches, intending to attack her.

She floats back, avoiding him.

It makes Rolf pause again. His brow draws in confusion. "What are you?" He crosses his arms.

The woman touches her throat and shakes her head no.

"Then what good does your presence bring me? Are you one of Silar's tricks?"

She shakes her head no and moves to a small bookcase. She points to the books. When Rolf makes no move to come closer, she stomps her foot and points at the books emphatically.

"You want me to read the books? I cannot read. I'm a warrior, not a scholar." He mutters.

She rolls her eyes at him when he says that. She makes a

motion around the room and then points at the books again.

"Lily." He hears her name whispered, despite having seen the specter not say a word.

"Are you a spirit?"

She makes a so-so motion, and points at the card pieces in his hand. She then motions to the books again with urgency.

Rolf's expression draws into a frown, but he comes forward. When he gets close enough, she points to specific books for him to pick off the shelf. "I do not see how this is of any importance. These look like those children books Lily has been reading to me." He looks up to question the young woman again, but she is gone. Putting the books back the way he found them, he plans to ask Lily about the girl and the books. There is something in these books the girl finds important.

Satisfied he has left Lily's room in the same state he found it, he quickly dresses and makes his way to his room. The girl appearing when the card was destroyed makes him want to confront Silar alone. If he was evil, he did not want Lily in the room to be used as leverage. His heart already weighs heavy that he believes he will have to kill her father. He paces in his room, trying to decide the correct path forward. Does he tell Lily everything and beg her to come home with him? Or does he confront Silar and expose him?

As if he had summoned the devil himself, Silar is leaning in the doorway. He watches Rolf pace in his dilemma before he finally speaks.

"You know, mutt, you are proving far more trouble than I expected." Silar closes and locks the door behind him.

XXVII

Three Midnights Gone

Rolf did not give Silar any reaction other than to cross his arms and look him square in the eyes. He would not be intimidated by this soft man. Lily was in danger, and no matter how much he wanted her happiness, he would not allow it to cost Lily her life. She is precious to him. For six long years, he waited patiently for her. He has cracked her tough exterior to trust him and make her fall in love with him. As the older man closed and locked the door, he got an uneasy feeling that he had made a grave mistake in breaking the card. This was only elevated when the mousy haired girl appeared by Silar's side, her head lowered.

"While this is troublesome, not all is lost," Silar muses as he brushes his fingers along the apparition's cheek. "Thank you, Rolf. Now Sarah does not have to work as hard to bring you and my sweet Lily together. She has been taxing herself because of your resistance."

Rolf narrows his eyes and inhales sharply. He had not attacked the apparition because she appeared to help him back in Lily's room.

"Oh, come now, mutt. Do not blame her. She foolishly threw herself into this game before you became a thorn in my side. Now, you will be a good boy and you will claim what is rightfully yours. Preferably before midnight. I need my daughter under my control." Silar pats Rolf on the head, like he is an animal.

Rolf tries to throw a punch, but stands still, motionless.

Silar turns and lets himself out of the room, only pausing in the doorway to look at Sarah. "Do not let him rest until he has sunk his fangs into my daughter's neck." With that, Silar closes the door.

Rolf lunges forward and throws his fist into the door, causing the wall to shake. He thumps his fist against the door again and begins to pant. His eyes close and he tries to calm down to think.

Gentle hands touch his shoulder. He leans against the door breathing hard. He struggles to work out how he could have been so blind as to walk into this trap. Every muscle in his body rigid from the effort to not turn around and face his tormentor.

"Your vile tricks won't work, witch. You are wasting your efforts. I lived six years yearning for my mate without breaking my oaths to her."

With a sad look, the mousy-haired girl comes closer. Rolf turns to face her, his back against the door. His expression is cold, and he crosses his arms to close off to her getting any closer to him.

She reaches up and brushes his cheek. Her mousy brown hair shimmers longer and into coppery strands that remind him of fire. Her eyes lose their dull gray shade for a green as vibrant as the fields of the Isles.

Rolf inhales to calm himself and regrets it instantly.

Lily's scent of mead with the hint of wood smoke surrounds him.

His body reacts without hesitation. His manhood grows firm, and his heart beats faster. The aching need to bury himself fills him.

Her calloused fingers slid under his shirt.

He looks to the ceiling, trying to ignore the specter tormenting him.

"Rolf," Lily's voice bounces off the walls as he feels the tightness around his manhood. His gaze whips down to see his own hand stroking himself in his pants. He rips his hand from himself as if he were burned.

"No!" He roars at the figure of Lily before him. His animalistic bond with Lily fills him with confusion. Why would he be so cruel to his mate? "You are not Lily. No matter how much you look like her." His voice is uncertain and breathless as he continues to pant. He should run. It always solves the problem. So, he forcibly turns from the vision of Lily and tries to rip the door open. It does not budge. He turns back and sees the window. He stalks toward the window and tries to shift. His body shimmers, and the flicker of his white wolf appears, but he is right back into human form. He growls and turns to face the vision again.

******

I had not seen Rolf all day. He wasn't at our studies. He wasn't at lunch. He didn't show up to dinner, and he did not come to work on his homework with me. For the better part of the day, I was distracted and aroused. All I could think about was Rolf throwing me over the side of my bed, yanking my panties down and fucking me like he had nothing to lose. More than once, I got my knuckle rapped by the pencil in Mr. Sparrow's hand.

After lunch, it was like a fog of teenage hormones had lifted. I could breathe easier and focus on something other than the thought of Rolf's massive manhood. I was halfway through my afternoon lessons with my father when he abruptly left me in his office. By the time dinner rolled around, I was flush cheeked and aching again. This was dumb. I was going to just take care of this when Rolf came to work on his reading.

Only, he didn't come.

The little green goblin in my head was roaring about how Miss Bryant was conveniently missing all day as well. She reminded me that I was not pretty, and how could Rolf love me when I have taken everything from him.

I spent an hour in the shower in a mix of self-loathing and arousal so intense; I'm convinced I'm going to die if Rolf doesn't mate with me. I exited the bathroom, still in a towel, when I felt the prickling sensation of someone in my room. I thought I had locked my door, but I see now it is standing wide open. I creep closer and ease it closed. The nagging sensation of being watched increases. I hesitate at the door, debating fleeing the room to go find Rolf, or my father. A tiny part of me fears it is Nick back from the grave to curse me.

"Mine," his voice is hot against my neck when Rolf manifests behind me. It sends burning electricity down my spine and I gasp. I turn to face him, only his body presses closer against me and holds me against the door. He yanks the towel from my hands, which makes me yelp. His hands are rough and needy as starts at my hips and gropes his way up to my breasts. I give another shy yelp and try to cover myself, but his hands are there and he growls in my ear. "Do not cover yourself or I will spank you."

"R…Rolf," I stammer. I had been dreaming about this for the past three days non-stop, but now I'm frightened of what is happening between us. Something feels off.

"Silence, witch," he hisses in my ear. His body weight presses against me. His hands knead and pinch my nipples until they are painfully taught in his grasp. Then one hand snakes up to curl around my throat. His fingers press firm enough to let me know he could squeeze the life out of me, but he doesn't tighten them enough to harm me. His muscles against my back twitch and his erection is rigid.

His other hand slides down and he thrusts his fingers between my curls to find my arousal slick and wet with readiness. My skin is flush with his fiery touch. I bite against my lip as a moan escapes me. Rolf had never been so rough with me before. Turning my head to the side, he is feral with lust. His steely blue eyes are fogged, and he is struggling to get his pants off. He means to take me against this door.

"Rolf," I begged. My voice sounded timid and frightened. I didn't want my first time to hurt. I already knew he was going to bite me and it would hurt in its own right. I wanted him to be consumed with desire, but I did not want him to fuck me like a whore against the door. I squirm and try to free myself, and then I feel him freeze.

His body goes rigid, as if he has jolted awake from a nightmare.

His fangs are extended, and he is in a morphed state of animal and human. He was going to mark me. He had a hold of my throat and had my head held to the side in submission. Had my voice penetrated his fog? He hesitated because of something he saw. Fear wells in me that he is about to reject me. He lets out another growl and pushes away from me.

I don't know what to do and I'm aching and wanting, leaning against the door. By the Gods, why did I want him so bad right now?

Rolf storms over to the bed, snatches the quilt off it, and turns to face me again.

I have turned my back to the door to watch him and hug myself. My cheeks flame red and I look anywhere but at Rolf.

"My flower," rolls off his tongue in a gentler tone. I watch him as he approaches. He wraps the blanket around me, trapping my arms at my sides. He then hoists me right over his shoulder with a grunt, clamping an arm around me to hold me in place.

"Put me down! Rolf! Don't you-."

He slaps my ass hard.

"I told you silence, woman. No more excuses. I'm taking you to where you belong with me, and I'm claiming what is mine. Three days have passed." His voice is husky and thick with command.

I squirm in futility, but the truth is I don't want to escape.

He barges us right out the door and is moving fast enough it's hurting my stomach.

The thrill of being caught wells and before I can truly protest this mistreatment, he is setting me to my feet. The clearing is small and hidden amongst the trees. As he peels the blanket from me, he flicks it out and lays it on the ground, leaving me to hug my naked form.

I watch him for any signs of the brute I just encountered in the bedroom.

He is still raging hard, and his jaw clenches. But, he otherwise appears to have all his faculties.

I start to speak, but a look from him silences me. He strips out of his clothing and comes to stand right in front of me. This is the most awkward and romantic thing that has happened between us. "Lily Viggodatter, I claim you as my own. I will cherish and protect you for all our days. What do you say?"

My heart hammers in my chest. The butterflies took off in my stomach, and I gasped in surprise. I slid my hand into his and eased closer. "Rolf Ivarsen, I claim you as my own. I will honor and adore you for all our days. I say yes." It felt almost silly to me to be talking, but it was enough.

The joy in his smile before he kissed me sent the rush of excitement through me again. He pulls me against him and the kiss deepens. His lips bruised mine with how fiercely he kisses me. His arms slide down and he pulls me to him as he is dropping to his knees.

I try to run my fingers along the soft curls on his chest and he catches my wrists. He kisses me again, tugging my lower lip between his teeth as he leans me back. My wrists in his hands are guided above my head, where he captures them both with a single hand. Leaving his other hand to come back down and ease his pants down. His movements are frantic and needy. He was not going to be denied any longer.

I didn't want him to be.

He springs free of his pants and with a grunt he shifts his weight over me to pull my thighs further apart.

I wriggle underneath him, causing me to arch when he keeps my hands pinned to the ground. Were it not for the blanket he thoughtfully kidnapped me in, I would be bare in the snow. He gives me no warning, and he thrusts himself into me.

I cry out and he devours my cry with a kiss.

His hips thrusting hard into me. He was commanding me to take him without saying a word. His other hand finds its way to my breast again, and he squeezes enough to draw a whimper from me. His gaze never leaves mine as he thrusts into me.

Our breathing becomes labored and sweat beads on his skin, in spite of it being January in Boston.

I would be shivering were it not for the inferno blazing between us.

I throw my head back and moan, breaking our eye contact. I feel his hot breath on my neck as he pants against me. I bring my knees up, trying to gain any semblance of control, but only find it makes him pump faster.

"Mine," he groans against my neck.

"Yours," I moan.

He peppers biting kisses along my neck and chin as he smiles down at me. I was submitting to him.

I could feel the pleasure ripple through his body and into me through our bond. I moan against my lip still caught between my teeth. I was going to climax soon, I could feel the pressure build and the way my body burned for more of his touch.

He nuzzles me and then he licks the skin where I assume he will mark me.

Fear wells inside me again, that he might still stop and reject me.

His fangs sink into my throat and all I see are stars. Blinding white stars that dance behind my eyelids as I let the volcano of my orgasm explode through me.

My skin is alive with sensitivity. I'm vibrating with energy and I struggle against Rolf's hold on my wrists, aching to run my fingers through his hair and pull him into a wanton kiss.

He denies me both by pulling out of me and rolling me over onto my stomach. I whine at losing contact with him. Before I can verbally complain of his lack of touching me, he brushes against me again. He releases my wrists and places his hand between my shoulder blades to push me down.

Sliding his hands along my sides he draws my hips up to him.

I obediently pose for him, gyrating my hips to rub along his still very erect manhood.

"Good girl," he murmurs as I milk him.

It was madness how much I wanted him to keep doing this.

His grip on my hips tightens, and he pumps with gusto. Leaning over me to hold me in position while he pistons into me.

My muscles ache and everything is sore, but I don't want him to stop. I want this feeling of unbridled desire to last forever. To feel everything he feels. I push back against him.

He groans as he erupts into me. His fingers bruising as he clings to my hips, then shudders behind me with the force of his orgasm still raging through him. His body relaxes, but he does not pull from me this time. Instead, he leans into me and then rolls to his side, pulling me with him.

My cheeks flush crimson when I realize he means to stay inside of me. It wakes the greedy, lust-filled monster inside of me and I begin to throb around him again.

"My sweet, insatiable flower," he murmurs against my temple in a kiss. His arms pull me back against him and settle, sufficiently holding me against him. Seconds later, he is snoring lightly.

My eyes catch movement in front of us, and it makes me tense.

Shimmering into view is Sarah. I gasp and start to scream, but I see her put her finger to her lips.

There is a light behind her, but I can't make out what is causing it.

From the light emerges Nick. He wasn't in dog form, though. He was a tall, slender man with silvering hair and vibrant green eyes. It doesn't matter that he wasn't a dog, I knew it was him.

Echoing in my mind is the thought of forgiveness.

She takes Nick's hand.

I had so many questions to ask. I wanted to hug Nick. Then I felt horribly embarrassed to be naked in front of them.

They both smile at me.

A sense of serenity surrounds me. Then the light was gone, thrusting us back into darkness. The moon is the only light in this part of the woods.

I thought I would be colder than I am, and uncomfortable out here. The cool air felt soothing against my hot skin.

Rolf is a raging inferno as he pulls me tighter into his grasp.

My body aches and is bruised from his rough claiming, but I soon join Rolf in sleep.

hot and Cold

The bitter sting of cold air kisses my skin and I close my eyes tighter. My body aches all over, as if I had been in a fight and was beaten until I couldn't move. My legs and arms cramped as I tried to hug myself but couldn't move. My cheeks sting from the wintry air kissing them. I flutter my eyes open to the silent whisper of snow falling. I gasp.

In an instant Rolf is awake, his wolf form positioned over me like a white furry blanket.

At first, there was something out there about to attack us and the reason I could not move is I have been hurt. My wild imagination gives way to the realization that I'm freezing cold. My body cramps and contracts from the exposure to the elements.

The longer Rolf crouches over me the better I feel. He's still a raging inferno, even in wolf form.

I try to lift my hand to pet along his belly, but it only brings me pain.

Rolf tilts his head down to look at me and a low whine escapes him. He shimmers above me and returns to human form. Panic fills his beautiful gaze. "Lily," his voice is urgent above me. "Lily, please say something."

"C... Cold," I say between my teeth chattering.

He springs into action and flips the now damp quilt around me and scoops me up.

The snow falls heavier and I bury myself in the blanket and against him as he carries me back to the estate house. I can hear his thoughts tumbling in a frantic plea to Mani and Freya to not take me. They are followed by how much he loves me and how stupid he was to bring me out here.

"N-No... Not stupid."

He doesn't respond to me as he bursts into the house like a madman. My room was far closer to the entrance than his, so he took us there, making a beeline for the bathroom. He sets me down on the ground.

I lie on the tile, thinking how shiny they were from this angle. My body shakes and my fingers are a reddish-purple color, making the melting snowflakes turn from white to giving my skin an iridescent sheen. I whimpered when he ripped the blanket off of me and hoisted me up.

He cradled me as he stepped in the shower and sank to his knees, holding me as the steaming hot water poured down over us.

I gasp in pain and surprise. It felt like he was pouring ice over my skin, and then it burned. I shivered against him and his arms held me tight enough to squeeze the air from my lungs.

"Can't... breathe..." I squeak against his chest. Relief floods me.

Rolf's emotions barrel into me like a freight train. He showers me with kisses and continues rubbing my arms and body to chase the frigid feeling away. I look down at my toes and they are dark looking. That does not bode well. "Rolf, my-."

"Unhand her mutt. Before she loses all her extremities," my father says with a fierce roar. He barrels into my bathroom looking as panicked as Rolf and I feel.

Rolf snarls at Silar, and the rage overpowers everything else. "You will never touch her again," he says as he roars back at Silar.

With a loud crack in the room, I see a vibrant blast of blue light erupt from my father and hurtle toward us.

Rolf dropped me to the floor of the shower entirely as he put himself between me and the blue light.

I scream and then Rolf slumps down, unconscious.

My father reaches into the shower like we weren't both crouched here naked and turns off the water.

He then drags Rolf unceremoniously out onto the floor, leaving him there. Then he comes for me.

It isn't anger on his face I see. It is fear.

He grunts as he picks me up. While my father is tall and muscular, he is not a weightlifter. I easily weigh a hundred and fifty pounds. He carries me from the room and dumps me onto the bed.

My feet are not responding to my brain. I cannot wiggle my toes.

"My feet," I cry.

"I need blood, Lily. To heal you." My brain is foggy and I don't fully process the implications of what he is saying.

Why would he need blood to heal me?

"Then take mine," Rolf says somewhere behind me.

I close my eyes and lose the conversation going on behind

me as I start to shiver again. Had I been in my right mind I would have warned him that blood magic is dark magic. Or that by willingly giving the blood he could put himself in great peril. "…I will kill you," is the next thing I hear from Rolf's mouth.

"She is no good to me dead," My father says. His voice is calm and soothing against the raging emotions slamming into me from Rolf. "Lily, I need you to relax. Come, my darling, uncurl your body."

I want to listen to my father and I try to roll onto my back, but I'm exhausted and I close my eyes.

"No!" I hear both men shout at me, but I just want to go back to sleep. I'm in my bed and it's warm. I will be alright.

******

It was dark when I woke next. I felt warm and safe with a heavy weight pressing against and on me. I wriggle to test that I can and my body still burns and aches, but I can move my toes. I can also move my fingers. I inhale and then nestle against Rolf.

"Mhmm, my flower, keep that up and I will have to remind you who you belong to." His voice is raspy and deep.

"I'm sorry I ruined our night," I murmur to him.

"No, Lily. I was thoughtless and put you in harm's way. I wanted to be under the moon so bad I was reckless and did not consider you not having a wolf to keep you warm." His arms wrap around me and he pulls me closer.

I can sense there is more, but for now, I'm content to remain in his arms. I realize we are both under the blankets and I'm in pajamas. Whatever happened between Rolf and my father resulted in Rolf being in bed with me and my father nowhere to be seen.

"He said he had to meet with other coven leaders in London. That he would be back in three days. That was two days ago."

I still wasn't used to Rolf being able to hear my thoughts, and I scrunch up my face at him.

"You can not like it all you want, but it is done so we can protect one another, my flower. With practice you will communicate with me in my mind as well." Rolf sits up, and he plants a soft kiss on my forehead before he frees himself from our pile of blankets.

He strides to my bookcase.

Wanting to get a better view of what he is doing, I sit up in bed.

He squats down, runs his fingers over the books to retrieve three of them. Anger and regret radiate from him. With an easy gesture, he comes back to the bed and sets the books down in my lap.

"Your spirit wanted you to read these."

"My spirit? Oh! Wait. You saw Sarah too?" I had not touched the books yet. I could not fathom why Sarah would want me to read children's books.

"You name your spirits?"

I giggle at Rolf, then grow somber. "Sarah is, I mean, was, a member of my father's coven. She lived here when I was younger, I mean, like a few weeks ago. She was the one I was practicing on."

"I thought you said you did not kill that girl? Did you lie to Alpha, Lily?"

"What? No. She was sleeping. Nick took it away, remember?" It irritated me that he accused me of such a horrible thing.

"I'm sorry. It has been a long week, my flower. Tell me what those books mean. Why did your spirit think they were important? She pointed to those specifically."

"I don't know, Rolf. These are children's books, like the ones with green eggs." I pick up the first one and I open it with caution.

Pens and Prophecies

As I turned the pages, the book shifted in my hand. No longer was it an Amelia Bedelia book, but a leather-bound journal with old parchment style pages. The handwriting on the page is flowing and neat, my mother's handwriting.

My lip quivers and I look up at Rolf, who is staring at the book with a concerned look. I missed my mother terribly. For all the fights and all the anger I had for her; I wish she were with Rolf and me right now. She always made it better and fixed things. I felt like the worst daughter ever as I watched the words ink back into visibility.

The thing about a witch's journal is it can be a trap. Unsuspecting victims flip open the pages and get drawn into the memories and thoughts of the witch never to be seen again.

Rolf growls in the background, but it sounds like he is far

away. Then his presence is near me. His arm wraps around my waist as I continue to stare at the words in the journal.

I felt twisted and curved, like the letters on the page.

Rolf sucks in a sharp breath behind me.

I want to close my eyes but I can't look away from the words, no not words, now shapes. The queer feeling of moving through memories makes me shudder.

We now stood in a room I recognized at Grandma Finley's home. It's the room with all the dolls. Or it was. This looks like a bedroom. I watch my mother stroll in. I take in her dark auburn hair and pale skin. The twinkle in her eye and the style of clothing she has made me furrow my brow. She looks like she stepped right out of one of those old war movies.

She turns and is talking to someone I cannot see, but her voice slowly fades in like someone heard my thoughts and turned up the volume. I watch in fascination as she argues with who I can only guess is Grandma Finley, but she looks much younger, too.

"That's my grandma." I say to Rolf.

We are drawn around the room to avoid colliding with them as they argue, and then pulled through the house as my mother leaves the room. Our movement is fast and hard to adjust to as it feels like pages are flipping through the air.

Then we are in the main room of my grandmother's cottage. Waiting, in an impeccable suit, is my father. He looks the same as he does now, with a hint of salt and pepper against dark hair and eyes that could look right through your soul. This dolled up version of my mother leaps into his arms and they embrace. They look so happy to see each other.

"Focus," I hear my grandmother's voice echo around the room.

Rolf's grip tightens around me as he must have heard it.

I narrow my eyes at the young lovers. I then see it. The

small gesture my father makes as he brushes my mother's curls back and gifts her a necklace.

Before I can move closer, we are ripped from the scene entirely, and the twisted curve feeling happens again. I hear my mother's voice reading across the pages about how in love she was. How her magic blossomed and grew under Silar's careful tutelage.

Then the voice becomes somber and angry.

We are pulled into the kitchen of Grandma Finley's home and Grandma Finley looks older. When I turn my head to my mother, she looks the same, only her hair is loose around her shoulders and she is wearing a little go-go dress with matching boots.

In walks my father, dressed to kill, and also looks the same age.

The three of them argue about covens and rituals. My father is some kind of authority figure. But my grandmother is standing against him. She looks tired and worn. My mother is worried for her, based on the words echoing from the pages, but then my grandmother tries to bind my father.

There is a flash of light and my mother's voice screaming as we are ripped through the memories faster.

The voice of my mother frantically fills my head as she talks of coming to Boston. Of how their marriage was blissful until she learned of the talisman he gave her. She had been so foolish and blind to his true intentions.

The prophecies her mother ranted and raved about all splayed out in the room of Grimoires.

We are in my father's estate, standing in this stone room lit by candles.

My mother is sobbing as she holds the necklace in her hand and reads over the pages. Her thoughts were full of rage and revenge for what my father had done to her.

What that was, I couldn't understand.

Until Sarah walks in. Sarah! But she was close to my age. How is this possible? She comforts my mother and tries to soothe her. Sarah tells her it's destiny and how much my father loves my mother. Sarah takes the talisman and passes my father as he enters and squats in front of my kneeling mother.

They argue and my mother tries to hex him, only to be thrown against the stone wall, like there was a protective shield around my father.

"A blood bond," I gasp.

My father had bound my mother to him through blood. Fear wells inside of me at this revelation. She could never stand against my father, no matter what happens. It is terribly dark magic, and all but enslaves the victim to the wielder. How did my mother get him to release her?

On and on we went, without realizing the other two journals joined the first, and we were passing from memory to memory. The words are filled with panic of all the signs that my father is practicing dark magic.

She doesn't know how he is doing it, but he is not letting her age like she should while her mother is aging rapidly.

People are disappearing, and anyone who tries to help her disappear suddenly turns on her.

How my father insists on her learning time magic. She is sure the man she fell in love with is devolving into madness.

I cry for my mother. I can hear all her fear and anguish as she pours her heart into her journals. Decades of a life with a man she thought she was in love with.

We are ripped from the twisting and turning travel one last time. My grandmother looks weak and frail, not at all like the woman I knew as a child. My mother sobs against her and begs forgiveness. There is a thunderous roar in the distance and my grandmother smiles softly at my mother. A horrible dread fills me as I watch my grandmother's eyes roll in the back of her head and her voice booms through my mother's journaled words.

"Born at the cusp of the millennium. Power beyond control. All will be right as it should be. What has been done cannot be undone. Love is the price of freedom."

My mother's mournful words about the death of her mother breaks my heart. The woman I know and love as Grandma Finley had been the remains of a spirit for my entire life, not just the night Viggo went with us.

I wail as I rip us from the journal.

Rolf's arms are instantly around me as he turns me to face him. His massive chest is like a rock in the storm of my emotions.

I cling to him and I sob, my mother's thoughts still screaming in my head.

"Shh, my flower. I will let no harm come to you. Shh. It will be alright." Rolf's voice is gentle and low against my temple as he rocks me in his arms. The drumming of his heart soothes me, and I understood the warning in the prophecy.

I was what she saw. Everything has happened as it should, and that brought a small comfort to me.

My father had targeted my mother and created me to be a catalyst to his plans.

I felt betrayed and frightened. What would my life be like had Rolf not chased after me?

"Rolf, we have to stop my father. We cannot let him complete whatever plan he has."

"Whatever you need, Lily. I am your sword and shield. I would break down the gates of Valhalla if it meant your happiness." He kisses my forehead again and brushes the tears from my cheeks.

Even with his confidence and calming demeanor, I take several minutes to calm down. I kiss him softly when I'm finally calm enough to think. "First, I need you to tell me what happened after I passed out. How do I still have toes? What did my father do? Don't leave out any detail. Then we will decide how to leave this place."

"Can we not just go, Lily? You opened the portal to here. Surely, you can open it back to our home." I see his eyes fill with hope and it is then I realize just how miserable he is here.

I cast my gaze down and my cheeks flush. "Rolf, I don't know how to open the portal to a specific place. What I did to come here was different. I cast the spell to take me home, and it brought me here." My voice loses volume as I finish the sentence.

"Then we will steal his books of magic and hide somewhere until you can do it." He takes my chin and lifts it again. "Lily. I am not angry with you. I love you. I go where you go, always." He leans in and gives me a chaste kiss.

Best Laid Plans

Rolf told me that he doesn't know what my father did to save me other than it took a lot out of the man.

I found this perplexing. I don't remember what they were doing either.

Rolf had carried my father back to his room after the ordeal.

I had danced with death according to Rolf's recounting. He felt me slipping away from him and was beside himself. His guilt washes over me and I watch him in silence. The thoughts of being a failure to me and feeling worthless in this place are strong.

I crawl into his lap without a word. I wanted him to know I was not angry with him, nor did I feel like he was a failure. I mean, I'm only eighteen. If we were perfect, it would be weird.

Nothing of Rolf's life still applies. He can't just invade people's homes and take what he feels he should. All the harshness of his time has been eradicated.

I take the time to sit in silence with him, regardless of the urgent need to get out of my father's home. His arms wrap tight enough around me he might squeeze me to death.

"You are amazing, my flower. I do not deserve you."

"I can hear you!"

He erupts into laughter as I shout in our minds. I knew that Mom and Viggo had been doing it. But this is great! Now we don't have to give away anything. I hop up out of his lap and start quickly packing things into a backpack. Mom's journals, my journal, and Latin workbook. "Okay. So, we need to get the Grimoire that focuses on time magic. Maybe a couple of others. I know what they look like and provided we are quick, we won't be noticed."

"You plan to keep them hidden in his own home?"

"What? No. Of course not. He would find that out too fast. We're going to have to leave, Rolf. It will take time for me to learn how to do it. Magic is not fast and easy. There is always a price." I recite the infamous phrase ingrained in me since I was in diapers. "If I get it wrong, it could kill one, or both, of us. We will need a safe place to study."

"Why not your home we stayed in before?"

"The apartment? It's gone, Rolf. My father took everything out of that apartment and likely told the landlord my mother had moved out. He wanted all of her things here. He was looking for her Grimoires."

"What is a Grimoire?"

I stop and look at Rolf like he had grown a second head. The bemused look on his face tells me he heard my thoughts on the matter. "It is much like me forgetting you are not a wolf and leaving you naked in the snow."

I feel the stab of guilt again and roll my eyes. "Guess you'll just have to keep your sword sheathed next time then."

Rolf laughs again, and it breaks him from his tense mood.

I felt giddy for the first time since coming back to New York. "Alright, my sassy flower, where can we go then? Do you have any other kin we can turn to?"

I pause, tapping my nose in thought as I watch him. "Not that I know of. I mean, we could probably try to find Ember Tree coven members. But they would be reluctant to let the daughter of Windraven in their folds. They alienated my mother for marrying him."

"And you do not trust your father's coven?" I see Rolf's expression change and hurt wells up inside me. He is testing me.

"I do not. They are bound to my father, as he is the head of the coven. To turn on a coven member is an unforgivable act. I'm only affiliated to the coven by birth. I'm not officially a part of the Howling Wave coven. They are guardian witches and warlocks." I turn from him and pack the last of the items I want to take with me.

"Lily." He says with a sigh. "I did not mean to hurt your feelings. I was-."

"I know what you were trying to do," I cut him off before he made up an excuse. "Still hurts that your trust in me is so low."

"Lily," he says again. This time he stands and tries to pull me into his embrace. I give him a narrowed look and step out of his grasp.

"You can't just hug your way out of it. I'm your mate. I have given you everything of myself. Yet here you stand, interrogating me to see if I'm in on whatever my father has planned." I sling my backpack onto my back and cross my arms, pouting at him like a child.

He rubs his hand over his face and lets out a small growl.

I feel the conflict in his emotions, as I'm sure he can feel the embers of my anger starting to flame into fury.

He cuts me off.

I cannot feel his emotions, nor hear his thoughts. I actually flinch at the sudden vacancy in my head.

His eyes narrow down at me and we are having a standoff in my bedroom.

"Don't lecture me on being mates. You did not trust me to make it right and brought us here. I have a right to question that motive. I made my oaths to you years ago, and yet, the moment Luna tries to come between us you run. I have nothing but you, Lily. No clan. No magic. No power other than what I can physically best. I cannot even do what I was born to do here. But please, tell me how you have been so wronged. Tell me how a girl who stank of death comes back to the place that gave her that scent without a fight? How you have allowed your father, at every turn, to do as he sees fit. Even defend him to me when I can smell him, Lily. He reeks of darkness and death. It surrounds him like a cloak. Tell me you are not using me, mate. That your love is true."

I closed my mouth with his final statement. I was crushed. I said nothing as I stared up into his steely blue eyes. I could not stop the tears as he cut me to the core with his lack of faith in me.

His nostrils flare in anger and he presses closer.

I take a step back, retreating. I didn't want to hear anymore. I wanted to get out of here. If he felt that way, I would not keep him here. I swallow hard and wipe my cheeks with my forearm. Maybe I'm not worth having a mate.

"C'mon. We need to get the books. I know where we can go. It's a safe place." I go to open the door and his hand slams the door shut, trapping me in the room.

"We are not finished." He says with a hint of authority in his voice.

"What else do you have to say, Rolf? Nothing I say will matter. You don't believe my words are true. What's the point? I thought you were different. I believed you when you promised to love me forever. But I see now it was only there. Not here. I will find a way to send you back to your home. Then I will stop my father on my own."

"Woman," he roars at me. He takes me by the forearms and forces me to face him.

I kick him in the shins and struggle against his grasp.

"No! You are my mate. You belong with me!" He roars at me again. "You are going to be the mother of my pups. You are going to keep our clan healthy and alive. You are going to be an amazing leader to our people. I am a warrior, Lily. I was born to raid. To hunt. To lead. There is nothing here. This time is full of miscreants and lay-abouts. Do you not want me? Is that why you ran? That life with me would be so terrible? When I go home, you are coming with me. It is your home too."

"NO!" I scream back at him. "No, it isn't! The spell I used was to take me home. *Home*, Rolf. The portal opened, and it brought me here. It brought me back twelve hours from the time I left. Like nothing had ever happened! Don't you think it would have deposited me right back at your village had that been *my home*? You stand there and accuse me of being the devil's spawn your entire fucking clan accused me of being. You claimed me as your mate. You promised to cherish me! And now, you're not even sure I'm on the same side as you. So, what? Last night was just another conquest for you? Now that you have me bound to you, you can do whatever you want? If that's the case, then take it back! I don't want it." I claw at the inverted mountain shaped like a wolf's fang.

His eyes widen, and he catches my hand before I can do any real damage. He pins me to the door, my wrists held captive in his hands above my head. He rests his forehead against mine. I did not need the mate bond to know he is seething with anger. "You don't mean that." He pants out. "Mani and Freya bound us together. You are my soul, Lily. It will murder me to lose you. It doesn't matter, the time or place. All that matters is that you and I are together. And after all this shit I have seen from your father, I had to know…"

"Rolf," I droop a little in his grasp, feeling defeated. "I don't belong there. From the moment I woke there, your clan has shunned me. They branded me evil and made sure I knew I was not welcome. Why would I want to go back to that hate? What happens if they turn on you for marking me? I am not a wolf. I'll never be good enough. It is why your father hid me in Ingrid's hut. Besides, I told you already, I can't take you back there. Not without my mom's help. I don't know the spell. I only know how to get home." I let the weight of 'home' hang in the air. I hate this animosity that has grown between us.

Rolf sacrificed everything he knew to be with me.

Could I not do the same? I don't want to fight with him. It makes me feel sick to my stomach and isolated. He is the other half of my soul, and to not be united would likely kill me as well. I couldn't move as he held me pinned to the door, and I shifted awkwardly, the backpack forcing me to arch in a weird angle.

"Look me in the eye, Rolf Ivarsen." I wait for him to ease from my forehead to look at me. I want him to see the truth. "My love is true. I pledge an oath to you. I will follow you to the ends of time and call home wherever you may be. I am sorry I lost your faith in me."

Silence is his reply.

I hold my breath as he stares at me with that intense gaze.

He still has me cut off from knowing his thoughts and feelings. As the beats of my heart thump, my faith in him accepting my oath and not abandoning me wanes. I don't look away from him, too afraid he will be gone when I look back.

All the fury drains from him. He sighs. "I am sorry. I am an idiot. You have trusted me this long. I should have trusted you in this. Your father disturbs me deeply. I had to know that you were not under his influence. He came to my room, Lily. I don't know what foul spirit he leashed upon me. But it was not pleasant, and I nearly gave you to him because of it. I will not risk you again."

All the fight had drained from both of us.

He lets go of my wrists and we head for my father's study.

I had a plan forming in my head, but I didn't want to voice it here.

Rolf keeps his hand in mine as we make our way across the estate.

I'm not so dumb as to think this has resolved everything. I conceded the point of when we would live. I didn't have the heart to tell him that I likely could never take us back to his time. From what I remember of the night Viggo came into our lives, the magic was extremely taxing. I needed my mother more than ever, and I can only hope that there is a way to reach her at Grandma Finley's house.

We round the corner to the hallway that leads to my father's study and two warlocks stand outside his office door. They haven't noticed us, and I pull Rolf back around the corner.

"What is it?" he says in my mind.

"There were no guards before."

"Okay. Can't you just put them to sleep, or something with all the magic you have learned?"

"*The last time I tried to put someone to sleep I murdered my dog, Nick, remember?*"

He gives me a perplexed look, and I roll my eyes.

"*Remember how I said you cannot do any of the things you did before?*"

"*Wait. Are you saying…?*" The hopeful look on his face causes me to bite my lip to not laugh out loud.

He rolls his shoulders and starts stripping down in the hall.

I can only imagine what the two men at the end of the hall are going to think when a very naked man comes storming down it to attack them. I scoop up his clothes and stuff them into my backpack.

"*Yup. Show me what you got.*" I didn't have to tell him twice as he rounded the corner to run.

Warlocks and Vikings

I wish I could have followed to see the scene unfold. I lean against the wall and look at the ceiling, waiting for him to knock them out so we could get into the study.

"What the fuck?" I heard from one.

"Put some clothes on! Hey! What the-."

Then there is a loud growl and a snap.

I cringe as Rolf most definitely broke something.

The first one shouts in pain and the second one shouts at Rolf.

As if a genie granted my wish, Rolf's white wolf comes barreling into view as he flings the warlock he had locked in his jaws.

It sends the man careening into the wall and snapping his neck, killing him instantly.

Rolf doesn't even look back. He takes off running toward

his room.

If there was any doubt in my mind about my father dabbling in dark magic, the spells I hear ripping from the second warlock cured me of it. I cover my mouth to keep from screaming as the stench of brimstone and sulfur reaches my nostrils. My eyes are transfixed on the terrified blank stare of the dead warlock in front of me.

I had lived among Viking werewolves for six years. There were raids, and violent encounters. People died. But due to my status as a pariah in the clan, I had been spared most of it. I gulp and tears form in my eyes as I start to shake. I couldn't leave him with a stunned expression, so I carefully stepped over him and closed his eyes. It was the only thing I could think to do.

After which, I vigorously scrub my fingers along my jeans to get the clammy feeling of his skin off them. I force myself to turn away from him and bolt for the study, now fearful his soul might haunt me. I yank open the heavy, solid pine door and slam it behind me.

My father's study looks eerie in the dark. I had only been in here during the day, with him. In the sunlight, it looked like a fairytale library with his grimoires sprinkled throughout the other books and maps. There are trinkets of wonder decorating various locations around the room. Some older than the United States itself. I fumble for the light switch and bring to life this magnificent place. I knew where the grimoire I wanted was before, so I walked forward with determination. I realize our grave mistake when I reach the shelf. Every book on this shelf is a plain leather-bound book with no indication of title, or content.

"Crap," I mutter.

"Okay. I can do this." I psych myself up and I set my backpack down. I rub my hands together, and begin to weave them in the air, calling upon the ley lines to guide me.

"Show me what is true," I bellow in Latin. The whisper of magic slips from my fingers like a lover's kiss blown to her suitor. It encircles the books, weaving its way lazily around them.

They flicker and dance with the magic, as if they had been pulled into a silent waltz. Only for my little blue wisp to then be devoured by shadow.

I bite my lip as the shelf resumes its dreary brown stacks of grimoires. Well, maybe not so dreary brown. I feel the call of the magic in front of me. Enticing and sweet. It beckons me forward, begging for me to touch just one book. I'm aware that this is an enthrallment spell. It's meant to cloud my senses and dull my mind to the point I make a choice that results in disaster. I close my eyes and breathe deep, hoping Rolf is having more success than I am.

My hand hovers dangerously close to one of these nondescript books before I'm able to expel the enthrallment. I could feel the rage coming from the shadows and my confidence swells.

******

Rolf sped down the hallway leading to his room.

Behind him, the man shouts words in Latin, and violent green flames slam into the wall over his head.

He nearly loses balance as he skids through a corner, and his claws cannot gain purchase on the shiny hardwood floors. He knew he needed to buy his Lily enough time to find her books. Were this an honorable battle, he would have turned and decimated his foes by his strength alone.

There is no honor in fighting with Hel's fire. Whatever gibberish this warlock was shouting at him sent flames and conjured weapons.

He slams into the wall, thanks to the shiny floors just outside of his room, and one of those conjured weapons slices clean into his midsection. He lets out a snarl and knocks the door off its hinges to leap into his room.

The warlock slides into view and before he can sling another spell at the white wolf, Rolf leaps at him.

The warlock lets out a gurgled scream when Rolf's teeth sink into his throat, ripping it out. He spits the dripping chunks of flesh out, and Rolf's pristine fur is now painted with blood around his muzzle.

With a hiss of smoke and a popping noise, there are five more around him, three witches and two warlocks. It is too cramped for them to throw spells at Rolf.

In wolf form, he's massive, and he uses that to his advantage. With a shimmer of light, he is in human form again, and pulls a warlock in front of him to take the blast of the binding curse flung by a witch.

A burning sensation hits his back, and he growls, ripping the arm off the warlock in hand before he throws him into the screaming witch. He turns, and swings the arm like a club at the witch who burned him.

She shrieks, now covered in the splattering blood.

Another shimmer of light and he shifts into wolf form, his fur staining further with blood.

A hand grabs him and he slams the body into the wall. Then he sees the opening. He could hear the whistle he ignored a few minutes ago.

It meant more were coming.

"Just keep him away from the girl," one witch shouts. "Don't kill him."

Rolf snarls, his ears folding flat. They were going after Lily and he would not allow that. He knocks the one witch over and runs for it, heading to the study without looking back. He could outrun them with ease, but they keep popping in right behind him.

The estate is getting ruined. Curtains are singed. Plants are uprooting through the floorboards. Furniture is blown to pieces with the crash of a spell.

"Tell me you found them." He calls to Lily in his mind.

There is no answer.

"Lily. We have to go. There are too many of them. They are trying to separate us."

There is still no answer from his mate, giving him incentive to run faster.

Turning down the corridor where this began, he hears another pop behind him. "He killed Angelo! I don't fucking care what Silar wants. I'll kill him!" A woman shrieks behind him.

Rolf plows into the study, sending the door careening off its hinges.

I stand stock still, my fingers hovering over a book. My body is rigid and the dark tendrils encircle me as a lover who is drawing me in for a kiss.

He snarls, shifting into human form and his hands grip into a chair, lifting it like it were a cushion. He hurtles it toward the floor-to-ceiling window, causing it to shatter. He snatches my bag from the floor, leans forward like he was positioning for a football line up and when he comes back up, he grunts with me on his shoulder. Once he is satisfied that I'm secure, he pushes forward and leaps out of the opening he made to make the run for the tree line.

Behind us there's screaming and shouting.

He will never make it in this form.

"Rolf! Put me down!" I shout at him and begin to struggle. I'm disoriented and confused. Why are we outside? What happened back in the study?

"LEFT!" I scream as a fireball flies toward us.

He veers right.

"Your other left!" It just barely misses us. I struggle again and I feel his grip tighten around me.

"Rolf! Put me down and shift! You're too slow!" He makes a tumbling motion and both of us head for the ground.

I'm going to be sick with the way he folds us into a ball. I don't know when the bag gets thrust between us, but I grab hold of it, and gasp in pain. Then I'm blinded by the light of him shifting into wolf form and I'm half on his back. One hand clinging to the bag, the other gripping onto white fur.

He doesn't slow down one bit.

I'm forced to drag myself onto his back the rest of the way.

He whines at the awkwardness, but then we're running faster than I have ever run in my life.

I bury my face into his fur and hold on tight enough my fingers ache. If we can get to the tree line, we can hide. It's too thick for them to see us, other than there is snow on the ground and they can follow our tracks.

"Find a grove for us." I say through our connection.

He shifts his weight and heads in a different direction. Then we are past the tree line. The thickness of the forest around my father's estate forces us to slow down. He doesn't stop. His emotions are conflicting, but all lean toward wanting battle. His blood lust is strong, but he knows to stop means death.

The smell of sulfur and brimstone still fills my nostrils, which tells me the dark magic is all around us. Coupled with his conflicting emotions to run or to fight.

When he finally stops, he drops to the ground, which sends me tumbling. He shifts back into human form, snatching the bag from me and turning to face the direction we came to stand guard.

"We need a way out of here, now, Lily." His movement is erratic. Every tiny sound makes him jerk in motion.

I step closer to him and try to stop him.

He growls at me.

"Rolf! Look at me." He snaps his gaze to me.

I reach up to either side of his face and pull him hard to me with a kiss. I feel the confusion, anger, lust, and fear roil through him at what I'm doing. He had to be touching me for the spell to work, and I was afraid I would do it wrong if we only held hands. So, I did the only thing I knew how to keep him close. I kissed him. My lips press firm to his as I focus on Grandma Finley's home.

His arms wrap around me tighter and he growls against my lips in a more sensual manner.

The world twists and fades to darkness. The murderous shouts of the warlocks begin to fade. Then the sweet pine aroma fills the air as the darkness fades.

I open my eyes to look up at Rolf. We're standing in front of an old cottage, now overgrown and hidden. The moonlight shining down on the two of us.

He tears his gaze from me to look around. "What is this place?"

XXXII

Mind Your Manners

Rolf's hands are still clinging to my waist and our bodies are pressed close from my unconventional traveling method.

I don't answer him immediately, as I'm listening for the tell-tale sign of someone trying to get through the wards. I smile at him when we are not set upon by warlocks and witches of my father's coven. "We are at my grandmother's home."

He relaxes and tries to draw me into another tender kiss.

"Nope! Nuh uh! Don't even try that, mister!" I push against his chest only to feel him tighten his embrace.

"We were victorious. Let me celebrate crushing our enemies with you, my flower," he purrs against my throat before he kisses it.

His kisses are laced with an addictive substance that makes me want more and his raging hard-on presses against my thigh as he peppers my neck with those kisses. I tremble when his lips brush over my mate's mark. He can't see my smirk as I trail my hand down his chest so I can then bop the head he is currently thinking with.

This wins me a disgruntled whine as he releases me to leap back and protect his most precious possession.

"I said, no," waggling my finger as I pointed at him. "Plus. Ew! You are covered in blood! Not sexy."

"I think it is sexy," he sulks.

I roll my eyes. "We will have plenty of time for that once we figure out how to get inside. I need to make sure the wards will hold, and you need a bath. There's a lake just down that path. Get cleaned up while I work on getting us into the house."

I turn my back to him to face the vines covering my grandmother's home.

He gives me a small whine before I see his dirty wolf dashing off.

I would never let him see it, but I pout too. There is something sexy about him smiting our enemies and then wanting to claim me again. I peel off the backpack and get a good look at myself. I have blood all over the front of my clothes and on my hands where it transferred from Rolf to me. I try not to vomit. Maybe I should have joined him in the lake? I shake my head and take a deep breath, trying not to think about where the blood came from. I needed to concentrate.

The Earth has swallowed up the house over the decades. How could I have not known she was a ghost all that time? The memories of the journal are haunting my mind, but the one phrase,

"Cor terrae aperi mihi," rings in my mind as if Grandma Finley were standing right beside me and teaching me the spell. It seemed out of place in the memories of my mother, but I realized the journals contained more than memories and I'm glad we brought them with us. They were all I had of my mother and grandmother at present.

If we could not gain passage into the house, we would have to find another place to go. I hear a rumble of thunder in the distance and it pulls my gaze up to the sky. There is not a cloud in sight, allowing the white light of the moon to bask everything in a gentle glow. It could only mean something is colliding with the wards around this place.

"Focus," the wind whispers to me and I bring my gaze back down to the cottage.

I purse my lips and roll my shoulders as if I were a boxer getting ready for the next round. My fingers begin the gentle swirl to create the focusing circle, then push to the center and toward the house, "Cor terrae aperi mihi." I ask the heart of the earth to open to me.

My fingers continue to move in the steady motion of keeping the circle intact, as the flicker of red and green light sparks from my fingertips. Over and over, I make the request. My energy is waning. I had expelled a great deal of magic in my father's study trying to find the right Grimoire. While we could sleep outdoors here, the thundering rumble in the distance is enough to warn me having shelter would be wiser.

"Cor terrae aperi mihi." I speak it firmer, pouring more of my energy into the spell.

The vines engulfing the cottage tremble and shift, as if I had woken them from a long slumber.

The scraggly garden shudders like a strong wind passed through. The thrum of the ley line courses through the ground like a river of energy waiting to be tapped. It's tempting to draw extra power from the ley lines.

My mother fills my head with a warning she would tell

me as a small child. *"Those who seek to control power, often find the power controls them."*

I did not understand the phrases when I was a child, but standing here now, I get an inkling to what she was warning me from. I exhale and inhale slowly, repeating the phrase again.

The vines that had been resting peacefully, spring to life like a nest of vipers. They slither and twist over the ground with great speed.

Fear wells inside me, but I can't move, or I will break the spell. I repeat the phrase again with conviction.

Like massive cobras, they strike, wrapping around my wrists and ankles as they lift me into the air. There are hundreds of vines everywhere. They engulf the house and now me.

I struggle and jerk to free myself.

"You sure about that, Lily?" My grandmother's voice flits through the air. *"Looks to me like you're not minding your manners."*

I thrash and kick. My attempts to scream are muffled as the vines wrap gracefully around my face. The thought of maintaining the spell is long forgotten in my panic.

"You dare trespass here, daughter of Windraven." I hear another woman's voice I don't recognize.

Instinctively, I frown and shake my head, or try to, as I'm held in place. Boy, do I wish Rolf were here right now. He could resume his blood lust and free me. How long does it take to take a bath in a lake? Then I remember what Mom said about the binding spell that I nearly killed Viggo with. All resistance stops and I hang limp in the vines binding me. Tears roll down my cheeks as I submit to their strength and resist my instinct to fight. I force myself to breathe slowly and remain still.

The vines from my face cautiously loosen.

"Answer me, daughter of Windraven." The woman's voice sounds impatient and all around me.

"Viggodatter. Not Windraven. Don't mistake me for my father." My voice is full of sorrow as I forsake the father I had so longed for as a child. In this panic-filled haze, I realize I always had that father in Viggo, and never in Silar. Rage fills me with this revelation. My flesh and blood is only using me for his own gain.

"I am Lily Viggodatter!" I shout to the vines.

As if saying that is a magic spell, the vines retract, dropping me to the ground. *"So say you, child. But we shall see. You may pass."*

I sputter and gasp as I kneel on the ground. When I look up, the vines have retracted enough to expose the house to me. All the vipers have resumed their lush green state of rest along the ground.

Stillness fills the air until I hear the bounding steps of Rolf in wolf form returning.

I push myself to my feet, exhausted. All I want to do is take a shower and go to sleep.

"Lily?" He asks, his rumbly voice laced with concern.

The sticky sap from the vines covers me. My hair drips with it, and my skin feels like someone poured syrup on me. "I'm fine. Grab the bag." I don't give him any further explanation as I walk up the steps and through the screen door. Marching straight to the bathroom I remove all of my ruined clothes and start the shower. I hope there is still running water.

Delight radiates from me when there is a hot, steamy stream pouring from the faucet. I don't linger in the shower as I forgot to tell Rolf not to touch anything and am now worried that he might have been hexed. I'm not used to being able to link to him with my mind.

"Rolf," I called, expecting silence in return.

"I'm down here." He shouts from the main room.

I pull the fluffy towel around me tighter as I descend the stairs. What I see makes me bite my lip, as it looks hilarious.

Rolf sits cross-legged in the very center of the room, hugging the backpack. Still naked.

"I dislike this place, Lily. Where have you brought me? It smells foul." He shudders and makes a disgusted face. This is the first time I have seen Rolf squeamish.

"Awe, my big bad wolf's afraid of a little magic?" I wink at him as I saunter the rest of the way down the stairs.

"I'm not afraid. I enjoy keeping all my appendages, thank you. You do not disrespect a witch's home." He chuffs petulantly.

"Rule number one of Catarina Finley's home. Ask before you touch. Rule number two. Mind your manners." I come closer to Rolf and offer my hand up while holding the towel closed with the other.

He eyes my hand like it is a viper and I have to bite my lip again to keep from laughing out loud.

"You just wait, Lily Viggodatter. You'll get yours for mocking me." He takes my hand and stands. As if the house has made its decision on Rolf, the ominous vibe ebbs away.

"See, Grandma approves." I wink at him as I lead him back upstairs.

He snorts at me. I pause in the hallway, trying to decide which room to take him to. I could take him to Grandma's room, but I feel weird about sharing a bed with him there. There's the doll room, which is even creepier of an idea. If he thought the main room was foul, I can't imagine how he'd react to the dolls. That left the room at the end of the hall.

We pass the other rooms and I hold the door open for him

to the guest room. Inside, it is the quintessential grandma guest room, complete with floral patterns on everything. The brass bed frame shines bright when I flick the lights on. I don't question how everything works. I mean, my grandmother was a ghost my whole life, and I never knew it. I'm going to just assume she knew how to create power.

I move to the dresser and fish out a t-shirt. Mom always had clothes for us here. It even still smells like her. I pull it over my head, discarding the towel before I hop into the bed.

Rolf stalks all around the room. He checks every nook and cranny he can find. He is still hugs the backpack as well.

I prop up onto an elbow to watch this entertaining endeavor. "What are you doing?"

"Securing the perimeter," he mutters at me.

"Rolf, we're safe. I promise. Nothing in this house will hurt you, provided you follow the rules."

His eyes narrow at me in suspicion. "How can you be so sure?"

I pout at him, jutting out my lower lip. "You don't want to sleep with me in the bed?" I sniffle for good measure. I bat my eyelashes at him as he takes in the full measure of me laying there in just a t-shirt.

He sets the backpack on the floor at the foot of the bed and tests it as if he believes it isn't there. When he feels it is a solid object, he climbs on board. "You're too trusting," he grumbles.

"That's what I have you for," I lean in and kiss him.

All of You

I was in the in-between, the place where you are no longer dreaming but aren't awake. I had spent the hours nestled into a soft bed with Rolf, with nothing between us but my mother's t-shirt. My dreams were filled with images I didn't understand, but they were of another time and another place. Something about it said home to me. There, I only saw Rolf as the conquering invader with a strange mark ever claiming his prize. A smile forms on my lips at the very thought of belonging to Rolf across the tides of time and it blossoms happiness inside of me.

His fingers brush over my skin. His calloused and rough fingers gingerly trail along my arm, as if he is learning every inch of my body. He follows along the faint scar on my arm that I earned from being careless near the forge of our village. His fingers dance from freckle to freckle kissing my fair skin.

He slowly swirls around my nipple, causing the pink nub to spring to life. My skin gets goosebumps from the sensation. His emotions are full of a curious wonder, laced with guilt. Unbridled love washes over my senses as his fingers brush along my chest to wake up the other nipple.

I shift so I'm more on my back, remaining open to his silent mapping of my skin. My hand is pinned between us, and I feel the smoothness of his manhood against my fingers. I'm not ready to admit I'm awake yet, wanting to see where he goes with this.

His hand cups the first breast, tugging on the nipple between his thumb and forefinger to keep it taught while he enjoys the rest of my soft flesh.

"Mhmm," I hum. I'm convinced the bond between us heightens every single sensation and the more I become aware he is watching me, the more I worry he will not find me beautiful. His kneading hand releases my breast and trails down my side.

"So beautiful," he whispers. "Thank you, Mani and Freya."

His fingers circle my belly button, then pet the spring of copper curls blanketing my tender sex.

I swear he's grinning down at me as his finger presses between the folds of my womanhood to tease my clit. At first, nothing happens, other than I feel his fingers pressing and rubbing against me. I make a pouting face and shift a little. I'm not sure what to do. Do I move? Do I lie still? Do I touch him? Does he like this? Does he think I'm beautiful like this?

Then it started to feel good. His fingers moved firmer in their motion. Why do I feel like he's listening to my thoughts with amusement?

"Because I am, my flower." His voice is soft as he leans down and kisses my lips tenderly. My cheeks flame red and I squirm more, but his hand does not relent. Leaning into him made the sensations feel different and better.

His finger dipped into me briefly, only to come back and rub the same spot that was starting to cause me to have a hard time thinking.

"It's cheating when you read my mind." I pout against his chest.

His laugh is soft still as he kisses my temple, but he does not stop touching me. "Lie back, my flower. Let me show you how beautiful you are." His body shifts and guides me back to my starting position. His fingers rub me faster.

I admit I like it, but I'm shy about what he sees.

"Touch me," he whispers against my lips. "Learn how I feel."

My fingers curl around his manhood, which is hard, and he gives a small grunt when I grip too tight.

"I'm sorry," I gasp in mortification.

"It's alright. It's not going to hurt you and responds better to gentle touches." He winks.

"You're teasing me." I pout again.

"Only a little. The way you blush makes me want you more." He kisses against his mark on me and I melt to him. "Lily, I want to apologize for our mating." He stops touching me.

My eyes widen, and my heart's racing. He regrets mating with me and now that he knows I don't know how to do anything, he wants someone else.

"Stop it," he commands, and it sends a jolt of sparks right through me. "You are the only one I want, ever. I regret how rough and careless I was with you, my sweet mate. You are perfect and I never should have defiled you in such a manner. I should have been gentle and made you enjoy every second. For that, I am sorry. I would not take one second of being your mate back. I have waited a long time to call you mine, Lily."

"But I liked what we did." My cheeks flame hot. "And I liked what you were doing… there," I motion to my vagina, but still find it awkward to talk about.

The stern look he gives me all of a sudden says he knows exactly what I just thought. "Get out of my head!" I swat him.

He pulls me close and kisses me softly again, "Lily, we are mates. You are not my whore to do with however I see fit. I want us to be close in all things. I want you to beg me for the sweet nothings as much as you beg me for the claiming. I want your happiness. I do not need to fornicate with you to love you. But I hope to the Gods you do not withhold that from me."

"What do you like? I mean, other than my happiness?" I genuinely wanted to know. He is essentially a stranger. We had barely seen each other in six years, and in the past week, it felt like a lifetime of being together. He was the first boy to make me feel special, and I wanted everything to be perfect with us.

"You." He gives a wolfish grin and I swat him. I was trying to be serious, and he is teasing me again. He laughs and then eases from the bed, kissing my forehead.

"Where are you going?" I sit up and pout at the loss of warmth in the bed.

"I am going to explore this place and get the lay of the land to make sure we are safe here."

"What about… that," I motioned to his erection.

"Mhmm… This?" he cocks his head to the side to gauge the depth of my question and my cheeks flame red at him making it bounce in front of me. "We should wait a little, and get to know each other again, my flower. I want you to want every part of me as I do you. When you believe our bond is true, you can have me again."

I sulk. I feel like he is teasing me, but then he turns and

heads out of the room, still naked, efficiently cutting off any discussion on the matter. I fling myself back on the bed and stare up at the ceiling.

"What just happened?"

My body aches for his touch, and my skin is warm from being flush with shyness and embarrassment. I close my eyes, imagining his fingers touching me again, and the ache intensifies.

"Careful flower. Thoughts like that might get you in trouble." Rolf's voice fills my mind.

Now I know he is teasing me and I huff. I concentrate as hard as I can on sending him the very image of me pleasing myself at the thought of him. Two could play this teasing game until I feel him block the link again.

"Cheater," I mutter as I get out of the bed.

Once dressed, I decide to start with the doll room to see if any of the magic lingers. The dolls had all gone limp when I was here before, but that doesn't mean they don't have magic. I stand in front of the door and hesitate in opening it. It somehow feels like I'm desecrating sacred ground by entering. I swallow any fear of this room and turn the doorknob. The door swings open without a sound and my eyes widen in shock at the scene before me.

Listen to the Beat of My heart

I stand in the doorway, dumbfounded. Glass shards mixed with frilly lace and creepy marble eyes sprinkle across the wood floor. Their satin dresses are shredded, patent leather shoes with limp socks hanging from them make me shudder. I carefully step into the room and close the door behind me. I don't know what I expected to find in this room, but this was not it.

"Lily," I hear a soft voice cry to me.

My eyes dart around the room looking for the source of the noise. A small part of me hopes to see my grandma again, but I see nothing but destruction at first.

"I'm under here," I hear the muffled voice again and I recognize the voice.

"Babette?"

"Yes, please help me." Her soft French accent gets louder

and I precariously make my way across the room to where she might be. I dig through blankets and doll corpses until I see her perfect porcelain hand. I free her and she stands, looking me over head to toe. "Oh, Lily, you have grown into such a beautiful woman. Your grandmama would be so proud!"

I smile at her compliment and help her back over to the bean bag chairs where I sat as a child. "What happened in here?"

"Your grandmother was a powerful witch, Lily. There are many who would take what she has bequeathed to you. Your father, included in that. If you are here, then it is as your grandmother feared."

"What do you mean?"

"Your grandmother left insurances to guarantee you would be safe here. She had hoped your mother changed the path when she brought Viggo to meet her. But alas," she sighs as she looks at the doll graveyard around us, "we will not have much time to get you where you need to be. First you must clean up this mess. Then we will need the Ember Tree's Grimoire."

I head back to the door to go get a broom and a trash bag.

"Where are you going?" She asks me in an incredulous tone.

"To get things to clean up with."

"Non! You are a witch. You will put all the dolls back together." With a wave of her tiny hand the door locks and it makes me jump. "You may leave when you have cleaned up this place."

"Put… them back… together? Like Humpty Dumpty?"

"Non! How crude. You would leave them cracked and broken looking? Non! I will not tolerate this. You will put them together properly. You are of the earth as much as you are of fire. I feel it through you. Something as simple as mending porcelain should come second nature to you." She crosses her arms and looks put out by the fact I don't know what to do.

"I see," I say even though I don't. "I don't know the spell."

"What is it with you witches and needing spells? It is magic! You have been harnessing it your entire life. You no more need a spell than I need to eat. Just listen to the Earth sing to you and you will know what to do." She points at the mess on the floor.

I blink in disbelief. I have never seen my mother do magic without a spell. Or my father. How do I listen to the Earth? I sigh and bite against my lip. I don't know why, but I close my eyes so I can hear better. All I hear is the creaking and groans of the house as wind blows around it. Out of nowhere, I'm struck by something wooden.

"Ow! Hey!" My eyes pop open to see Babette with a ruler. Where did she get a ruler? I watch this nearly three-foot-tall porcelain menace brandish the tiny piece of wood at me.

"You listen with your spirit, Lily. Not with your ears. Do not make me tell you again. Have you forgotten everything?"

"It's been a while," I huff. Then yelp as she whacks me again.

"So? Magic is a part of your soul, Lily. Not some mystical force around you. Just because you have been taught otherwise, does not make it so. Forget what your father knows. He was holding you back."

I rub where she whacked and take a deep breath, looking around. "Fine," I grumble and squat down to touch one of the shattered faces. I had no idea what I was doing, or how I was going to hear the Earth sing, but I wasn't getting whacked again, that's for sure.

Again, silence fills the air. My anxiety rises as I don't think

I can do it. I focus on the little shard of glass in my hand and exhale slowly.

Nothing happens.

Then I feel it, a small pulse from the fragment of porcelain in my hand. My eyes widen and then I'm slapped with the ruler again. "You lost focus, again!" She barks at me in the French accent.

"I was focusing. Then you distracted me! Ow!"

She whacks me again. "If you have time to argue, you have time to focus. Now, fix the doll."

I give her a dirty look and return to looking at the shard. I close one eye again, keeping one open to dodge any incoming rulers, but fail at that, too. "Ow! Stop hitting me," I snarl and the ruler bursts into flames.

"Very good!" She claps her little hands together, ignoring the pyre of ruler on the floor. "Now put that focus into fixing the doll. The Earth is about life, Lily. Feel life growing in you, around you, everywhere. Even in the broken pieces of these dolls there is life. Listen."

I huff in frustration and sit down cross-legged, like a petulant child.

"The Earth is also stubborn and unbending. Hence you get a mountain you cannot move. You will never grow as a witch as long as you fight that which is natural."

Now Babette sounds a lot like Ingrid. I sulk and shake my shoulders to gain some sense of focus. Placing the shard on the ground I rest my hands on my knees and relax.

Babette walks to the other side of the room, taking up her perch on the shelf my grandma kept her on. She goes lax and becomes the porcelain doll again.

"At least she won't whack me with a ruler, now," I mutter.

I pan my gaze along the room, sad that all these beautiful dolls were gone. Each of them had names, and personalities.

They had little cliques and rules. It was a whole society in this tiny room where I first learned magic.

All of them were my grandmother in some fashion. I felt her then, or at least an echo of her. The thought of her warm arms around me brings me to focus on the shard of porcelain I had picked up previously. The soft thump of my heart beats in my chest, like a drum in the distance. The whispered hum of the ley line below the house grows louder.

My breathing slows and the drums get louder. A chorus of drums beat in this room. The rustle of leaves whistle like piccolos outside the window.

Ringing fills my ears as the shards all float into the air.

Listen to the beat of my heart like the drums of war.

The voice whispers through everything around me. The pieces whirl and twist, finding their mates and pairs. Tiny fingers piece back to hands, hands to arms, until they are whole again.

Silky strings of the clothing sigh as the pieces whisk to move out of the way.

I close my eyes again and the symphony of noises fill every inch of me. The old wood beneath me creaks and groans from age. The vines enshrouding the house hiss in anticipation. I feel the clay is soft and malleable in the ceramic. I hear the loud thud of the stone beating in defiance to fading away.

I don't know how long I was lost in this cacophony of sounds. It was drowning all else out as my soul sears to life in a way I had never experienced before. I thought I had been made whole when my magic returned in 1287, but I had been wrong, so very wrong.

"Lily," Rolf's concerned voice over me. The Earth sang through him louder than anything else in this house.

I flutter my eyes open and realize it's dark. When did I fall asleep? "How did you get in here?"

"The door was open." he looks at me oddly. "Are you unwell?"

I take a moment to survey the room as he helps me up. Much to my surprise, the graveyard is gone. Scattered about the floor are the dolls of my childhood, healed from their wounds, though strewn about like a child discarded them. "I..." I start to explain but realize I don't even know what happened. "I'm fine. No. I'm better than fine. I'm great. I... I fixed my magic."

"Your magic was broken? I thought your mother lifted that curse on you when you turned eighteen?"

"I was not cursed, Rolf. I was warded. It's like binding your hands behind your back. You're not handless, you are just bound. There is a difference. But yes, it was broken, and now it is not."

He nods in understanding and finishes helping me to my feet. "If your magic is fixed, it means we are able to go home?" He looks so hopeful.

"Rolf," I look at the floor in shame, "I cannot create a portal back. I'm sorry."

He sighs. His emotions roil through me from disappointment, anger, and grief for what he has lost to blossom into pure love.

It confuses me how he skips through the spectrum of feelings in such a short time.

He gives a sharp nod and breaks into a sappy grin. "Then my home is here with you, my flower."

XXXV

Pursuit of happiness

"What do you fucking mean, they vanished?" Silar roars as he throws a tumbler full of whiskey into the fire.

"The wolf was so fast. We lost them in the woods. By the time we found where they should have been, there was nothing in the clearing."

"What do you mean, where they should have been?"

"The tracks. They just stopped."

"Did you look for magical tracks?"

"They used some kind of transportation spell. We can't get a lock on where to go."

Silar sighs as he knows exactly where Lily would run to that would prevent someone from knowing where she went. He storms out of the room, leaving his coven members dumbfounded. If his guess is correct, not even he could get beyond those wards. He has been trying for years and has lost quite a few coven members to the wards surrounding Catarina Finley's land in upstate New York.

A few minutes later he is in an underground chamber. Lined along one wall are cages full of fluffy rabbits. He gently reaches in and extracts one, scratching it behind the ears as he approaches his altar. Dark words seep from his lips as he plunges a dagger into his sacrifice.

He ignores the gore as he pulls the entrails loose. As the steamy innards smear and ooze on the altar, he begins to see the path Lily has tread. Until the entrails explode, leaving him and the altar, covered in gore. While he does not get the final destination, the ward that stopped him flickered and the small village of wolves revealed itself.

He knows now what he needs to do in order to get his daughter back.

He leaves the altar and quickly heads back into the main estate, summoning his coven. Still covered in gore, he addresses the witches and warlocks. "My beloved daughter has been corrupted by a pack of wolves and they have absconded with her! I have divined the location of this pack. Summon the finest hunters, as we will deal with these pests properly. Time is of the essence as I fear for Lily's safety." With that, he dismisses them, and gets himself cleaned up.

Hours later, he is standing before six men, pleased with the efficiency of his coven in finding these hunters. They are a motley crew. He likens them to mercenaries more than hunters. If they're half as good as the coven believes them to be, Lily will be home in no time. Her precious Rolf will no longer be a problem for him.

"Under no circumstances are you to harm the girl. She is to be brought back alive and well kept. This is non-negotiable and I will require a blood oath."

"I thought you fancy pants warlocks didn't believe in

blood oaths?"

"When it comes to sending a nefarious group of gentlemen to collect my young daughter, I will do everything to guarantee her safe return. While I do trust you will get results, I do not trust you to not mistreat my daughter."

The leader's face breaks into a sinister grin. "Fair enough. It will cost you triple the price."

"That is acceptable, and I will pay a bonus for every wolf you kill. If you bring me a snow-white pelt. I will pay you twice again."

"We're hunting the white bastard, huh? Oh, this should be fun. What has that old wolf done to you?"

"You will find this one to be not so old. You will need to keep your wits about you."

******

The months passed in blissful happiness. I worked each day with Babette, learning more about how magic comes from within rather than from the spells I weave. While words can hold magic, it is the spirit behind the words that gives them power.

The doll room became my classroom and my work room all in one. The limitations of the magic in Babette kept her trapped within the confines of the bedroom. The other dolls had all been carefully returned to their designated homes on the shelves. Babette is the only one to still wake when I come into the room.

After I confessed to Rolf that there was no going back, I noticed a small change in him. While he whole-heartedly throws himself into our relationship, the longing for his home in his emotions breaks my heart. He has adapted and spends his days patrolling the surrounding area to get familiar with it.

We agreed to fix up Grandma's home and make our life here.

In the evenings, I continue where Miss Bryant left off in teaching him to read and write. Under my tutelage, he excels. Each night, he reads me a chapter of the romance novel we discovered in my grandmother's office.

As the nights have progressed, I have had to explain fewer and fewer words. I'm so proud of him. He grumbled about how warriors don't need to know how to read until we hit the chapters that made my cheeks blush. Then, he was excited to re-create said scenes, and eager to read me the next chapter after that.

As our supplies dwindled, Rolf began hunting for food. I was not sure if there was any civilization anywhere near where we are. I don't even know where here is. I have never come here via normal means, as my mother always teleported us.

Rolf mentioned there is a small village several hours away but didn't think it a good idea to go there alone. He wanted to check it out first, and make sure they were friends, not foes.

A few weeks before Beltane, and I'm working with Babette on the spells in the Ember Tree Grimoire. Specifically, I'm learning how to renew life in dormant plants. Most of the training in the room has been learning the incantations. Once Babette is satisfied with my annunciation, I will be turned loose on the garden.

Rolf had been gone since just after dawn.

"Lily, you need to prepare to leave this place." Babette blurts out of the blue.

"Why? We have everything we need here."

"Non. You are destined for a different path than the one that ends in this cottage."

"What other path could there be?"

"The path that will show you the way when it is time. Promise me that when it shows itself to you, you will not hesitate. Your life could depend on it."

"Babette, what aren't you telling me?" I narrow my eyes at the doll. "OW! Where do you hide those?" I ask as Babette whacks me with a ruler.

"Not important." She whacks me again. "Lily. You are hiding here and it will not do either of you any good. Your beast is already restless. And that which you hide from will find its way to you, regardless of what you want."

I frown at her and resist the urge to cross my arms and sulk. "But nothing can break through the wards, right? We're safe here."

"Just like a mountain eventually bends to a river, nothing is forever."

The sense of dread fills me as Babette toddles across the room away from me. I want to scream and shout how it's dumb that people just throw themselves into chaos instead of hiding. Or that this is better because I'm still learning. I don't want to face my father, or to figure out how to go back in time. This has been the only place I have been happy.

"You are not happy here," she counters, as if she has heard everything I was thinking. "You have solace in a time of need. There is a difference. Your happiness awaits you, but only if you pursue it."

I storm out of the room in anger. I don't want to hear what Babette has to say. It's not fair that I'm fated for some forsaken destiny where I can't just live happily ever after with Rolf. This storming continues all the way out to the garden. The thunderclap in the distance mirrors my mood.

I pace in circles in the half-dead garden, not bothering to bring any plants back to life. It feels like such a waste if I'm just going to leave. "Why teach me anything at all?" I mutter as I continue to burn a path through the weeds. "I'm happy," I whine at the air, sounding anything but. I wanted to live the life all the kids on TV did, or how they are in that stupid romance novel.

"Rolf's not happy," I mutter. It's a blessing and a curse, being linked to another being the way wolf mates are. I plop into a sitting position in the center of the garden with a huff. Everything is making me more emotional than usual, and I feel like I'm on the edge of setting the entire world a blaze.

This makes me pause in my tantrum.

I lean back to rest my hands on the ground, digging into the dirt just enough to feel the connection. I gasp.

Pain and anger rush up through my hands and into my very core.

The wind whines in fright. Another thunderclap rumbles in the distance, but the skies are not dark and threatening, like they should be if a storm is rolling in.

The hair on the back of my neck stands on end and I'm labored to draw breath. Something is happening to me. No, not to me. To someone else. The only person I could think of that would affect me is Rolf. I go to stand and the vine-like weeds encircle my wrists, holding me in place.

Listen.

The feminine voice hisses. I have learned that the voice belongs to the Earth and when she speaks, you listen, or there are dire consequences. I stop moving and calm down, returning my hands to the dirt. I let all the emotional turmoil course through me and close my eyes to help me focus. Slowly, the images blur into view. I turn my head back and forth to see better. I still can't see very well, but I hear growling and whining. There are voices shouting at each other, and then I see the little girl slumped over, half her skin gone.

I want to puke at the sight. Who would hurt such a young pup? How can I see this? As I turn my gaze down, I see the white fur on my paws. Then, the rage that fills me is not my own, but Rolf's.

As our gaze turns, the battle before us is enough to make him seethe. I realize the Earth has connected us through our bond, and I'm seeing what Rolf sees. Suddenly, the connection is severed and I'm back in the garden, alone and untethered.

I don't hesitate as I bounce to my feet. There is not much time, and Rolf needs me. I don't know how I know this, but everything in me is screaming that Rolf is in danger and that this place is no longer safe. I sprint into the house and gather up what supplies I can carry.

If violence had found Rolf, then Babette wasn't lying and we couldn't stay here.

I shove the Ember Tree Grimoire into my backpack and I turn to look at Babette.

"Oh, Lily. I thought we had more time. Be my brave girl. Remember that acts done with a pure heart and for love will always triumph." She puts herself on her stand, and then the essence of my grandmother dissipates from her.

I don't have time to stand there and cry, like I want to,

The Earth literally pulls me to move faster.

I race out the door and run toward the forest. I don't think about where I'm going, letting the ley line guide me. That's when I feel the sudden blast of pain explode across my chest.

XXXVI

how Do We Rewrite the Stars?

Rolf had come across the traps two months ago. He thought nothing of them at first. He took it to mean there were others within this protected place who hunted and were not as skilled as he. Then he found the first one, a young man, only twelve or thirteen, with half of his skin missing. His scent held the familiarity of Rolf's pack, which only made his rage grow. He carried the boy to the edge of the forest near the village for him to be found but had to turn back to get back to Lily without suspicion.

The days passed, and he revealed any traps found. Laced with silver and wolfsbane, these traps fueled him to track these hunters. They are too knowledgeable to be regular hunters, and Rolf almost found himself in a pit designed for someone of his stature. As a wolf, he's huge, being closer to the size of a horse than a wolf. His white fur is a rare gene passed from the descendants of Fenrir himself.

Lily was sleeping when he left her this morning.

He wanted an early start so he could find where they are camping. Their scents have been growing stronger, and while he had found no other wolves skinned, he has been scaring pups back to the village every day to prevent it.

Their confusion at seeing the white wolf has been enough to keep them away from him.

Every instinct in him screams to go demand their Alpha do something, but without proof of hunters he could see where the pack might think he is the villain. No wolf likes strangers on their territory.

Then he finds her, a pup no older than ten years in age. She is curled on the ground as if it would protect her from the pain with her skin peeled right off of her. The gruesome sight of muscle and bone left to be picked by foragers.

The silver that shimmers through the muscles and veins has him seeing red. He goes to step closer and the very Earth reaches up and entwines around his hind legs. He lets out a frustrated growl, not understanding why the Earth would hold him here to see this?

Confusion and rage wash over him. Then he feels shock and horror. The urge to be sick consumes him, and he realizes he is feeling Lily's emotions. The jerking motion of trying to figure out what she sees makes him force his muzzle down to show her he is in wolf form.

There is a gunshot in the distance.

He thrashes against the vines and they go lax, severing his connection with Lily. He tears through the forest, wolfsbane and silver permeate his sense of smell. The shrieking yowl of a pup echoes and he pushes harder. When he leaps over the fallen tree, he sails through the air a mass of snow-white fur and snarling teeth.

"No! Pop-Pop! RUN!" the little girl shrieks, but it's too late.

He crashes into a man wearing a leather duster, shifting into his human form as he collides with him. He snaps the hunter's neck before he can get another shot off from the pistol in his hand.

"It's him!"

"Fuck! He's not old!"

"Shit! Ow! She bit me!" The third turns to chase the little girl as she breaks free of him and shifts into her wolf form. The little tawny wolf snarls at the men from a few feet away.

"Forget her. He's the goal," the leader barks at his men. The man that had been holding her points his pistol and fires at her with an eerie precision that makes her yelp and fly back.

Rolf doesn't understand what the noise is, or what the metal thing in the man's hand does. All he sees is the pup flying back and the fear radiating off of her is palpable. He lets out a howling roar, sending the war cry into the ether as he sprints forward and throws himself at the man that shot the girl. In the distance, there is a rallying cry from several other wolves.

Rolf shifts in his tackle and rips the man's throat out. He grunts as there is a sudden pain in his shoulder from another loud clap of sound. He isn't thinking as he turns and goes for the second man.

Another loud crack and he feels a pain in his back. His claws elongate as he shifts into human form again, ripping the man's arm out of the socket.

A third loud crack causes Rolf to roar in pain. He leaves the second man to bleed out as he turns to face the source of the loud noises.

The third man has ditched his pistol and is pointing a shotgun at Rolf.

Rolf leaps forward, intending to shift midair when the man raises the shotgun up and pulls the trigger.

Buck shot sprays through the air, like little silver pellets of death.

Rolf blinks in disbelief as it sends him flying, the pain white hot and all over. He can't breathe and is on his back. His ears ring, and panic fills him as he can smell the wolfsbane now worming into his blood. Rolf claws at his chest in a frenzy to get the searing hot pain to stop. The silver now burning everywhere it touches him.

The man stalks toward him, cocking the weapon in his hand.

What sort of madness is that thing? His eyes grow wide as he looks up at the man now pointing it square at his face.

Rolf relaxes, sadness filling him. He will never get to see his beautiful Lily again. The image of her flashes in his mind. Her coppery hair shining in the moonlight. How soft her pale skin is to his touch. The way she laughs when he teases her. How she curls to him for comfort. Her sweet scent fills his nostrils and as he closes his eyes, he whispers goodbye before he musters the strength of the Gods and pushes to attack this monster one last time.

******

I arrive at the clearing, and there is blood everywhere. My chest burns and my body aches. I have vomited twice, feeling the bond between Rolf and I unravel. I can't stop crying and my heart is breaking. I am going to die right here if I don't get to him. I can fix this. I will rewind time. I will never make him come here. We will live happily ever after if I could just find him.

"Rolf!" I scream. "Rolf! Where are you?"

I move from body to body, frantic for any signs of life. There are the remains of men, all ripped to shreds. My hands tremble as I try to find a cell phone or wallet. I keep my hand over my nose and mouth to deter the stench of death. Whatever happened in this clearing has left Rolf's life fading. I sob, unable to tolerate, carnage and vomit again.

On my hands and knees, I pray to Mani and Freya. I beg them to help me find and save Rolf. My magic is in chaos around me.

The Earth trembles at my touch. As if she could sob with me, the skies open up into a monstrous storm. The wind howls and rain falls like tiny daggers against my skin.

My hands burn with the desire to raze this entire forest to the ground to find Rolf and murder any who hurt him.

The elements swirl around me and I can hear the howling cries of wolves mourning the loss of a loved one.

As if the Earth knew I needed to move, I'm jerked to my feet. One foot in front of the other with no knowledge of where I'm going, other than I know it will lead me to Rolf. I feel his soul call to me. The faint beating of his heart moved slower and slower. I will never find him in time on foot. The wind howls louder around me, whipping my hair into a frenzy of copper waves. My hands move to make the symbols for a portal. "Accipe me ubi cor meum!" I scream to take me where my heart is.

******

"Lily, you told me we could not interfere. That to intervene would alter the timeline." The silver-haired man stands with his arms crossed in my path.

"If you don't move from out of my way, you're going to die right now. Or have you already forgotten?"

"It was you!" Rolf's eyes light up.

"No. It was Lily." I clarify. "I just made sure you didn't die before she got there."

"You meddled then." His eyes narrow at me.

"Do you want to live or not? We don't have much time before she appears next to him."

"Pop-pop! Nanny! Come quick! The stranger wolf that looks like Pop-pop is hurt bad!" The tiny pup that comes bursting into our home is wide-eyed and frantic.

Rolf gives me a narrowed gaze, but there's morbid curiosity in his eyes. He doesn't believe the young wolf we are about to attend to is him.

I use the opportunity to flee with one of our great-great-grandchildren to go to stabilize Rolf. I can't heal him, or I will never learn how to do it. I remember how I felt on this day. I was sure I was going to die with Rolf.

The pup stays with me until I step into the medical clinic. I try to enter the room where Rolf is dying but am stopped by our great grandson, the current Alpha. "You cannot go in there, Lily. You know that."

"I need to stabilize him." Panic wells in me. I might not be able to help Rolf at all.

"No. You need to leave before either of them sees you two." He motions from me to Rolf who is not far behind me.

"Are you willing to let that boy die?" I growl at him.

"I am Alpha and I say you cannot enter. Your presence here is enough, Lily. You are his mate and that bond is strong, even if you are not the Lily that will be in that room with him. He will survive. We have excellent doctors, great grandmother. Do you not remember telling me about this very moment when I was younger?"

I throw my hands in the air in frustration and I go to open my mouth to freeze the young Alpha in place, only to find

Rolf's hand over my mouth. I narrow my eyes at him, and then huff.

"Pout all you want, my flower. But look," he motions with his free hand as the flash of light dies down and there I stand, my copper hair a holy hot mess around me.

My younger version is not even thinking about what she is doing as she puts her hands on her dying mate.

I watch as she works, and then allow Rolf to lead me away. We could not remain without altering the timeline.

XXXVII

The Life of an Alpha

I sob and thrust my hands onto his decimated chest. The words won't flow from my lips. Healing magic is tricky and dangerous. His soul is fading, and it's crushing me. All I want is for him to live. I call on the air element to help me rip the silver from his body.

The tiny buckshot pellets of silver suck out of his chest and float around us in bloody shimmery balls before they fall to the floor.

He continues to fade.

"Rolf! Please! Please don't leave me. I will do anything. Please just wake up."

His heart's beating in my ears, louder than any drum. Pain courses through me as it radiates through him. The sting of silver as it holds his wounds opens, the poison of the wolfsbane that they are coated in slithering through his blood, preventing his healing abilities from kicking in. My eyes close and then the clank of a silver bullet hits the floor. It's followed by the other bullet that had been lodged in his system. I'm wildly using the magic to do whatever I can to heal him. There is no control, no patience. No respect. I don't care if the Gods punish me the rest of my days. I will do whatever it takes to save Rolf.

"Don't touch her," I hear a male voice bark behind me. "Just step back."

All the medical people around us obey instantly.

"Rolf," I cry his name like a prayer.

I begin to fade as I literally pour my very soul into the unconscious Viking beneath me. I don't care that the longer I try to wake him the more it drains me. My fingers are covered in blood and splayed over his chest.

"Onus tuum porto," my words echo in a scream off the sterile walls of this room as I cast the spell to bind my soul to his beyond the mate bond and draw all the remaining poison into my body.

I collapse against Rolf.

******

Silar stares out the window, watching the sky.

The amount of powerful magic surging through the ley lines could only mean Lily is performing magic.

His duties as the guardian of the New England area have not gone away in the years since his brother's death. He remains still, staring off into the distance. Sending the hunters may have helped him twice over. If they murdered the mutt, she may exact revenge, which would taint her soul enough to perform the summoning spell.

The wind howls with her cries and he resists touching the

ley lines to manipulate her magic. He has no idea what she is trying to accomplish, other than the amount of power she is using to do it is great.

"The hunters are dead, sir."

Silar raises a brow and looks over his shoulder. "Oh? How do you know this?"

The young woman bites her lip and shifts uneasily in Silar's presence. "The Alpha threw their heads at us."

Silar frowns. "Did you bring the heads?"

"Sir?"

"Their heads, bring me their heads." He sounds irritated and with a slow breath he turns to look out the window again. If the hunters are truly dead, then why is Lily still in distress?

He reluctantly moves away from the window and turns to his grimoires. He slowly turns the pages while he waits for the girl to return with the heads of the mercenaries.

Between the three of them, he would have had to pay them for five pelts. By their size, he would guess they are from children. They got what they deserved if that is the case. Though, it is a surefire way to draw out the alpha of a pack. Too bad for them. They did not take his warning to heart.

The young Rolf is proving a worthy adversary for a mutt.

He's resigned to having to do everything himself when the girl returns.

One hand holding the bag at arm's length and the other covering her nose and mouth.

"Leave them," he motions without looking up from the grimoire. When she drops them and flees, he chuckles. He leaves the small vial of blood sitting on his worktable and comes to the bag to retrieve the three heads.

He squats down and pulls the first head out of the bag. The expression on the leader's face makes Silar smirk. Arrogant fool looks like he pissed himself when they relieved him of his head.

"Dic quid meministi," he commands the head to tell him what it remembers.

******

"What did you do to my mate?" Rolf growls at Alpha Aaron.

"Rolf, you need to calm yourself. We did not do anything to your mate. She did this to herself." The older man sighs as he looks at the agitated younger version of his great grandfather.

"What do you mean, she did it to herself? No one would willingly knock themselves unconscious."

"You are a fool if you think a witch would not knock themselves unconscious to use more power. You are lucky that is the worst of it."

"Why would she need more power?"

Alpha Aaron gives Rolf the look every adult gives children when they are being dense. "Really? Maybe, oh I don't know, it was the magic to pull the hundreds of silver buckshot from your hide. Or, call it a hunch, to drain all the wolfsbane from your veins. I mean, honestly. What kind of wolf rushes a hunter head on with a shotgun full of silver?"

Rolf gets a perplexed look on his face as he reflects on the fight. He pieces together that the stick that made the thunderclap must be this shotgun the Alpha is referring to. He frowns and moves closer to Lily, taking her hand. He can feel her heart beating strongly, but it has been three days, and she has not opened her eyes once.

The Alpha sighs, watching the pup with his mate. It's terrifying and exciting to see his great grandparents so young. They have changed little over the years other than their appearance. Lily is still head strong, leaps first and asks later. While Rolf is ever the Viking warrior. He rubs his hand over his face, knowing he is about to get into another fight with young Rolf. "As soon as she wakes, you two need to leave. You cannot stay on pack land."

"What?" Rolf growls. "This is my pack! You cannot kick me out."

"This is my pack, Rolf. I am Alpha and have been for years. And I can kick you out. You bring death in your wake and I cannot, in good faith, allow more harm to befall my pack."

"Is not it the responsibility of the pack to protect all of us? We have nowhere else to go."

"It is the responsibility of the pack to protect the pack. You and she are not pack. As it is, your presence here has caused five pups' deaths and injury to my daughter. How am I supposed to reconcile with those pups' parents if I allow you to stay?" Alpha Aaron feels guilty for choosing this path to deny Rolf's request, but he knows that his great grandfather was one of the greatest Alphas of this pack and understands the hard choices an Alpha has to make to protect it. "You are guests here until she wakes and can travel. Then we will see you to wherever you want to go. So long as it is not on pack lands. That includes the cottage."

Lily had taught Aaron about this moment. Explaining that it will fall on his shoulders to make their younger versions continue their journey. She didn't explain to him all the details, but he knows it's imperative they don't stay. It is the one demand Lily made him promise to follow. He understands now why. If the younger versions stay, it will cause all sorts of problems. As much as he would like to ask Rolf how they can help him more, the older Rolf made him swear he would not help them outside of travel arrangements.

Rolf relents. He understands putting the good of the whole pack over the good for the individual comes first for an Alpha. "We will need to get to the park in the center of New York City. The large one with the forest."

The Alpha nods. "When she is ready, we will see you there safely. I don't want to see you on pack land again, or I will be forced to deal with you."

Rolf turns his attention back to Lily, taking up residence in the chair next to her hospital bed. He does not understand all the cords attached to her, or the beeping box on the other side, but the people calling themselves doctors say it is all necessary. He struggles with ripping them off of her and absconding with her back to the cottage. Even if the Alpha said he could not return there. He would like to see that wolf take on the vines, or the creepy dolls.

XXXVIII

Wake-Up Call

I don't know how long I slept, but I know Rolf's emotions teeter between sad and angry.

His raging emotions are like a tether in this ethereal nothingness I have found myself in.

I don't know what magic I used, or how it worked, I just know Rolf is safe, and alive. When I open my eyes, I'm blinded by a white light, which makes me groan. I want to move my arm to shield myself, but something heavy is on it.

"Lily!" Rolf shouts in excitement.

I squint at the bright lights blinding me. That's when all the sounds come rushing in. The beeps of the monitors, the hum of the lights, and the now excited shouts of Rolf all make me wince. It had been peaceful and quiet in the nothingness. I blink as nurses and a doctor come rushing in, pushing Rolf aside.

His growl is enough to make me sputter, "It's alright. Let them work," to him. I imagine he is beside himself with all these strange machines and oddly dressed people.

They have me sit up, grip their hands, follow their fingers, and they check all of my vitals.

Rolf's agitation floods into me stronger than before. His thoughts race through my mind like a race car. It's giving me a headache.

Why is he touching her? Is she alright? What does that do? I'll rip her arm off if she hurts my flower.

I laugh at the last one. "Rolf, they are medicine people. They aren't going to hurt me. Please don't rip their arms off," I speak to him in his language, assuming these people did not speak it.

"No, we like our arms, thank you very much," one of the older nurses retorts as she turns to face Rolf. "You either behave, or I will turn you out."

I watch in disbelief as Rolf quiets down. She must be the nurse that has been dealing with him while I was unconscious.

"Well, everything looks good here. Let's get some food in you, and see how you feel tomorrow, okay? I will give you some quiet time with your mate." The doctor looks between Rolf and me with a smile.

"Yes, sir," I nod.

Everything is situated, and the medical staff leave the room.

Rolf is back to me, wrapping me into the most heated kiss I have ever known. It's needy and wanton, sucking all coherent thought right from me.

I cling to him. I don't care that we're in a hospital room; I thought I lost him, and here we both are.

He climbs onto the bed with me, and we awkwardly shift

around until we're nestled together.

"Don't ever do that again, my flower," he growls at me. "I thought you were gone forever."

"Don't you get yourself shot with wolfsbane laced silver then," I retort.

"Deal." He kisses my forehead and I feel the sudden sadness fill him.

"What is it? Why are you sad?"

"Because, now that you are awake, we have to leave this place. The Alpha has agreed to take us to New York City but has denied us becoming part of our own pack."

"Wait. Our own pack? Alpha? What are you talking about? How long was I out?"

"It has been a week, Lily."

I've lost an entire week. I nestle to him more and the tidal wave of emotions between us is enough to make me cry.

Rolf kisses the tears away and holds me close.

I couldn't even fathom how to process losing a whole week. "What are we going to do in New York?" I ask after I pull myself back together.

"I don't know. I thought we might go back to that park and look for clues on how to get home. It is not safe here anymore, my flower. Your father is hunting for us, and he is the one who sent those monsters that skinned my pack members." The amount of rage rolling off of Rolf is enough to make me gasp.

If my father ever shows his face, Rolf will shred him to pieces.

"Rolf, I don't know the spell to use. My mother has it or had it. It wasn't at Grandma Finley's, and if my father had it, we would know." I nuzzle him, trying to explain why I could bring myself here, but not travel back. "We can't just open a hole through time and run around like fools. One wrong move and it could leave us trapped in the in-between. Or worse, send us to different places."

A foreboding sense of panic bubbles inside that my father will capture us and something terrible will occur. Looking at Rolf I keep catching glimpses of him in front of a portal, covered in blood. My panic is enough to cause the heart monitor to pick up pace.

Rolf's expression darkens, and he looks from me to the beeping monitor. His touch is gentle as he pets down my back, but his body is rigid. "Lily, we will have to try. I will not let anything happen to you. I promise." He kisses my temple again, and we stay snuggled on the hospital bed until they bring in food.

I'm ravenous and scarf the food on the first tray faster than a speeding bullet.

Rolf laughs and disappears from the room. He returns with two more trays of food, one for me and one for him.

We eat in amicable silence, and then resume snuggling. His earlier tidal wave of rage and agitation has shifted to the comforting sense of excitement and love.

I soon drift back to sleep nestled in his arms.

The nurses interrupt this blissful rest to force me out of bed.

Rolf is irritated and tries to protest, but the old battle-axe nurse takes him out of the room, reading him the riot act.

The cute, young nurse encourages me to get up and walk to the restroom on my own. While I'm not physically injured, I have been laying in a bed for a week. It takes a few seconds to get my body moving. Not being a werewolf, I don't have the luxurious healing abilities my mate does. I'm breathing hard by the time I get to the restroom, but grateful for the trip. By the time the doctor returns to check on me, I have had a shower, changed into new clothes, and have forced Rolf into a shower as well.

"Lily, I would like to ask you a favor," the doctor begins.

"Okay."

"When your mate was brought in, there was a little girl also brought in. She was injured with the same kind of bullets as your mate. We were able to get most of the bullet out, but its pieces remained, and the wolfsbane is still in her system." The doctor hesitates, looking from me to Rolf with an anxious glance. "Alpha has instructed us to notify him as soon as you woke, but I wanted to talk with you regarding this… matter, first. I wouldn't ask if I thought we could help the girl, but she's."

The weird sensation prickling under my skin tells me she's in grave danger. While the doctor has not come out and said it, he has inferred as much. I know what his favor is before he says it out loud. "You want me to pull out the wolfsbane."

"No! Absolutely not! I forbid it," Rolf snarls. "You saw what it did to my Lily before!"

I did not have time to process the tsunami of emotions rolling off of Rolf. They cause me to turn and vomit into the trashcan nearby. This brings both men to me, one soothing and one raging. I wave them off, trying to convey I'm alright as I vomit again. I could see Rolf's side of the argument. I don't know how I did it fully, but it must have caused me great harm, to have him panicked. On the other hand, I couldn't just leave a little girl to die from wolfsbane poisoning.

When the horrible feeling passes, and the two men get me settled back on the hospital bed, I frown at them. "Can I have a minute with Rolf, please?" I ask the doctor. We watch as the doctor steps out of the room, closing the door behind him.

"Don't try to change my mind. Lily, it's too dangerous. They will not even provide us sanctuary because of who we are."

"That's not a reason to not help that girl. If I can help her, I should. It's my father that caused her predicament."

"Then your father should help her," he snarls.

"Do you think he would truly help her? I'm his daughter and look what he has done to get me back."

"What if it kills you?"

"It won't."

"You can't know that."

"I can and do know that. I have se—," I stop and purse my lips. "I have a feeling it will be alright. Trust me."

Rolf's eyes narrow. He heard what I wasn't saying and I can tell he wants to question me more.

She must be touched. Didn't she say the old woman had visions? Why does she have to be so stubborn? By Odin, I should just take her over my shoulder and leave this place.

If he knew I could hear his thoughts as plain as day, he probably would be more guarded. Tit for tat, as he could hear mine, too.

What kind of people would we be if we only helped people who helped us? Yes, my grandma had visions. Visions no one would listen to until it was too late. You're just as stubborn, jerk. Besides, maybe a little good will in helping them will get them to help us in New York.

I laugh hard when his eyebrows shoot up to his forehead and his cheeks flame red.

"That's cheating," he grumbles.

"Uh-huh. Rolf, I will be fine. I promise." I get back up off the bed and come to him, wrapping my arms around his waist. When I bury my face against his chest, I feel his body relax and his arms go around me.

"My flower, you are everything to me. I dislike feeling like I cannot protect you."

"You protect me more than you know, Rolf. When I healed you, I connected with you more. There are… things I feel from you that are… intense."

He chuckles at my choice of words and kisses my forehead. "I will allow you to heal her. But if you start to look like you are in trouble, I will not hesitate to put a stop to it."

I linger in his arms until the doctor pops his head back in.

With a nod, I let him know he can return.

"What is your decision, Lily?" He purposely does not look at Rolf.

"Show me the girl. I'll see what I can do."

XXXIX

You Say hello I Say Goodbye

The doctor leads us from my room to what appears to be the intensive care unit.

The poor little girl looks terrible. Her skin is covered in dark veining, and the wound from the bullet itself is still open and raw looking under its bandage.

A pretty, dark-haired woman is sitting on the other side of the bed. Her face is red and blotchy from crying. She looks up from her daughter to the three of us entering and her eyes go wide.

"How... How did you... You're so young. Your hair... It's..."

"Luna, they have come to see if they can help Seline." The doctor doesn't answer the questions, and the woman is staring at me like she is looking at a ghost.

I bite my lip, and I move around the doctor to the little

girl.

The woman lets go of her hand and sits back in her seat, watching me with an apprehensive gaze. "They said you had left. I had lost all hope." She looks from the doctor to me with confusion written all over her face.

"Come, Luna, let's go get some coffee and let them see what they can do." He guides the awestruck woman out of the chair and to the door. He only pauses long enough to give me a stern look.

You have five minutes at most before she contacts the Alpha.

I'm not sure why the Alpha would be a problem, but I nod and turn my attention to the little girl who looks ghastly.

Rolf hovers nearby and the nervous energy rolling off of him makes me breathe harder.

I shake my head as if the physical action will soothe the mental connection. Her festering wound is as good a place as any to start. With delicate fingers, I remove the bandage and begin humming.

Rolf's hand rests on my hip as he tries to look casual, but I know he is getting ready to pull me away if something goes awry.

The hum of the surrounding elements grows with his touch. It amplifies my call to them to retrieve the silver first. The small whoosh of air flutters around my hand and the silver pieces dislodge from her flesh. My chanting is soft and steady in Latin, and all other things disappear from my vision as I focus on the little girl before me. After two minutes, all the silver flecks are sitting on the bed table next to us.

"Da venenum tuum mihi," I say as I shift my focus to retrieving the wolfsbane, and the water element resists. Water is wild and unwieldy. To connect with the element is not difficult, but to wield it, is a whole other matter.

At first, nothing happens with Seline and sweat forms on my brow, along with my hand trembling.

Rolf's hand tightens on my waist and his fear is rising, which is distracting to me.

I narrow my eyes and focus harder on the element. Feeling the blood flows through her like a brook bubbling down the side of a mountain. The drums of Earth's heart in her pulse and realize water will never give me what I want.

We come from the Earth, and our blood is its flow, not water's flow. My voice turns to a plea, "Da venenum tuum mihi," I call again.

Somewhere in the distance a man's shouting, "What do you mean you let her touch Seline? Are you mad?"

Focus!

"You damn well know who she is and what she can do. Did you want your daughter to die? We were out of options," the dark-haired woman shouts back.

Hurry up, my flower. The Alpha is coming.

My face pinches, and I suck in a sharp breath to pull harder. The inky heaviness of the poison moves like sludge in her veins. It's slow going and when the room door finally bursts open, I slump into Rolf's arms, my hands black from the wolfsbane coating them. I tremble and lean into Rolf, who scoops me up without hesitation and pulls me back from the little girl.

The Alpha, doctor, and Luna all barge in, but stop short looking at Seline in the bed.

Rolf cradles me to him and storms out of the room back to mine. He gently places me on the bed.

I flutter my eyes open to see him step into the bathroom. When he comes back, he has a wet hand towel and what looks like a small basin of water. "Give me your hands, Lily."

I raise my hands to him and watch as he carefully dabs

and wipes them until they are flush pink from the warm towel. The now dark looking cloth is tossed aside.

Rolf turns to look at me. "You should not have done so much."

"Yes, I should have," I sigh.

"No, they made their bed when they denied us. We owe them nothing."

"You're being stubborn. They are scared and there is something weird about us that makes them be on edge."

"This is our pack, Lily. They all smell like home, like family."

I frown and watch Rolf, trying to understand his lack of compassion on this matter. "Is it possible? I mean. What if the reason they are being so weird is we are supposed to be dead?"

He snorts and shrugs. "Then they should thank the Gods that we came back from the afterlife."

"You're cute when you sulk," I tease.

"I'm not sulking!"

"Oh, yes, you are. You look just like Ingrid did when she sulked at Alpha."

Rolf chuffs and crosses his arms.

I laugh, wanting to say more.

In storms a man with dark hair, and silver wisps clinging to his temple.

Followed quickly behind him is the dark-haired woman.

He stops short, seeing me lying on my side on the bed, and Rolf sitting on the edge, petting me gently.

I move to sit up and curl into Rolf, half expecting this man to berate me for what I did in the other room.

The woman steps between us and her hands are on her hips as she faces the man.

"You will not turn them out after what she just did for

you."

"You understand nothing, woman. Step aside."

"If you think I won't put you on the floor, Alpha, you have another thing coming. You will thank her for saving your daughter's life, and then you treat them with respect. Not cast them out like trash!"

"You want me to put our entire pack in jeopardy?! If they are not in New York by Beltane, there are severe consequences. You heard the old woman as plain as day!"

Beltane. That's the night my mother opened the portal and found Viggo.

I'm beginning to wonder if there is a way to recreate the spell without my mother's book.

"Then you will not only see them to New York, you will help them find a place to stay safely! You are not just going to abandon them. You are better than this!"

"Maybe we can find other witches in the city to help you? Someone has to help us. These two are going to offer us little," Rolf says in our link.

"Fine! Fine!" The man then moves around, who I guess is his wife. "You," he brandishes a finger at me. "Thank you." He then wraps us both right into his arms, causing me to squeak and Rolf to growl.

"Uh… you're welcome. Is she alright?"

"She's healing on her own now. Doc says it may only be a few days before she's awake," the woman says from a few feet away.

The Alpha eases back, and his expression darkens. "As much as I would like for you to stay, you cannot, as you heard my wife. Come on, let's get you out of here."

What he didn't say was 'before we're attacked again.' We gather up our things and follow the Alpha and Luna out.

"If we just flee to New York, her father will know exactly

where we are and will hunt us down."

"Oh pup," the Alpha laughs as he leads us to another building. "You are not the only wolf with a witch on your side." He opens a door and ushers us into what looks like a gymnasium. That's not what makes me gasp. As the gathered people turn to look at us, I see at least a dozen copies of myself.

Whose Lily is it Anyway?

Rolf steps in front of me and pulls me close behind him.

I can understand his fear. I have to admit, seeing multiple copies of myself makes me nervous too. What if the Alpha was lying and is going to kill us to just replace us with a copy? I wish my mom were here. She would make me feel better instantly.

The Alpha laughs and pats Rolf on the shoulder. "Easy, pup. They agreed to help because you have been saving their pups."

"You what?" I ask from behind him.

"He has been stalking around the woods and scaring the younger ones back into our town."

Not giving me enough time to grill Rolf on what else he has been doing, the Alpha leads us further into the room. He explains the plan and then the pairs of Rolfs and Lilys gather up with the escorts.

My eyes never leave Rolf.

So, this is what you have been doing while I was learning? Are you insane?

Lily, they are still my pack. Even if they don't recognize that. I was not about to let hunters skin anymore pups.

Skin?

Yes. The hunters were skinning them, likely before they transformed back into their human side. That is what you saw when you connected with me.

Oh. You're still insane! You could have been killed.

You were the one that said we should do the right thing.

He gives me a wolfish grin I want to slap right off his face.

"You ready, my flower?" He pulls me in close and rubs noses with me. It's his way of apologizing without actually apologizing.

"Wait, so how are we going to all leave without my father's coven knowing what we're doing?" I ask. "Oh! I learned how to make a transport portal!"

"Thirteen times, Lily?" Rolf asks with concern on his face.

"This way," the Alpha motions, and I raise a brow at his chuckling.

Rolf turns me and keeps his hands on my waist as we move forward. We descend from the gymnasium into a massive underground garage. Lined as far as I can see are SUVs with dark tinted windows.

"Welcome to the twenty-first century. Your chariot," he holds the door as he motions us into the back of the vehicle.

I climb in first and slide across.

Rolf eyes the vehicle with suspicion, then looks at the Alpha.

I giggle as he grins at Rolf and looks just like him.

Rolf slides into the seat next to me. The door shuts and the

Alpha thumps on the roof twice.

The vehicles pull out of the garage and race away from the little town. "Buckle up, this is going to be rough," the man in the driver's seat says to us.

Rolf looks confused, but I reach over him and pull the seatbelt across him.

"It keeps you in place if something happens to the car."

"What is the magic that makes this work?"

I lean back after clicking him in and pull my seatbelt on. "It's a combination of mechanical parts and liquids," I say as I struggle to breathe from fear. If my father has been looking for us this hard, then how do they plan to hide us? Will those people get hurt?

Rolf takes my hand and kisses the back of it gently.

"It will be alright, Lily. I promise."

I turn back to look at the vehicles following us, only they aren't there. I could have sworn they were right behind us. By the time I turn to face front, the vehicle lurches forward and punches into what looks like Star Wars hyperspace.

Rolf's grip on my hand tightens and a second later, we are bouncing onto a side street in Manhattan.

The driver pulls into traffic like we didn't just hop through magic in a truck and is humming when he pulls up to what I can only imagine is the safe house. "Lie low. Don't use magic. We'll send word when it's clear to go out again."

Rolf and I ease out of the vehicle and are greeted by the most gregarious woman I have ever met. She reminds me of Ms. Miller in the Chipmunk Adventure. "Oh, look at you two! By the stars! You look just like your grandmother!" She pulls me into a hug without warning.

I squeak. I have no idea who this woman is, but she makes me feel safe.

Rolf chuckles at my plight before he is pulled in and his

face nearly plants into her ample bosom.

"Come on in. We'll get you settled. Girl, you are too skinny. With a young stud like him, you gotta keep your figure," she winks at me, and I turn as red as a cherry while Rolf snickers behind me.

******

Silar redoubled his efforts to get the wards broken. Now that he knows where his daughter is, and who she is with, it's just a matter of getting through the wards. The day of the power surge he came to the edge of the ward. With a few precise spells, he sets a trigger along the entire ward. Should anyone pass in, or out, his warlocks would be alerted. Then he waits.

He waits for seven days.

Seven long days of patiently waiting for the girl to foolishly leave the safety of her grandmother's world. He couldn't be sure, but he imagines she will try to stop him and when she does open the portal for him, he will complete the ritual and set the world right. If he could just get her away from that damn wolf, he could convince her to help him. He has a back-up plan if she will not come willingly.

On the seventh day, fortune favors him. The little chimes alert him to something leaving the warded area. He sends warlocks to intercept them. Then the chimes happen again, and again. His office erupts into a cacophony of discord music. He narrows his eyes and looks up toward the ceiling, As if that is where the sound originated from.

The first warlocks enter his office. "It wasn't them. When we retrieved them from the vehicle, they transformed into wolves and attacked us."

"You were fooled by a transfiguration spell?"

"No. It was them. Then it wasn't."

Silar pinches the bridge of his nose, believing the two warlocks before him to be idiots when the next pair come in, injured and frightened.

"It… was… wolves," the young witch stammers.

Soon, Silar's office is full of several injured witches and warlocks saying the same thing.

He growls. "Out! All of you! Are none of you capable of retrieving a single girl? They are werewolves, not Gods. You know fucking magic!"

The witches and warlocks disperse, and Silar clears his table in a violent swipe, sending grimoires, potions, and anything not bolted down to the floor. He storms from his office and descends the stone staircase to the underbelly of his estate.

The small font at the end of the altar room shivers in response to his mood. The air howls around him like a wailing banshee. Ripping a terrified rabbit from its cage he thrusts it onto the stone altar.

In a flourishing motion, he raises the dagger, then plunges it into the white fur of the innocent creature. His voice booms in Latin for the seeing spell, and the blood pools over the altar and the rabbit twitches as its life flows from it.

Silar's eyes roll and he snarls as his vision is obscured. Visions of his daughter bounce before his eyes until, in focus, is an old woman with hair whiter than snow and piercing green eyes. Confusion washes over Silar's face as he stares at the woman. Then she turns her gaze and stares as if she can see him.

Silar rips himself from the vision, his nose bleeding, and his head feeling as though Thor's hammer had pounded against it. Falling onto his backside, he brings his hand to his head.

No witch is powerful enough to block a scrying spell.

Who is that white-haired woman? Silar wipes his nose on his sleeve as he pulls himself up and looks at the rabbit. Its body is shriveled and the blood drips on the floor. He stalks to the cages and pulls a second rabbit from them. Repeating the process, only, this time looking for the white-haired woman.

Again, she appears before him, with everything around her obscured. Her eyes stare at him like emeralds in firelight. She smiles, and he is convinced he is staring at Catarina.

"Who are you?" he shouts into the ether.

Her expression turns sad then and gives him a finger wave.

Silar is forcibly thrust from his vision and sent flying across the room. He lands with a thud, his nose bleeding, and his head feeling like it is split wide open. He was no closer to getting an answer or finding Lily. The fury of his roar echoes off the stone walls as he forces himself to his feet a second time. Then he staggers to the cages and retrieves a third rabbit.

When he stumbles to the altar and places the rabbit upon the bloody stone, he sways for a moment, his body battered and bruised from whatever that white-haired demon did to him. He brings his dagger down to evoke the spell again, only to be shot across the room, allowing the terrified rabbit to flee.

Silar sinks down the wall unconscious.

LXI

Third Time's the Charm

A few days after we arrive at Matilda Wrathburn's home, our things are delivered via a courier.

Matilda is the quirkiest woman I have ever met. She neither confirms nor denies if she is a witch. She has an altar, which she claims is a knick-knack shelf. There are herbs hanging in her basement, with a worktable, a mortar and pestle, and an entire room that Rolf and I cannot enter.

Rolf has been restless. He's not used to staying indoors all day, every day.

I try to placate him with the plethora of board games Matilda owns, but I discover quickly he is a sore loser. To preserve the games, I introduce him to the television. I explain how the people are not really trapped in the box, but it is recorded elsewhere.

He doesn't believe me, but thoroughly enjoys flipping

through the channels.

This is the first time the two of us could spend any time together without the interruptions and threats. It's Saturday morning, and I'm curled on the couch with a bowl of cereal in hand. The television is on NBC with the last bastion of Saturday morning cartoons playing on the screen. My feet are tucked under me and the bowl of cereal is precariously balanced between my torso and legs while I happily crunch away on the sugary goodness.

"Girl, you're going to be nothing but sugar, you keep eating that stuff! That's for my grandson."

"Maybe I enjoy being sweet," I say as I smile at her.

Her entire belly shakes with laughter. "I bet your pup upstairs would have something to say about that. I'm going to the store. Be back in a few hours. Don't burn the place down!" She waves as she turns and disappears from the double doorway leading into her living room.

I resume my breakfast and watch cartoons until I see Rolf appear in the doorway.

He quirks a brow at me and staggers into the living room until he settles on the couch next to me. "What is that?" He eyes my bowl with a suspicious look.

"Cereal. Want some?"

He sniffs and then raises his brow. "It is sweet?"

"It is," I offer him the entire bowl.

He takes a bite of it cautiously, like I'm springing Brussels sprouts on him. Then his eyes light up.

I take the bowl back from him and head into the kitchen.

"Hey, I was not done with that!"

"This is mine. I'm making you a bowl."

He follows me into the kitchen and leans against the door as I retrieve the box of cereal and milk. Pouring them into a bowl, I fish out a spoon, then hand him the whole thing. "And

Luna said you would never cook for me."

I snort in laughter. "I imagine she said you should never let me cook for you."

He laughs too and eats a few spoonfuls, milk dribbling into his beard.

I reach up and wipe my thumb along his chin.

He snaps fast enough he draws my thumb between his teeth, wriggling his brows at me.

"Brute," I tease.

"You tried to come between me and this deliciously sweet cream," he says releasing my thumb.

"Milk. It's milk."

"I have had milk, my flower. This is cream."

"You've had goat's milk. This is cow's milk. It's been harvested and made to last longer when stored properly. They add stuff to it to make it taste good." I repress a giggle at the idea of trying to explain pasteurization of milk to my Viking.

We finish our cereal in the kitchen, and I take the dishes, rinsing them and then putting them in Matilda's dishwasher.

"What does that do?"

I glance over my shoulder to see what he is pointing at. "Oh. It's a washtub that works without humans." How did mom do this with Viggo?

"Without humans? How is that possible? We aren't supposed to be using your magic, Lily."

I roll my eyes at Rolf. "It's not magic, it's technology. This," I motion to the dishwasher. "Has wires and parts that all work in unison to make the soap and water clean the dishes." I realize that while I know what a dishwasher is, I don't actually know how it works. I laugh and shrug. "Alright. Fine. It's magic. Just not mine. I haven't used magic since Seline."

Rolf and I migrate back into the living room and plop down on the couch.

He makes the mistake of leaning back to drape his arm along the back of the couch, so I curl right to him and nestle my head against his shoulder.

On the screen is a vibrant and noisy cartoon that I'm not even really paying attention to. I'm listening to the steady beating of his heart and playing my fingers along his chest. Even in human form he's a walking Wookiee and his muscles twitch as he tries not to react to being ticklish.

"These must be the cartons that Viggo complained about."

"Cartons?"

"These… brightly colored nonsensical images."

"Oh. Cartoons. They are for children and I like them."

"You are not a child."

"Adults can enjoy childish things too! You enjoy throwing your cousins into the river in the dead of winter."

"That is different. They deserve it."

"Oh, really? You liked the cereal you just ate," I shift up and jab where I know he's ticklish.

"Woman!" He squirms and tries to capture my hands. Then he goes in for his own attack, which makes me shriek in giggling.

Next thing I know we are tussling on the couch and fall square onto the floor with me underneath him. His boyish smile says he thinks he has me and he is pushing my shirt up to gain access to my bare skin.

"Man!" I gasp in laughter and then try to roll him over.

"Feisty." He taunts me and steals a rough kiss from me to distract me from my mission of rolling him over. His hands slide down and cup my ass to press us firm to each other.

"Mhmm," I groan in the kiss, and then bite his lip as I try again to roll us. I know he let me, but he does not relax his grip on my ass, as he growls in response.

Our jabbing and tormenting of each other becomes tugging and pulling, as what little clothing we are wearing gets sent flying. He leans up and nips a nipple while he gropes and pinches the other while I push out of my shorts and panties. He takes the moment to rotate us back around to him being on top of me.

My back arches and I rake my nails along his shoulders.

"Greedy flower," he murmurs against my breast. His fingers slip between us and the rough callous of his thumb brushes along my clit, sending tendrils of pleasure through my body.

"Don't tease," I pout.

"Hush," he growls against my lips before kissing me. His hand shifts and he plunges two fingers into me fast enough I arch up to him and gasp. He doesn't stop kissing me as he slowly retreats his fingers from inside me to thrust them in again. His thumb worked expertly over the nub to keep my body rocking between the sensations.

He hardens and I move to reciprocate when his fingers pull from me.

"No, bad flower," his voice is husky and deep. He brings his hand up, catching my wrist and eases my hand above my head where he holds it with the other, his firsthand trailing back down my flush skin to resume his intentional, sweet torture. "Now, be a good girl and enjoy this," he coos to me while his fingers thrust into me again.

It's not long before I'm gasping and writhing underneath him, a hot mess, and without any sense. My body throbs and aches to be filled. "Please, Rolf," I beg. I bring my leg up, rubbing along his to entice him into shifting his hips and thrusting his raging hard cock inside of me instead of his fingers.

He kisses against the small of my neck, where my mate mark lives, and I shiver.

I moan, my orgasm washing over me like a tidal wave.

Then his hand is gone, and I'm left wet and throbbing again, just long enough for him to roll us so I'm fully on my back. His hands release mine and he raises us, pulling my hips up toward him. Without hesitation, he parts my thighs more and brushes the tip along me before he plunges in.

His hips roll firmly against mine, pumping into me with abandon. His fingers grip tighter and he thrusts harder, winning a louder moan from me.

I bring my legs up more and he releases my hips to slide up and grip my shoulders from underneath. Our bodies press even closer and he buries his face against the small of my neck. The mix of growling and grunting reminds me of how animalistic he can be.

His lips smother mine in a primal and demanding kiss. This is nowhere near as brutal as the night he claimed me. His muscles are tight and his body is getting a light sheen of sweat to match mine from the effort. Another kiss and he leans up, resuming his grip on my hips as he kneels above me. The speed increases until I can only move as he moves. With a violent shudder, he groans and collapses against me.

I cradle him to me, feathering kisses against his temple and cheek. "We can't sleep here," I giggle.

"Huh?" he murmurs, as rests his weight on me.

"Rolf," I whine. "Matilda didn't say how long she will be gone."

"Hmph," he growls against me and pulls me closer to silence me.

I do what any self-respecting mate does when her alpha wolf won't listen. I bite him hard.

He grunts. "What was that for?"

I realize my mistake as his manhood begins to stiffen again, still inside of me. "I want to do this in the shower," I tried another tactic.

"Oh?" He perks right up, and I have to keep from laughing at how fast his manhood is back to full attention.

With a light cough, I blush and giggle. "Mhm hmm," is all I can get out before he is scooping me up while he stands.

We make it to the stairs before he takes me again. This time, I'm breathless and dizzy from the lovely afterglow.

By the time we reach the shower, I'm mortified that he is hard as a rock again.

"You're insatiable."

"I live to serve. And my service is your pleasure, my flower." He gets a bemused look. "So, I live for your pleasure?" He tilts his head, holding me against the shower wall as the steaming hot water rushes over us. "Yes. I like the sound of that. Let me hear how much you love this." He growls against my neck as he slides back into me.

Why is it Always Midnight?

Beltane 2012

Tuesdays are boring. Nothing eventful happens on a Tuesday.

Matilda has been little help as she has me cutting and grinding herbs at such a vigorous pace.

I have new calluses and my shoulders are sore.

Rolf has spent the last two days running like a fool in the tiny backyard of Matilda's walk-up. In his wolf form, he looks like a small pony trotting about in the yard. When he's not pretending to be a big puppy, he has taken to watching exercise programs on the television.

If I have to listen to one more 'eight more times,' I might murder someone. I've been plotting our escape for two days. I know they told us to stay put, but I had a dream about opening the portal, with Rolf battling someone behind me. I remember the words I chanted, and had another dream, or memory, of when I was four and I mumbled along with my mother.

It's just before dawn, and I'm meditating in the garden, facing the east. My fingers thread into the grass, and my eyes close as my face lifts to the waking sun. The hum of the city coming to life all around me puts me at ease. Even here the beating drums of the Earth's heart calls to me. She is strong and ever present and her connection with me this morning tells me my plan is the right one.

"I don't suppose I can talk you out of it," Matilda says from behind me.

"I don't know what you're talking about," I lied. The grass weaves tight over my fingers and when I try to pull my hands away I'm unable to get up. Fear wells inside me and fire builds in my fingertips.

"You burn my yard and I'll do worse than hold you in place, Lily Finley."

"Viggodatter," I growl at her as I struggle.

"Whatever you want, dear. You're Catarina Finley's grandchild, and I don't have time for semantics. You need to listen to me, or you have no chance of succeeding in your endeavor tonight."

I still as she walks to face me, then sit with her legs crossed in front of me. For a plump old woman, she is pretty flexible. I try to give her my meanest expression to show she can't intimidate me.

She boops my nose, which only makes me angrier. Her eyes flick from me to over my shoulder as I hear Rolf growling as he comes from the door.

"No! Don't step in the —," but I clamp my mouth shut and find that not only can I not move, but I can't talk either.

Rolf springs forward and as soon as his paws hit the

ground, the grass grows up, binding him right in place by all four feet. He growls and snarls, ripping at the grass, only to be bound tighter until he is on all fours in human form, naked, and held in place.

The appreciative look she gives Rolf makes me growl at her.

"Oh, hush up and listen," she laughs and turns her attention back to me. "You're a damn fool, Lily, if you think you can open that time portal without your mother's magic. Your father tricked her into delving into that nonsense and he hunted the rest of us when she fled to New York all those years ago. It took her a century to create that spell, and you think you're going to master it in a minute? I think not."

Rolf has changed back into wolf form. His head tilts as he perks up at what Matilda said. *You said you could not do it. What is she talking about?*

My eyes narrow and cheeks flush red. *I had a dream about the night I met Viggo. I remember some of the words. I was going to try tonight.*

You were going to what?! Were you going to tell me? You said it was too dangerous. No, Lily. You cannot be so reckless.

"You two finished? She is reckless and crazy, just like her mother. Love does that to the Finleys, apparently." She gives me a wry grin.

This makes us both whip our attention back to Matilda, as we didn't think anyone else could hear our mind link.

"I don't need to hear your thoughts to read your faces. Don't be so surprised. My house is old, and the walls have ears. I can hear just about everything, and you two are booking a one-way ticket to oblivion if you don't talk to Morrigan Finley."

"How do you suggest we do that?"

"You watch your tongue, girl. I may be old, but I'll curse

the shit out of you. I don't care if you are the De facto High Priestess. You want my help; you'll mind your manners."

My cheeks flame red, and I turn to look at Rolf who looks furious.

His ears are folded back, and his hackles are up.

I glance down and the grass wraps around his paws like socks holding him in place. I want to ask Matilda what she means about the High Priestess business, but she might be messing with me, so I tell her about my mother instead. "My mom is in 1281. I don't know how to reach her." My voice cracks as I feel like this endeavor is hopeless.

"She's what?" Matilda looks mortified.

"It's a long story. The short of it is, she took me back to 1281 on my birthday… in 2011. For me, that was six years ago."

"By the stars," Matilda frowns and releases us both. The silence grows heavy between the three of us. By the look on Matilda's face, I can guess she thought my mother was hiding in the present. "That explains why she missed the last gathering. Oh, you sweet girl. Come with me." She moves to her feet with more grace than a woman her age and size should have, and leads us to the room Rolf and I could not enter on our own. "Don't touch anything without my permission. This room is heavily warded to keep your father out. It is one of the six libraries of the Ember Tree Coven."

Rolf follows closely behind me and slips his hands around my waist.

This wins a laugh from Matilda. "I suppose that's one way to keep from touching anything. Now, where is it?"

I stand in the center of the room, and I cannot decide where to look first.

Old books are strewn about like someone read part way through and just abandoned the pages where they stood.

There are baubles and trinkets crammed throughout. I swear I see little eyes peeking from the shadows of a shelf. This room feels old, as if it exists before the use of electricity. There are no light outlets, but sconces for gas to fuel a flame, or to hold candles. The mix of stale paper with the spices of herbs permeates the air. The incense burning near the window billows up a tiny plume of smoke to add to the ethereal vibe.

"I know it's here somewhere. Where did she put it?" Matilda moves from one place to another, rummaging through baubles and books like she is a small child rifling through a toy box for the exact toy that she wants.

"What are you looking for, maybe we can help?" I ease from Rolf's grasp but keep hold of his hand as I move closer to the window. Outside looks normal, with cars and people passing by.

"No. You might set off the traps. Morrigan trapped everything. She was convinced Silar would use it against us. Don't blame her, mind you. I would be that paranoid too if I watched my mother deteriorate to keep me young and fertile. Don't know how Silar did it but getting the drop on Catarina Finley was no small feat. And your mother is every bit as powerful as she was. Ah ha!" She comes from around a corner, clutching a velvet pouch. She holds it out to me. "Don't open it. Not until you are ready to commune with her. Now, do you have anything of hers?"

"No," I frown. "My father had one of his warlocks clean out her apartment. Oh, wait! Her journals."

"No, no. Journals won't do. Needs to be something with jewels, or metal."

"Oh. No. The only metal things she has are with her in 1281." We settle down at the kitchen table and I sulk.

Rolf sits next to me, and his hand pets the small of my back in comfort. "Is it possible any of her things were passed down through the pack?"

Matilda's eyes go wide. "What do you mean passed down through the pack?"

"Really, woman? I can smell the wolf on you. You damn well know we are members of the same pack."

"You listen, pup. I don't know anything about whatever you are talking about, and I'm sure as shit not about to guess about things that would only put us all in jeopardy. You two, you need to fix what you broke, and complete your path. So don't you really woman me."

I could tell she is lying. She knows way more than she is saying. For whatever reason, she does not want to explain herself.

"I'll speak to you how I damn well please, witch. I am still the Alpha of the pack, even if you usurpers think you own it."

My eyes turn down to the newspaper in front of me while they are fighting. Their voices fading to the ringing in my ears. The longer I stare at the paper the worse it gets. The images are shifting on the page and the words are popping off the page. One image is clear on the page. The banner displaying my mother's locket, my leather bracers and two axes with the great big words of Vikings in North America. I swoon and Rolf catches me.

"My flower," he whines.

"What did you see?" Matilda barks at me.

"The paper… Locket…" I point to the newspaper on the table and bury myself against Rolf. The room still spins and the air whines around me. I feel a terrible pressure against my mind. It feels like someone has my head in a vise and is trying to punch their way through.

Matilda looks to the ceiling, and she draws a sharp breath before slapping her hand on the table. It felt like a thunderclap rippling through my bones, but the pressure subsided.

"How long have you been having visions?" She stares at me again.

"Not long. That was the first time where I knew what was happening."

"So, you are touched?" Rolf says calmly and does not release me.

"No. My family comes from Cassandra, the oracle in ancient Greece." I sigh when Rolf frowns at me and turn to look at Matilda without leaving the comfort of his embrace.

She is reading over the newspaper, her face lighting up. "We don't have much time. Come, let's get you everything you need. We only have until midnight."

"Why is it always midnight," I grumble as I follow her.

Bedknobs and Broomsticks

"Remember, when you touch the stone, the ward will drop and Silar will know exactly where you are. You won't have long. Ask your mother for what you need, then get away." Matilda is matter of fact about the entire thing, like we weren't about to do something terribly insane in the State Museum.

I nod and I get out of the car.

Rolf follows. He carries the pack on his shoulder and we look like a couple of young college kids getting ready to spend a few hours in the museum before closing.

I glance up as we move to the entrance, and the banner makes a smacking sound from the wind, as if the air itself were showing me what I saw in my vision. Rolf's hand on the small of my back comforts me and I lean into him.

He kisses my forehead before we continue up the steps

and into the lobby.

We walk hand in hand, enjoying the museum. As we step into the room for the Vikings in North America exhibit, it evokes an emotion I never thought I would feel for that horrible little village. I miss it, greatly. Even with all the awful things Luna did to me, I miss Mom and Viggo. I miss Ingrid scolding me for having too many emotions. The items are faded and tattered in places, but the sword at the far end of the room shines. As do the bracers, and other weapons and shields.

Rolf's hand tightened in mine.

I miss them too.

I'm so sorry, Rolf.

Do not do that, my flower.

I ran away. I took you from all your friends and family. I almost got you killed.

Tears roll down my cheeks as the guilt hits me like a Mack truck.

Rolf pulls me into his chest and holds me close. "Lily, you are my everything. I regret nothing and getting to spend my life with you is enough."

I don't care that we might look weird to people in the room with us. I had not expected to react this way to these relics. While Rolf's words are comforting, a yearning for home fills me. I promise myself that once we stop my father, I will use the spell to take us back to that stupid village.

When I ease from Rolf, he brushes my cheeks with his thumbs and kisses my forehead again.

We peruse the cases of items found. Weirdly, most of the items are what I remember as my mother's and Viggo's possessions. It fills me with a sense of dread for the rest of the clan.

We find the locket on display in a glass case that has a lid.

I could not very well just open the case with all these people in here. Rolf and I continue the tour of the exhibit until I find a door labeled maintenance. I take Rolf's hand and pull him into the closet, locking the door behind us.

Provided the museum doesn't check all the closets at closing, we could easily slip back into the exhibit and take the locket. The clock on the wall in the lobby had said four thirteen when we arrived and I knew we would not have terribly long to wait, but standing in the cramped quarters of the closet, pressed against Rolf, made it hard to concentrate.

It doesn't help matters that being pressed to me gives Rolf all sorts of ideas.

"You're a pervert," I giggle as the latest image of what he would like to do to me in this closet flashes in my mind.

"What does the word pervert mean?"

I open my mouth to respond and close it. Didn't they have the word pervert in 1281? That seems perverted, and I giggle at the joke in my head. "It's a person who thinks of things that are really…naughty for the situation. Like what you want to do with me against the wall."

"You're my mate, and I want you against the wall. What is perverted about that?"

"We're hiding in a broom closet, about to commit a crime in a museum, and you want to have sex with me against the wall next to all the…potions for cleaning."

"Yes."

I palm my face and giggle again. "I'm not having sex with you in this closet. We'll get caught."

"Not if you keep quiet." He wriggles his brows at me.

"Now you're a dirty pervert."

"Would it not give a convincing lie if we are discovered?" He smirks.

"And we still get kicked out for being here."

"I will render him unconscious, and we can lock him in this closet while we commit the crime."

"Rolf," I whine.

He leans down and kisses my mate mark, nuzzling me.

I blush and bite his neck.

"Keep that up, my flower, and I won't care if you scream to Odin himself as I take you." His kisses pepper up my neck until we are lip locked as he presses me against the wall.

I can't help myself as we make out, I do want more.

His touch ignites desire in me without effort. His fingers strum along my skin like a rock star with his guitar.

I moan into the kiss.

He nibbles on my earlobe, "You better keep quiet, my flower. Someone might hear." I bite his shoulder in response and he laughs against me. "Fair enough, my wildflower, I will not enjoy you."

He has the gall to ease back and lean against the closet door, leaving me breathless and excited against the wall. Dressed like he is ready to walk into a boardroom; he looks so smug watching me struggle to focus.

Oh, two can play this game. I level my gaze on him and give him a mischievous grin as I slide my hand down and under the hem of my shorts.

"What are you doing?" his gaze fixes on me with a predatory desire. He moves to come closer and I bring my foot up, planting it squarely in his center to keep him against the door, which elicits a growl from him.

"Mate," he warns.

"You don't get to touch me for teasing me like that. You'll just have to watch."

He whines, trying to move forward again and I push him back with my foot again, holding him in place. I know well enough he could easily move me, but he is choosing not to.

He's into this based on the surge of excitement rolling off of him. I grin at him and rock my hips with my fingers as I work myself over.

Then I stop, cold turkey. I'm aroused and aching now, but I need to focus, and he needs to behave. "Rolf, we need to concentrate. We have to get to the park by midnight." I release him from my hold. This is my second mistake. The first was teasing him at all.

"I know what I'm focusing on," then he is to me like a magnet to metal. His hungry kisses suck the air right out of me as his hands work to free me of my shorts.

I want it too, so I frantically unfasten his pants. It's a lot of grunting, struggling, kissing, and then his hands are cupping my ass, slamming me against the wall as he thrusts up into me.

His lips devoured mine to silence any moaning escaping from them. It's sweaty and dirty as he pounds into me, the unbridled need to bring me pleasure mixing with my desire to give him everything.

I cling to him, and his hand comes over my mouth to muffle my climax.

His face buries into the crook of my neck as he shudders and releases. Another few quick thrusts and then we're breathing hard, a tangled mess of limbs against the wall.

I expect a security guard to find us at any minute, but they never come. I finally look at the watch on my wrist, and it says seven twenty-eight. Our perverted shenanigans in this broom closet killed more than enough time.

With wobbly legs, I retrieve my clothing Rolf relieved me of. He looks so smug at me when we dance around for me to open the door. I crack it open and peek my head out. "Come on. It's clear."

The two of us race back to the exhibit. I fish the velvet

pouch out of my pocket, and remove the stone, placing it in my right hand. Then I wave my left hand.

"Fac me introire," I whisper, and the lock on the case pops, allowing the lid to open with a hiss. As soon as my fingers curl around the locket, my eyes roll until only the whites are showing and I drop to my knees, my hands falling lax at my sides, one holding the locket, the other the stone.

I'm no longer in the museum in 2012, but now in my mother's bedroom in the village.

It's dark which tells me it's night. "Mom," I called and she sits upright. When she sees nothing, she starts to settle back.

"Mom!" I shout again.

"Lily?" Morrigan calls in return and I watch her sit up fully.

"Mom. It's me. Hold the locket. Hurry!"

My mother springs out of the bed and rushes toward me. I realize I must be looking through the locket when I see her hand growing massively until I hear her gasp and we are standing face to face in nothingness.

"Lily, how did you do this? Where are you? Where is Rolf?"

"I don't have time for all that. I need your help. I need you to give me the spell to open the time portal."

"No, Lily. It's too dangerous. Your father could—," she shakes her head.

"I'm going to stop him. I read your journals. I went back to Grandma's cottage. Please, Mom. He's hunting us and the only way to stop him is to finish what you started when I was four."

LXIV

One-Way Ticket

Rolf watches Lily collapse to her knees, and he steps forward to help her when he sees her eyes roll and she stares ahead like she is in a trance. No matter how fierce a warrior Rolf is, he is disconcerted by the vision of Lily before him. He doesn't get to linger in his anxiety, as he can hear the telltale whistle of incoming witches. "We need to go, Lily."

There's no answer, nor any movement from his mate.

"Lily," he hisses at her again.

She still does not respond.

"They're in here," he can hear a man's voice call. "Kill the wolf, bind the girl."

Rolf had never been fond of his father's sword. He has always preferred the smaller, shorter weapons of axes. He has to rip the bracers off the wall to get to his axes. He slides the bracers onto his forearms, something telling him they will be useful. He tugs them tight with his teeth, then rips the axes off the wall. Alarms start blaring as he turns to face his attackers.

The whistling pop happens repeatedly. With a confident and eager stride, he puts himself between Lily and the would-be kidnappers. "I will give you one chance to flee with your lives." Rolf's voice rings across the room with the command of an Alpha. He stands tall and his shoulders square as he brandishes both axes out to the sides.

The witches and warlocks pause. A few even look at each other and backpedal a few steps. "You know we cannot do that. She belongs to the Howling Wind Coven, and our High Priest demands her presence."

Rolf throws his axe into the man, pleasantly surprised at the sharpness of the blade.

Chaos erupts like flames of a wildfire.

Spells start flying through the air and Rolf moves with supernatural speed into the fray of enemies. He had no hope of surviving this, but he would buy Lily as much time as he could. He finds he can't shift, but the bracers are blocking the spells. A shimmer of a shield bubbles on him when one collides. His eyes light up.

The warlock before him panics at the revelation.

He takes a spell straight to his back, which slows his movement, allowing them to close in on him.

Another spell sends him to his knees, and he drops the axe.

Another spell hits him and he struggles to get the bracers off.

"Don't let him shift!"

His gaze turns to see Lily still kneeling where he left her. His body twitches with the effort to keep moving in human form and a bracer hits the floor. He growls as his body starts to shift, and the other bracer's tether snaps.

"Shit! Hit him again!"

The greenish tint of the spell comes barreling toward him.

He shifts into wolf form, breaking the slowing spells. He leaps at the nearest warlock, tearing his arm clean off as he moves with the animalistic grace of a well-trained predator. He bowls into the enemies closing in and puts himself between him and Lily again.

There are too many of them for him to fight and protect. He broadens his stance, moving closer to his mate and baring his teeth. He would take as many of them with him as he could, but if she does not wake soon, they are going to lose.

LILY! WE NEED TO GO NOW!

"Repeat it back," Morrigan says again to Lily. Then she looks above Lily as Rolf's voice roars into the nothingness of the in-between. "Why can I hear Rolf?"

"We are soul bound," I say and then parrot the spell back for the third time.

"Soul bound? Lily, what have you done? Where are you?"

"I don't have time, Mom. I love you. I won't let you down."

"Don't forget. You need an offering, and if you are not clear, you will get lost in the ether. Time is not to be trifled with, Lily. If you fail, the consequences are great."

"I know Mom! I love you. I need to go."

I love you, my sweet flower. Do not let them take you alive.

I blink my eyes open and spring to my feet, almost colliding into Rolf's wolf. There is no way we are going to fight them off. The hex to slow Rolf down is taking hold. I grapple his coat between his shoulders with one hand as I whirl my other hand through the air. There is an explosion of flame that blasts out in every direction, like a shock wave of fire.

The alarms already blaring are now joined with the fire alarm as water erupts from the sprinklers, allowing my second circle of motion to create a hurricane of water with us in the eye.

"She isn't even using words! She can control the elements! Get out of here. She'll kill us all!"

Please Mother Earth, take us to where we need to be.

The third ring of magic I cast rips open the very fabrics of our world, the ethereal darkness of the in-between blossoming until the lush greenery of the clearing Rolf and I appeared in months ago becomes visible, like a vision of a painting. Spells are eaten by the vortex of water and flames. Smoke fills the room.

Go, Lily. I'm right behind you.

You are hurt, you first.

Woman!

Together then.

I tug at his fur, and he lumbers into the portal with me.

As soon as we clear the threshold, we are ripped forward. I cling to his fur. It is only seconds long, but it is agonizing, as they weight of the warlocks trying to rip us back through the portal to them grows stronger.

"Follow her, you idiots!" A witch screams as I collide with the ground.

With a sharp horizontal motion, I slam the portal shut to the echoing screams of people now trapped in the in-between. I'm covered in sweat and shaking. The amount of magic I used to save Rolf is draining.

His whine is enough to get me to let go of him and pull myself to my knees. I muster my strength as I place my hand on his furred body splayed out, "Redi ad te quod pertinet." I chant until he tackles me and showers me with licks and nuzzles.

"Get off me!" I giggle.

He does ease back onto his hind legs, then shifts. He sits before me, cross-legged and naked, raging hard.

"Of course, you would be hard from battle," I mutter and roll my eyes. "I need you to listen, Rolf. I only have the locket in offering. We will only be able to perform the spell once. Tell me now and I will take us home. No more witches and warlocks. No more curses. Just the village with our dumb Luna, and all the fat babies you can stand."

"No, Lily. We have come this far on the journey. We must see it through. To go home now is to surrender. It would bring shame to our families and deny us Valhalla."

I don't argue with him as his entire being is radiating the same emotions he just spoke. A perk of our soul bond is that we cannot lie to each other. "Alright. Then I need you to keep them off of me while I open the portal."

"Oh, is that all? Should be child's play," he gives me a lopsided grin, then pulls me into a heated kiss. "For luck, as you say." He stands and stalks a few feet away from me.

I glance at my watch, and it is a quarter to twelve. I can already feel the power surge waning from the height of Beltane. I kneel with my offering placed before me and I pocket the summoning stone. I place my hands flat on the ground and close my eyes and begin to chant the spell my mother just taught me.

The wind howls in anger.

The earth shudders beneath me.

The skies erupt into a deluge of rain.

In my heart, burns the date of Beltane 1821. I lose track of all sounds around me as I focus on the spell.

The only sign there is a battle is the adrenalin rush coming from Rolf as he rips through unsuspecting warlocks.

"Don't harm her," My father roars from far away.

I open my eyes to see sunshine blanketing over Central Park. "Time to go!" I scream at Rolf.

He plows into me as we are sent barreling through yet another portal.

My arms go around him as black spots start to fill my vision.

We land in the lush grass of the park, but it's the middle of the day and nothing looks like what it did in 2012. Before I pass out, I snap the portal closed.

Rolf's arms wrap around me, and I lean heavily on him.

"Well, this is most definitely not a sight I would expect to see," another man's voice comes from behind me that is strangely familiar.

LXV

I Am Who I Am

The chime of the wall clock irritating me is the first conscious thought I have. I open my eyes and get the view of the underside of a canopy bed. The vibrant and ornate drapes are neatly tied to the posts. The warmth of the fireplace fills the room, and a golden-red hue paints the intricate furniture in a soft light. The soft crackle tells me there is a fire nearby.

I sit upright, gasping and looking around for Rolf.

"Rolf," I call and struggle under the weight of the blankets half covering me.

I land with a grunt on the floor as I win the battle to free myself from the covers.

"Rolf," I call again with panic in my voice. I push off the floor and get to my feet, then sway. My body has a heavy sensation, like I have been swimming upstream for hours. The closer I move to the door, the heavier the sensation feels.

"Rolf," I whimper as I lean heavily against the door frame, sweat beading on my forehead from the effort of staggering across the room.

The clap of a book being shut behind me makes me turn my back to the door and search for the source. As he rises out of the chair, panic swells.

My eyes widen and the man who steps forward, standing before me is Nick. My Nick, who was a dog when I was a child, and this man when Sarah died. I take him in fully and I fling myself with great effort to him. "Oh Nick!" I begin to sob, because if Nick is here, that means we died, and this is the afterlife.

"Oh, honestly, Nicodemus. I leave you alone with the woman and you are already seducing her. How you Windravens became the guardians is beyond me." The sharp tongue of the woman entering the room makes me step back quickly.

I frown as I realize that I can move freely, but when I move closer to the door, a weight presses me into stillness.

"Madame, I did nothing of the sort. I am offended you think as such. She flung herself upon me, calling me Nick." His gaze narrows at me and my frown deepens. If he is not Nick, he sure looks like the ghost I saw that night. He puts space between us, and the guilt on his face when my lip quivers offers me little comfort.

"Come along, dear, let's get you back into the bed," the woman gives him a stern look and rests her hands on my shoulders.

I pull my gaze from the man not accepting he is Nick to get a good look at the woman. This is definitely not Sarah, and this woman is dressed in an outfit right out of the movies. Her skirts are full and the corset is firm, with long sleeves and a high collar. Her hair is neatly pinned on top of her head, dripping down in perfect ringlets.

"No!" I jerk myself from her grasp and try to get around her to the door. The pressure weighs heavily on me again and try as I might, I cannot force my body to move faster.

"Rolf!" I scream.

"Would you stop screaming," the man growls. "He cannot hear you. When he would not come along quietly, we rendered him unconscious. He is sleeping in the other room. By the stars, girl, why was he naked, and you barely dressed?"

I whirl around and his eyes go wide as the very air in the room crackles from the ozone, and the flames in the fireplace roar with my emotions. I can't think straight, as I can't feel Rolf at all.

They have somehow severed our connection.

"Give me my mate," my voice sounds foreign to me with how sinister it is. I should have been paying attention because the next thing I know, I'm collapsing to the ground. As the blackness vignettes my vision, I see the woman's skirts as she squats down next to me.

"Nico, she commanded air and fire. She is far more powerful than we thought," is the last thing I hear before I pass out.

When I come to again, I'm more cautious this time. I lie in the soft bed with my eyes closed and try to keep my breathing steady, like I'm still asleep.

"Carolyn, she will not harm us."

"You can't know that Nico."

"I can and do. There is something about her. She looks exactly like the new high priestess of Ember Tree. Last I checked, Ember Tree was still in the light. When they appeared on Whitestead's land, there was only fear. They were being pursued, Carolyn. You cannot tell me you aren't the least bit curious. She obviously has traveled through time. Look at the garments we burned."

"Curiosity killed the cat," the woman sniped at him.

"Hah. We should bring the boy in here with her, so they both calm down. The ward appears to be agitating them."

"Do you have a death wish, Windraven? She was about to burn down your entire estate with her little episode. And you want to bring that animal in here to strengthen her?"

"Now, you are being rude, Carolyn. He is a man as much as an animal. You would do well to remember that when speaking to a werewolf."

"Werewolf? Should we involve Ivarsen?"

"Ivarsen and his mate are dealing with something for me in Silver City. There appears to be a plague curiously targeting miners out there."

She sighs heavily. "You are a damn fool if you put them together or let those wards down. It's too dangerous. You should wait for your brother to get here. Silar always was the smarter of you two."

I'm not surprised by the revelation that the man in the room is my uncle. My mother had poured hundreds of years of knowledge into me in the short thirty minutes we had together. She explained everything in so much detail that I almost gave up on the entire endeavor. My grandmother has just been named High Priestess of the Ember Tree coven. She will meet a man with fire in his eyes and ten years from now my mother will be born. My father will meet my mother twenty-five years from now. It means the man standing in this room has months to live if I don't do something.

I sit up, which causes them both to start, but I hold my hands up. "My name is Lily Viggodatter. The man in the other room is Rolf Ivarsen, and he is my mate. You are in grave danger, Nicodemus. I have been sent here to protect you from death and to stop your brother from falling down the dark path he has set himself upon to bring you back." I watch the pair of them, knowing they will not believe me.

No one believes Cassandra. It is the curse of the Gods for the gift of sight. Though none of this is sight, it is still a prophecy to them.

Carolyn rolls her eyes and throws her hands in the air.

Nicodemus crosses his arms and frowns.

"She is a liar, Nicodemus."

"I am not!"

"Girl, I know very well you cannot be who you say you are. I know Lily Viggodatter and you are not her!"

"Carolyn, leave us." Nicodemus commands.

Carolyn turns and looks at him wide-eyed, then throws her hands in the air. "Fine! When she murders us all, I will taunt you for all eternity."

"Go talk with the boy."

I see the look between them, and he means for her to interrogate Rolf to see if our stories match. Once she is gone, he moves to the wardrobe on the other side of the room. "This is my mother's room when she comes to visit. You and she are nowhere near the same size. I have never met a woman as shapely and tall as you. But I think," he glances over his shoulder at me, "this one will do."

He retrieves a beautiful-looking dress made of dark green satin. He follows this with a boned corset, bloomers, and a petticoat. Laying the items on the bed while keeping an eye on me, "First, let's get you appropriate for male company other than your mate. Then we can talk about your claims."

"You have to believe me, Nick. I swear. I don't know how it happens, but… but… my father kills you. And it happens this year."

The man stops and frowns, looking at me. "Why do you

keep calling me Nick? I do not know you, madame. And my brother has no children."

I wipe the tears from my cheeks and look down at my hands, defeat washing over me. "You were my… familiar. When I was little. You took a killing spell away from my friend Sarah when I accidentally cast it."

"I can assure you, Lily, I am not a familiar. I imagine traveling through the portal you created has blended your memories somehow. People who tempt fate by trespassing through time only find madness. A mad witch is dangerous, and I am sworn to protect magic from that madness."

His voice is gentle, but I can hear the edge of threat in it. "I'm sorry. I must be mistaken then," I mumble, then get out of the bed. I notice his body tense, and it makes the tears come faster, forcing me to wipe my face on my sleeve.

His shoulders slack, "Goodness, do not cry. We will sort this all out." His eyes are transfixed on me.

I hiccup and try to rein in my emotions. Without Rolf here, I feel empty and broken. Whatever is keeping me from feeling our bond is terrifying me.

He then eases closer cautiously and pulls me into an awkward hug.

It does nothing to help me with the void of missing the other half of my soul, but the small sign of comfort is enough to get me to stop crying.

The surge of jealous rage that fills the room makes me gasp in fear. "Get your hands off my mate before I remove them for you," Rolf snarls from the doorway.

LXVI

Love Me Like You Do

"Well, I know for certain he is at least related to the Ivarsens, none of them like you." Carolyn follows Rolf into the room as he stalks toward me and Nicodemus.

Rolf means to rip off Nick's arms.

So I turn to face Rolf, putting me between the two men.

His gaze shifts from Nick to me and he is blazing in jealous anger. Even without the connection between us, I could tell he believes Nick has done something nefarious with me. His chest rises and falls as he breathes in deep.

I frown at him. Did he think I would be so loose with my love? It's not like Rolf to show jealousy.

"Mine," I say to him in his native tongue, touching his heart.

He snorts and growls at me. His emotions and distrust cut me to the core.

I did not ever think there would be a moment where Rolf does not believe me. I pull my hand back and quickly turn from him, snatching up the dress. I take it behind the screen in the corner of the room, hiding from all of them as I try to remain silent in crying.

Rolf's emotions are a mix of guilt and rage still, but I am in no state to soothe him. He obviously believes that I would even look at another man how I look at him.

I pull the petticoat on first and tie it into place. The overdress is harder to deal with, but after some wriggling and squirming I get it settled as well. There has been silence in the room the entire time I'm dressing. It's like the three of them have frozen in time.

When I appear from behind the screen, I hesitate, hugging myself.

Rolf's expression still shows his anger, but when I don't come to him, there's guilt in his eyes.

"Now that you are decent, let us talk like civilized people and sort this out." Nick's voice cuts across the tension.

Carolyn snorts and shakes her head. "I am going to contact the firebrand. She will help with this." Brushing by Rolf she leaves the room.

Nick moves to the chair he was in when I woke up and takes a seat. He motions for Rolf to take the other, who stalks toward it and sits abruptly.

Nick and Rolf watch each other with narrowed gazes, as if they are sizing up for a rumble.

"He is my uncle," I say to Rolf in his language. "The one my father kills when he comes through the portal."

Rolf's head snaps up and looks at me. "You closed the portal. This man is not your uncle. Lily, do not lie to me."

I lift my chin then, fury welling up before I can tamp it down. "You know what, Rolf Ivarsen? Fuck you!" I switch back to English, the air changes, and fire grows again. "How dare you accuse me of being unfaithful! His name is Nicodemus Windraven. He is who we are here to save, you jackass. So, if you stop thinking with your fucking Alpha male ego for two fucking seconds, you might see that you're fucking hurting your fucking mate for no fucking reason!"

The mirror in the corner shatters as my voice pitches and I stomp my foot, causing the entire room to shiver. "You said you were mine! I said I was yours! You don't get to treat me like this. If you think so little of me, we'll find another offering and I will send you home to your fucking Luna and her sister!"

Nick's eyes widened.

Carolyn comes running back into the room.

I want to punch Rolf, kick Nick, and run away.

Rolf's to his feet and stalks toward me, anger still blazing in his eyes.

"You do not get to flaunt yourself to other males. No one can touch you, Lily. You're mine." He's still in his native tongue, and he takes hold of my forearm as if he means to pull me off my feet.

"Nuh-uh. Nope. I don't think so!" I slap him. "You don't own me, Rolf. We are equals and I am your mate, not your slave. I will do as I damn well please."

"You would lie with him?"

I slap him again. This is only making him angrier. "That is not what I said you filthy pig of a wolf. What I said was he is my uncle. My mother told me I had to save him to stop my father from becoming evil. So, you either get over whatever has you suddenly unsure of my love, or I am going to ask him to help me send you home." My voice lowers and fills with sadness. "Because our oaths mean so little to you." My chest rises and falls as I stare at Rolf. My entire world hangs in the balance with whatever he says next. How could he think these things about me? What have they done to my Rolf?

He whines like I have kicked him.

The hurricane of emotions between us is making it hard to hold my composure. I don't wipe away the tears rolling down my cheeks again.

He steps closer and I brace myself for him to say goodbye. He looks upset and distrusting, but afraid as well.

I haven't seen fear in his eyes like this before.

His eyes search mine as he gently wraps his arm around my waist, pulling me even closer. Then he leans his forehead against mine. "I am sorry, my flower. I love you more than life itself, Lily. When I saw you in his arms, I lost my mind because I could no longer feel you. I thought you severed our bond." His words are hushed as he explains himself to me. "I would die without you by my side. Please do not banish me to that hell."

My brow furrows, as I know exactly how he feels. When I woke, I could not feel him either and was terrified he had been killed. I ease back, frowning as I turn to Nick. "How did you sever our bond?"

"Not severed, masked. There is a difference."

"Okay," I roll my eyes. "How did you mask our bond?" I ask, dripping with irritation.

"Let's just say a certain old witch taught me a few tricks. It comes in handy when bonds supply power to magic. Now, if you young lovers are done with your quarrel, we can understand why you came to my city in the state you did."

I spend the next few hours regaling Nicodemus with our harrowing tale, starting all the way back to when I met Viggo.

Nick listens patiently, his face a stoic frown the entire time. His curiosity is piqued when I mention my mother's journals and grandmother's cottage. He asks me question after question about the cottage.

I give Rolf a quick glance, and I purposely leave out certain details about the cottage. I feel like the wards have always been in place and neither Windraven could get by them easily.

We finally leave the room for supper, and I'm fascinated by his estate. It's ornate and intricate, as if it has a life of its own while being an inanimate object.

Rolf doesn't stop touching me the entire time. He either holds my hand or rests it on my waist.

Nick shows us the entire estate. It's a massive square building with a courtyard as big as a football field in the center. There are trees and even a small pond contained within. He introduces us to the staff and explains that we are distant relatives that had been set upon on our journey here. That we are to be treated accordingly. He then asks us, for our own safety, not to leave the confines of his home until he can assure it.

We are both aware of the veiled way he tells us we are being kept here on purpose.

Dinner goes on uneventfully, and Rolf continues his possessive touching throughout the meal. His hand squeezes my knee occasionally to remind me I am his. The conversation is light and mostly about what Nick does in the area. How the ley lines converge near here, on the Whitestead estate, and how he and his brother have been appointed guardians of the area.

After dinner, Nick shows us back to the room I woke in, and he smiles gently at me. "Do not worry, young Lily. We will take care of everything, and I assure you it will be fine."

It's strange the way he phrases that.

Rolf doesn't seem to act oddly, so we retire into the room.

When we nestle into the bed, I feel content and safe in

Rolf's arms, like the first night we slept in Grandma Finley's cottage. Rolf's body stays tense and the slightest sound has him stirring.

I try to soothe him but find myself unable to stay awake and soon enough, I drift fully to sleep.

LXVII

True Love's Bite

September 1821

Nicodemus sits at his desk, looking out the window toward his courtyard. He watches the girl run and chase the massive white wolf around. Her musical laughter is a distraction. Then the squealing laughter when the wolf catches her is even more of a distraction. One thing is clear between the two, they are very much in love. The beast of a man cannot keep his hands off her, and any time Nicodemus tries to get her alone to further probe her mind, the man is there, growling at him. From what he has gleaned, she is telling the truth of her story. She believes she is Lily Viggodatter and was sent here to protect him. He also discovered she believes she is the High Priestess of Ember Tree.

Her magic is off the charts and is in all four elements. The rarity of such a witch has left most of his community believing it is only in prophecy. He has retrieved every scroll, parchment, and book recording, and anything of witches who control all the elements.

Even his mother has questioned what he is doing, and why the pair of them are being kept here. She wants to ward the girl and send her to the asylum and be rid of the boy. Nicodemus has placated her with assuring the girl is no threat under his care, and this way they can make sure no other witches come barreling into the Whitestead estate where the ley lines converge.

The wolf shifts into his human form and then scoops Lily right up onto his shoulder like she weighs nothing. They disappear into the crop of trees toward the center of the courtyard.

Nicodemus chuckles and turns his attention back to his desk. Missives and spells stacked in front of him make him sigh when Carolyn walks in. "I finally have word from the firebrand. She kept me waiting all this time."

"She must like you. I have heard of people being trapped on her land for years. I do not see Catarina Finley with you, though." He arches a brow and leans to look around her.

"You are funny, Nico. She said she is not at your beck and call, Windraven. That if you want her help, you come to ask her yourself. She then gave me this," Carolyn steps forward and hands him a letter with a wax dripped seal of the burning tree.

Nicodemus raises a brow and gently pops the seal. He half expects a curse to sling itself from the page and is disappointed when nothing happens. He reads aloud, "Heed the flower's warning. Height of light's waning. All will be as it should be." He then throws the parchment onto his desk.

"Why? Why do seers do this? Why can they not just answer my questions when I ask them? All I needed was for her to come and confirm that this girl, who claims to be her grandchild, is related to her. But no. I get that," he points at the paper.

Carolyn snorts at Nicodemus's rant and crosses her arms. "Are you that dense, Nico? She answered your question. Or are you planning on keeping that pretty little flower in your garden forever?"

"What, by the stars, are you talking about?"

Carolyn sighs and points to the window behind Nicodemus. "Nico, her name is literally Lily. How much more of a flower do you need?"

Nicodemus gives Carolyn the dirtiest of looks. "It is never that plain with a seer."

"Oh, this one is."

"Anytime you think it is that simple. There is always a catch."

"Well, that is all you are getting. She refused to leave her home and told me if you summoned her again on this matter, she would involve your mother."

"Threatening to involve the High Priestess? She must be serious on the matter."

"Well, then I suppose we should decipher the rest."

******

"Rolf," I giggle as he carries me toward the crop of trees that we spend every evening under.

"Quiet you, I caught you fair and square," he pats my butt to emphasize his command.

I don't have to wait long as he sets me to my feet, then pulls me into a heated kiss. After we got past our first few days of hard feelings and jealousy, these months have been blissful with him.

Nicodemus brought in a marksman to teach Rolf about modern firearms. He also insisted we spend time together making sure my magic was not tampered with during time travel. The afternoons are spent studying old texts, and then I pass the evenings with Rolf in the courtyard before dinner. We laugh and talk, but the conversation is never anything more than trivial matters.

Tonight, Rolf has no intention of talking and has become an expert at hoisting my skirts to gain access to what he wants. With an easy motion, he is pulling me down to the blanket laid perfectly on the ground he claims me for his own. His eyes never leave mine as he silently wills me to give myself over to him. After he satisfies his lust, he relaxes down on me, not removing himself from his nestled position.

It's distracting when he does this. All I can think about is how quickly he is ready to go again, and how sensitive everything is. The slightest movement and I'm sent into a tizzy of sensations.

His warm, hot breath against my neck where he nips me as he chuckles sends shivers down my spine.

I frown, in spite of how much I'm enjoying our romp, his emotions don't match his actions. There is anger and frustration, mixed with a healthy dose of suspicion. Without opening my eyes, I pout. "Am I no longer satisfying you?"

"Hmm, no, my flower, you are perfect and sate my every need." His lips press to mine in a tender fashion.

"Then why are you angry?"

"I have not heard you talk about your father once in some time," his voice is low and hesitant.

"Nick is taking care of it."

"What is he doing to take care of it?"

"He is monitoring for any surge in power, and any new warlocks in the area."

"Do you truly believe that is enough, my flower?"

"He is the guardian of the area, Rolf. It's like… Alpha with magic."

"No. That's the High Priest's role. Guardians are simply powerful enough to manage most magic."

I crack an eye open then and look at him with a suspicious gaze.

"I listened to your lessons," he grins at me.

"Nick has written letters to all the covens, and he is helping me make sure my magic is not tainted or blocked again. Nick has been amazing at showing me things. He's so patient, and fun to learn from."

It's then Rolf bites me. Not nip me, not playfully tug at my skin, but bites me, hard, right where he marked me as his mate.

I cry out in pain, and struggle against him, but am not getting far as he is buried deep within me and has me pinned under him.

He releases my throat and licks it gently to seal the wounds he just created.

I look up at him in a mix of rage and fear as I bring my hand to my neck. Slowly, the rose-colored fog lifts from my mind as I blink at my mate. The panic and urgency I felt when we arrived starts to fill me again as I realize I have been passive for months now on this matter. "I'll kill him," I growl as I try to get up. Then I gasp as Rolf swells inside of me and begins to pump again.

"I love it when you talk about battle." His hands slide down to part my hips as he thrusts.

My body tenses, unable to decide on the action I really want to take. I want to fly out of this courtyard and burn this place to the ground for what Nick has done. I also feel my own lusty desire raging at Rolf being aroused by my temper. He did this on purpose.

"By the Gods," he moans against me, "I did."

The next few minutes are a heated battle of me wanting to go murder Nick and staying to enjoy Rolf's rough claim. When he erupts in me again, I'm sent over the edge as well.

Left panting and a filthy mess, Rolf rolls off of me and shifts back into wolf form.

I stagger to my feet, and I realize what Rolf was doing. "Clever brute," I grumble at the white wolf.

His tail wags and I shake my head. "I'm still going to turn him into a toad."

His tail wags harder. "I cannot believe I let him do that to me. Oh, he's going to pay!"

Rolf happily trots with me as I storm into Nicodemus's office.

"You filthy warlock!" I cast a binding spell on his chair before he could move. The ornate woodwork comes to life, and wraps around him, holding him in place. "You have been making me…" as I struggle for the word, "docile!"

"Safe," he barks back at me. "I have been —,"

I whip my hand into the air, closing my fingers to silence him, just like my mother had done to me all those years ago. "No. No excuses. You have been keeping me from doing what I was sent here to do. And keeping us from going home. For what? Your precious coven? Or stupid rules? You are going to die if you don't listen to me. Silar Windraven will get here and when he does, he intends for me to summon a demon. Why would he do this, you ask? Well, Nick," I stomp forward to get right in his face. "Because you are murdered by dark magic before he gets here on the Winter Solstice. You have wasted months we could have been preparing to prevent this."

His eyes are wide in understanding, as if everything I just said clicked in place. He goes as still as the dead in the chair, not struggling against my binding or my silence spell.

I release his mouth and move back to stand next to Rolf, who is still in wolf form.

"Until today, I did not believe you were of Catarina Finley's line. I apologize, Lily Viggodatter, for doubting you. Please, release me, and we can discuss this properly."

LXVIII

Come With Me Now

Winter Solstice 1821

True to his word, Nicodemus, Rolf, and I sat down and began to prepare for my father's arrival. We all agreed to not include the Silar from present as it could cause untold problems with the very fabrics of time.

I could see the stress it puts on Nicodemus to have to lie to his brother, but it was his choice to make, and I commend him for it.

The plan is simple.

Nick and his other guardians, along with Rolf and me, will be at the entry point and when they begin to push through, we will push them back and hold them in the in-between to prevent them from opening another portal.

The problem with people like Nicodemus is they think they always know best. This hubris allows for silly mistakes.

Like having a secret real plan with Carolyn when a werewolf is near enough to hear what is going on.

Two nights before the Winter Solstice, Rolf comes storming into our room and reveals their intention to keep us prisoner until it is all said and done. He wants to confront Nicodemus and Carolyn. Thankfully,

I'm not as angry as he is about being betrayed. I could see their side of the argument. They don't trust us, and if we are on my father's side, having us there would put them at a disadvantage. So, I convince Rolf to play along as if we don't know. Then we make our own plan to stop my father, one that does not involve his brother at all.

The morning of Winter Solstice comes, and it's a beautiful snowy day in New York. The sun creeps over the horizon, casting an iridescent sparkling over the snow. Even with Rolf having had his way with me until I passed out, I'm roused with the sudden sense of dread.

The power draining the ley lines beats angrily in my chest. I could feel the very earth trembling in fear. I slip out of the bed, letting Rolf have a few more minutes of rest while I dress for the day. I wish I could leave him here, trapped in this room where he would not potentially be murdered in front of me. Fear that my magic will not be strong enough to bind my father without him present causes me to not entertain that betrayal further. As I'm finishing getting dressed, the second pull on the ley lines nearly knocks me to my knees. "Rolf, it's time," I kiss his forehead.

He eases from the bed with a grunt and does not bother with clothes. After he rubs his hand over his face, he pulls me to him and kisses me with such passion it wins a content sigh from me. After which, he shifts into wolf form.

We move to the center of the room, and I run my fingers through his fur one last time. Then I draw the power to create the transportation spell. Focusing on the field we arrived in and calling upon the elements to guide me. It swirls into our vision, and then we're both being pulled through with a loud hiss.

The field is in absolute chaos. Witches and warlocks litter the ground as they throw hexes and curses back and forth. The snow is falling heavily, and the wind is howling in rage, causing near white-out conditions.

The portal is already closed.

Rolf doesn't hesitate. He moves forward ripping into witches and warlocks without caring whose side they are on.

That wasn't our agreement and I scream for him to stick to the plan. Which, of course, gives away that I'm on the battlefield.

Nicodemus roars for me to flee.

My father shouts for me to be taken alive.

Rolf snarls and rips the arm off another warlock before he returns to me and nudges me to run.

My legs feel like Jell-O. Each step is labored, and the skirts are getting heavier from the wet snow on the ground. Even with stockings and leather boots, I feel the bitter sting against my skin. That doesn't frighten me as much as I'm having a hard time connecting with Rolf. It's like his bloodlust is overpowering our bond and making him fight like a berserker.

"How did they get here? You said they were warded, Windraven!" Carolyn shouts.

I move as quickly as I can to make sure my father is close enough to follow me. It's hard going as I'm forced into combat with the warlocks and witches near us.

Both sides are attacking me.

My father's in the effort to detain me, and Nicodemus's as they believe I'm a liar and a traitor.

Rolf takes at least two direct hits in curses I'm forced to dispel.

Sweat beads on my forehead from all the effort and abuse of magic.

Light and dark, it's taking its toll on all of us.

Vines rip up out the ground and pound at anyone within their radius.

Fireballs are sent sizzling toward people's heads while the very snow turns to daggers paper cutting against my cheeks. What stops me in my tracks is the massive stones that line this field are now rumbling and moving. They shudder from their beds of soil and soaring across the field to land on a group of warlocks with a sickening thud.

The tiny witch near where they started is swooning from her efforts.

Which gives the warlock opposing her enough to raise up the wall of snow and turn it into large shards of ice that he sends with expert precision to pierce through her.

The ground is stained with the bloodbath. The pristine snow turned crimson and brown from the battle. The sun creeps ever higher into the sky, unaffected by the squabble below it.

I'm so lost in the battle that I have lost track of all the men important to me. I'm snapped from my nightmarish revelry as a hand clamps firm on my forearm and I hear a snarl.

The source is Rolf staring at me. Violence and anger pulsing from him like a storm cloud. His arm poised to rip my arm right from its socket.

"Rolf," I scream.

He does not move for several seconds and I can't feel him. He staggers back and frowns at me, releasing me. "We need to leave this place," he whines. He jerks, as if he has been hit by another curse.

My hand goes to his chest, dispelling the magic.

There is too much, too close to us. We are not going to survive if I don't do something.

I close my eyes, my hand still resting on Rolf's chest, and I summon the Earth to me. Coupled with air and fire I send an impact wave out from the two of us. A loud thunderclap booms and flames shoot out in a circle as the Earth ripples angrily. Anyone within a ten-foot radius of us is sent bowling and now on fire. There's more shrieking and the wind whistles around us like a banshee wailing.

I don't look back. I have to just trust this will work. I rip open the second portal. I'm sick with how much magic I'm using, but there is a dangerous surge of energy that can only be the dark magic that tainted my soul as a child. I don't care; I use it to my advantage. This is for the greater good, and I need to muster the courage to see this through.

Rolf runs through and I wait until I see him safely in the courtyard before I follow him. It is not until we are in the peaceful snow-covered center of the Windraven estate that I look back.

My eyes meet with my father's. He looks furious and excited all at once while stalking toward the portal, I tease like I'm going to close it, though I have no intention of doing so, and he rips it open further. I can't make out what he is saying, but it is obvious he is giving orders to someone I cannot see.

Relief washes over me as he takes the bait and follows us through. I thought for sure he would just force me to perform the ritual there. I retreat, with Rolf in tow, until he is far enough away from the portal, and I seal it.

My father stops in his tracks and looks back at where the portal was. His eyes narrow and he slowly turns back to face me. "Lily, whatever you think you know, you are wrong. Help me undo the damage. He is my brother. Help me save him."

"Liar! I know everything! You're a monster!" I summon the buried grass up from under the snow and it twists into violent bindings that wrap around my father like a devil's snare. The very curse I flung at him when I was a child, only he is not fast enough to deflect this time.

"Very well." He sighs, not acting like he was being squeezed to death by grass vines.

The back of Rolf's hand connects with my face, spinning me hard enough I lose my balance and hit the ground.

My nose is now bleeding, and my eyesight is filled with stars as I fight passing out.

Only for him to pick me up enough he backhands me again.

It sends me flailing the other way and I whimper, trying to crawl away from my mate, who has gone violent and mad. "Rolf," I whimper. My father entirely forgotten as my mate attacks me.

He stalks forward and picks me up by my throat.

As my feet leave the ground, he squeezes my throat enough I'm sputtering and choking on my blood. I kick and struggle to find purchase. I get a good look at Rolf; all I see are the solid black eyes of a man enthralled.

Rolf is being controlled by his own blood. My father is a master of mind magic and with Rolf's blood, he can force him to do anything.

LXIX

The Mark of the Beast

Rolf stalks toward my father with me held in the air, clawing at his arm to get him to release me.

Between panicking and lack of oxygen, I'm growing weaker in his grasp.

"Rolf, it's me. It's Lily. Fight it. You have to fight it." I beg.

He throws me down at my father's feet.

I gasp and sputter, bringing my hand to my throat. My face is bruised and swelling from Rolf hitting me. My heart breaks as whatever my father has done to him has stolen my mate from me. When I turn my gaze up to him, pitiful and bleeding, he stares back blankly.

He waits for the next command.

My father kneels and gently takes my chin, "I wish it were not this way, Lily. You were supposed to be twelve, when you still thought I was the hero. Your mother was wrong. If there were any other way, I would do it." His touch is gentle as he retrieves a handkerchief and wipes my face. But his eyes are dark and full of regret as he stares at me. "You have a choice my dear," as he guides me to my feet.

I raise my hand to curse him.

Rolf snatches it, pulling it behind my back and twisting it up. The pain is white hot, making me scream. Rolf presses against my back, and my arm threatens to break.

"Do not break it, mutt. We need her to complete the ritual."

"I'll never do it," I growl through gritted teeth.

"Oh, but you will. You see, my dear, you have a choice to make. The first choice is to perform the ritual and give your loving mate the minuscule chance to survive. The second choice is I kill him now. Which is it?" He crosses his arms and waits.

"Please don't make me do this. Please. I love him. We're meant to be together." I sob and wince as Rolf drags me toward the center of the courtyard.

"Very well," Silar says with a sigh.

Rolf releases me, and I fall to my knees again from his shove. He claws at his chest and growls instead of attacking me.

The pain that radiates from him suddenly hits me harder than when I saved his life. I gasp and cling to my chest, an invisible force squeezing my heart. My eyes lock on my father as I realize he is allowing our bond to feel the suffering he brings to Rolf.

Panic, fear, and rage wash over me as Rolf is aware of what he has done and cannot control himself. "Lily," he croaks as he drops to the ground in front of me, clutching his chest.

I want to be defiant and brave. I want to say I could let Rolf die and fight my father. But the truth is I'm not that brave, or strong. Rolf is everything to me. He makes me laugh when I don't want to. He makes me mad when he teases me. Until we came here, he never treated me roughly.

Our eyes meet and tears are streaking the bloodstains on my cheeks, making me look even more demonic. His hand cups my cheek and I feel his life fading from him as my father continues giving him a heart attack.

"I'll do it," I scream and fling myself onto Rolf. "I'll do it. Please don't hurt him anymore. Please. He is all I have."

"Good girl," my father murmurs as he moves around us, drawing the circle and then the intricate patterns for the summoning ritual. It burns into the ground, little flames melting the snow down until the ground is branded with the dark spell.

I no longer feel Rolf as I look down at him. His eyes hold the inky black blank stare again as he stays compliant under me. I brush my fingers along his face, and then lean down to kiss his lips, "I love you. I won't let you die."

My father thrusts the ornate dagger into my hand.

I gasp. My body goes rigid as the tiny pricks in my palm draw my blood into the weapon. Flashes of visions dance before my eyes. I have held this dagger before. The vision of six-year-old me snooping in my father's study and finding the bejeweled silver weapon on his workbench plays out. Then the visions of a stone room where he teaches me the chant, "Sanguis gratis datus. Animus donatus. Te voco."

My mouth moves in the wailing cry of the words over and over telling the universe I have given the blood freely, and am now presenting the soul below me, Rolf's soul, as a gift to summon the one who can undo time.

The earth thunders beneath me.

The air wails above me.

Sleet whips down from the sky in brutal strikes.

My entire body glows with the embers of unholy flames buried inside. It leaps from my body and re-ignites the intricate brand in the ground. I hear nothing but the symphony of death I'm shrieking into the sky. My hand tightens around the dagger, the blood droplets splattering down onto Rolf as I bring the other hand around the first and hoist the dagger above my head. My very soul is ripping into a million pieces as Rolf's fear suddenly pushes through my senses. I hesitate above him, trying to bring myself to stop, only to find I cannot move at all.

An unseen force holds my hands above my head, like I'm bound to the air.

All I can do is repeat the chant over and over. I can't stop myself no matter how hard I try. Nothing but the wisps of magic float in the air.

A man's face appears through the veil and watches with a mischievous look. No, not a man, a demon. His two perfectly gilded horns protrude from his brow.

My eyes widen and I feel the blood replacing my tears as I stare at him, held prisoner by some force and the ritual trying to complete itself.

The illusion shatters. The demon's face is gone, and everything is quiet for a second as the air throws Rolf from the circle, causing backlash to me and I collapse, lying where Rolf's body was a moment before, the dagger still piercing my hand.

"You... You aren't supposed to be here! You can't be here!" My father shouts.

"No, brother. I am exactly where I should be." Nicodemus, dirty and battle-worn, kneels next to Rolf and touches his bare chest.

The blackness that oozes from Rolf's chest and up Nicodemus's arm looks like a snake coiling around its handler. Slowly and quietly, it traverses up Nicodemus's arm and then right into any opening it can slither into until it disappears.

"No! Nico," Silar growls. "You damn fool! What have you done?"

Nicodemus staggers to his feet and then backwards, away from Rolf as he gives his brother a lopsided grin. "I did what was right."

Nicodemus throws a curse at him.

That was all the invitation Rolf needed, he leapt through the air in his wolf form snarling at Silar.

I can't move. My body feels heavy and drained. Rolf's rage is the only thing giving me strength as I watch him and my father battle to the death.

Rolf is a streak of snow-colored fur, then a violent, raging Viking warrior. Then back to the wolf as he moves around my father who is flinging magic like candy out of a piñata.

My father screams in pain when Rolf's jaws connect and rip flesh from him.

Rolf yelps when a spell blasts right into him.

I can't tell who has the upper hand, but the two of them are locked in such a fierce battle that even the Gods would stop and watch.

Nicodemus is barely moving. The blackness is spreading through his veins like he has been injected with ink. It spiders up his neck and along his cheeks. He shivers and rolls onto his side as he tries to fight it. The handsome and dashing Windraven brother looks like a man possessed. "Silar," he calls in fear.

I sob. The force that holds me down fades, so I push to my knees.

It was all the distraction Rolf needed as he rips into my father's throat.

"No!" I shriek as my father's final spell sends Rolf flying, his body shifting back into human form as the inky darkness begins to spread over him to suck the very life from him. All three men lie on the ground dying. This is not how it is supposed to be.

My mother promised me that we would come here and Nicodemus would be saved. That we would stop my father from becoming evil.

I struggle, looking dumbfounded as Rolf lies still, staring at me. His fingers outstretched for me.

My father's body twitches as he gurgles and chokes to death on his own blood, his throat completely shredded.

Nicodemus lies still, his skin has turned blue in the snow.

"Rolf," I sob. My entire world has been shattered. There is only one way I can think of to fix this.

Rolf's eyes widen as he watches me raise my hands in the air, as I had done before over him. The brand on the ground ignites in flames again.

The wind wails with my chant.

The ground shakes under me.

The sleet resumes its battering course from the sky.

"No! Lily! No!" Rolf whines.

I plunge the dagger through my heart.

Lightning flashes and thunder claps as the golden portal rips open the fabric of time and space.

Casually strolling through it is a man easily eight feet tall, with broad shoulders, midnight hair, and two golden horns curling forth from his brow. His eyes dance with fire and his pale skin shimmers in the sunlight. He squats before me and sighs. "What a mess you have made, little flower."

He shakes his head and reaches down, ripping the dagger from my chest and prying it from the palm it had embedded itself in.

My hand falls limp on the ground.

He sits me up, with his hand on my neck, holding me like a doll.

"Now, little flower, you can only save one. Do you save the man who saved you?" He turns my head to Nicodemus.

"Do you save The man who sired you?" He turns my head to Silar.

"Or is it truly love and you save the man who claims you?" He finally turns my gaze to Rolf.

"And last, but not least, or do you save yourself?" At which point he turns me to gaze into his eyes.

The only word that slips from my mouth is, "Rolf."

Anger flashes across his face. "Martyrs," he mutters in disgust and casts me to the ground. With an easy stride, he strolls to Rolf and leans down touching his forehead.

The last I see of my beloved mate is the steely blue of his eyes as he disappears into the sunlight.

My father's body shrivels and dries in the pool of blood, turning to dust as the magic that has sustained it, vanishes.

The demon steps before me again and then laughs as he reads my confused thoughts. "Oh, little flower. You cannot change time. What should be will be. But…" He sighs, like I had caused him a great inconvenience.

I see the tiny puff of air as I breathe my last breath. I close my eyes, never knowing what the rest of his statement was going to be.

Wherefore Art Thou?

January 1, 1288

Rolf groans and rolls to his side. His head pounds and all he can remember from the dream he was suffering through was his Lily was dressed strangely and afraid of him, covered in blood. When his eyes flash open, he gasps, and he jolts upright. He is naked, and clean. No signs of blood anywhere. His body hurts as though he has been in battle. His hands go to his chest and there are scars peppering it, but how he got them is lost to him.

Viggo and Morrigan's scents fill the room, but there is no scent of Lily anywhere to be found.

"Lily," he groans and there is a sharp pain in his chest, like a hole in his heart. "Lily, where are you?" He shoots out of the bed and comes storming out of the home Viggo and Morrigan have built.

The shriek of a child draws his attention down and he is met with a small boy clinging to skirts.

Rolf's eyes drift up and turning to face him is Morrigan Ivarsen.

She smiles brightly and closes the distance between them. "You're awake. How are you feeling? What happened to you? I should go get—,"

"Where is Lily?"

"Don't you know?" Morrigan's expression turns sad, like she knows more than she is letting on.

"Do not toy with me, Morrigan Ivarsen, or I swear by the Gods I will—,"

"You will what, pup? Take your hand off my mate before I remove it for you," Viggo steps in between Morrigan and Rolf.

"Where is my mate, your daughter?" Rolf snarls at Viggo.

"She was not with you."

"Rolf!" Sacha's high-pitched squeal fills the air and as Rolf turns, he is forced to catch the young girl leaping at him.

"Get off me, woman. What have you all done with Lily?" He sees Luna not far behind Sacha, followed by his father.

"So, you have returned. Get the romp out of your system? Where is the girl? We want to discuss what happened last night."

"Last night?" Rolf looks in confusion from one person to the next. The only person who does not look like they have gone mad is Morrigan and he stalks forward to force her to talk, only to be blocked by Viggo again.

The elder wolf gives him a low growl to remind him he is the beta and will whip him soundly if he harms his mate.

Rolf turns his confusion onto Luna and Sacha. "You did this," he growls. "What have you done with my mate?"

"Mate?" Luna frowns. "Last I checked you are still just a —
," she stops as her eyes settle on Rolf's shoulder. There, in the vibrant colors of his mark is the Ember Tree coven's symbol, blazing like the tree is on fire.

The entire crowd around him gasps.

"Lily marked you?" Morrigan murmurs.

"And I her. We are fated mates, as I told you all years ago. And she," jabbing a finger at Luna, "has been torturing her since. Now, what have you done with my mate?"

"Pup, we have done nothing with her. The last I saw of her you were clinging to her on the other side of the portal. What have you done with her?"

"Portal?" Rolf looks in confusion. "That sounds like witchcraft. The only witches we know are my mate, and her mother," he now turns a suspicious gaze on Morrigan.

"If you went through a portal, it means Lily got her magic back…"

Viggo now turns a stern gaze on his mate, having had the conversation with her when he returned with Rolf a few hours ago. "You were always a terrible liar, my love."

"Good enough to convince them I ever had control of Lily's magic."

This wins a chorus of gasps from all the wolves around Morrigan.

"You know where she is," Rolf accuses.

"I know where she was. If she did not come back with you, then I can only assume she is still there."

"Where is there?" Rolf demands.

Morrigan frowns and bites her lip. "1821."

"Send me to her. This instance."

"I cannot."

"Liar. If you know when she is, you know how to get to her."

"I do. I still cannot."

Rolf shoves Viggo out of the path and gets a hold of Morrigan.

Viggo snarls and leaps on Rolf to protect his mate.

"Enough! You will not harm a member of this pack, Rolf Ivarsen. Especially not one carrying a pup." Alpha puts himself between Morrigan, Viggo, and Rolf. With his back to his brother to deal with his son he says, "I do not know what you did last night. Or where that girl is, but we will find her and bring her home. Now go find yourself some clothes before I have you thrown in the river."

The command from Rolf's father cannot be denied, and Rolf storms away, still full of rage.

Turning to face Luna and Sacha the Alpha narrows his eyes. "What you did to Lily and Rolf was unacceptable, mate. It was cruel and vindictive to an innocent girl. A girl, I remind you, who is a member of this pack fully, by blood and by oath. More than you can say for your whore of a sister. I suggest you send Sacha home before she gets herself in further trouble. Or you have the boy that has impregnated her step up and mate her."

Luna's eyes go wide and she nods in silence, not wanting to feel Alpha Ivarsen's wrath.

Sacha turns as red as blood at being called out. Her shoulders droop and she looks to the ground in shame. "Yes, Alpha," she stammers out and then runs toward the pack house. Luna runs after her, after giving him the deadliest stare.

This leaves Alpha to turn and face Morrigan and Viggo. "I do not know what game you two are playing with my son. But end it."

"The reason I cannot send him to her is she is no longer there. He did not listen to what I said. I said I knew where she was, not where she is. If he is here, she fulfilled her destiny. After seeing the mate mark still active on your son, there is a chance for them. To send him through time would destroy that."

Alpha rubs his hand over his face. "Witches," he mutters. "Let me get this straight. You believe that your daughter is somewhere out in the world for him to find someday?"

"Do you believe it? You saw the mark with your own eyes and how it burned, as if to call to him."

"Brother. Why would we lie about something so sacred? We were as stunned as you last night when Luna announced Sacha," Viggo says.

Alpha grimaces. "Fine. I will deal with the boy." He points at Morrigan and closes the space between them. "You will use whatever means to get me something I can tell him. I will not have him moping like a lovesick child around the village. He is to be Alpha and needs his Luna."

"Yes, Alpha," Morrigan mumbles.

Alpha heads to the docks. "Erik," he bellows when he arrives.

The old raider stands to greet him. "Yes, Alpha?"

"I have a moping pup for you to whip back into shape. Remind him what it is to be an Ivarsen."

"Oh. Those Celts are always good for making a man forget his woes."

Alpha snorts in approval and nods. "I'll send him in the morn to ship off with you." Then the Alpha takes his time returning to the pack house. He stops first at Luna's room and enters without knocking.

"Get out," she growls.

"No. You will listen. I am the Alpha, and I make the decisions. You are lucky I did not send you back to your father for what you did."

"She is not a wolf, Ivar. She cannot be Luna. She will be the death of this clan."

He closes the distance, his hand going around her throat as he pins her to the wall. He leans in closer and growls against her ear. "If she returns and brings death upon this clan, I will kill her myself, mate. Until then, you will treat my son, your next Alpha, with respect by honoring his mate." He nuzzles her, "Or do I need to remind you what happens when you step out of line?" He pushes away from her, leaving her against the wall as he storms out of the room.

His final stop before he resumes his daily duties is Rolf's room. As he opens the door, he hears the snarling and whining as Rolf destroys every non-living thing inside.

"Sit," he barks at his son, then closes the door behind him.

"You are better than this, Rolf. Look at you. You are acting like a foolish pup, over what? A missing girl? She is probably hiding in one of the Gods forsaken caves the natives use. Or the natives have her. Whatever happened last night, you were brought back covered in blood and gore. Who did you kill?"

Rolf opens his mouth to argue, but his father's final words make him frown. He looks down at his hands and his breathing becomes erratic. "I did not kill her. I would never hurt her." Doubt rings in his voice from the horribly vivid nightmare he had had about his Lily.

"Well, you have killed someone. You are leaving with Erik in the morning. Do not question me on this."

"Yes, father." Rolf is still, staring at his hands. He is now terrified that he has hurt his mate and she has fled from him.

Epilogue

Beltane 1269

"Breathe!" The old woman coos to the younger woman.

"You breathe, ya fat sow," the younger woman spits back as she draws in a heavy breath. "Ow! Don't hit me, I'm having a baby."

"I'll thump ya as often as I like, ya wee harpy, if ya keep talkin' to me like that. Now push."

The screams that erupt from the small woman are drowned out by the drums beating at the ceremony not far from her cottage. Her dark red hair clings to her temples where it has escaped her braid. She's hunched up, her face pinching in pain as the contraction works its way through her body while the older woman is between her knees and ready to bring the infant into this world.

The man approaching the village gets a small smirk upon his lips at what he hears. He is not too late for the birth of his daughter. He picks up his pace and lets himself into the small cottage. He has to duck to fit through the door, but his shoulders are broad, and his hair platinum blond, tied neatly at the nape of his neck. A leather patch covers one of his eyes, and his beard is long, and braided.

The women turn their attention from the task, and the old woman looks at him in confusion.

The younger woman growls, "What the feck are you doing here?"

"Now, now, Catarina. That is no way to greet the father of your child. I would not miss this for all the Gods." His smile is gentle and full of mirth. He leaves the walking staff he carries and his cloak near the door, and comes to her side, brushing her hair from her face. "Here, let me help you," he kisses her temple.

The older woman watches in fascination. She has never once seen this man before, and Catarina has absolutely refused to talk about who impregnated her. It has half the village up in arms about the baby.

The superstitious lot calmed when they realized she would be born near Beltane, not Winter Solstice. She is about to say something when Catarina lets out another wail, and it forces the old woman to bury her head between Catarina's knees.

"This was not part of the deal." Catarina hisses at him.

He waves his hand dismissively. "I do not care what deal you think you made with my son, Catarina. This is my child and I will see it born. You can either allow me to be here, or you can suffer when I force myself. You would not want the latter, witch."

There is a snort of laughter from the old woman.

"Quiet you! I swear, you're all against me!" Catarina flops back. "Fine! Do what you will, pig. You've already done this!" She motions to her round belly quivering with the contraction that pulls her right back up and into pushing.

His massive hand pets along her back, soothing her.

The radiating warmth that he pushes over her skin eases the pain. Catarina grits her teeth and screams again. Only this time, there is a matching wail, much higher in pitch. Catarina falls back, exhausted.

"It is a wee lass," the woman boasts. With experienced hands, she wipes the infant clean and makes sure her mouth is clear of anything before she places her on Catarina's sweat-kissed chest.

"She is perfect," he says in awe. "What will you call her?"

"She is my perfect little flower. I will call her Lily."

The old woman lets out a small squeal of shock when she takes Lily to finish cleaning her up. "What, by the Gods, is that?"

"What? What is it? Let me see," Catarina whines.

When the old woman turns and shows the infant's shoulder, there is the burned imprint of an inverted mountain shaped like a wolf's fang.

Caterina's eyes narrow and she snatches the infant from the old woman.

"Leave us," the man growls and the woman hurries from the room.

"What is the meaning of this, old man?"

He shrugs, "Call me a romantic. All happens as it should be." He then stands and leans over the two. He plants a soft kiss on the now sleeping infant's forehead. Then he turns to Catarina. "I will be here if you need me." He leaves the woman to her child.

Catarina smiles down at the infant and pets her as she lets out a sigh, "See, I told you love would save the day."

Biography

J.R. Froemling was born in Indiana and currently resides in Illinois with her husband (Mr. F). She has a Bachelor of Science in Information Technology, a Master of Arts in English and Creative Writing, and is currently working towards a Master of Science in Marketing.

She got her love of writing in the early 2000s when writing fanfiction for a Star Wars community online. For several years she facilitated the online writing community before branching out to author her own stories.

Want to find out more about J. R. Froemling?

jrfwriting.com

www.ingramcontent.com/pod-product-compliance
Lightning Source LLC
Chambersburg PA
CBHW030711190726
48286CB00001B/277